# One Lie Too Many

## Moma Escriva

To Joanne ~
Longtime friend ~ Enjoy!
Love, Moma

# Acknowledgements

Fifteen years ago, I decided to write a novel. And, as we writers know, the words don't always come as easily as we would like. But thanks to the encouragement I received along the way, the book is finally done. I owe my thanks to so many; Barb Froman who believed in me enough to threaten to kill me if I didn't publish, Lisa Nowak who gave me tons of writing and publishing advice, Beth Miles, Esther Wood, Pat Lichen, Orice Klaas, Alice Lynn, Helen Wand, Sharon White, Jackie Ackerman, Roxie Matthews, Linda Appel, Rose Leferbre, and all the wonderful women in Chrysalis Women's Writers Group who inspired and supported me. I also want to thank my wonderful crazy, zany Bunco gals, Phyllis, Helen, Sharon, Sally, Donna and Robin who would buy my book just because they love me; and my dear friend Patty Dutcher, who was with me from the beginning of this journey. I want to thank, Diane Angelo who took the barest amount of information and created the perfect book cover. Finally, thanks to my beautiful children who always believed I could do it, and to my husband Joe, relieved that I actually did finish it.

# Let's Have a Party

THE EARLY SUMMER morning sunlight slipped through the slats of the window blinds, hinting at the start of a pleasant day. I'd hoped it'd be a good sign for me as I approached the kitchen table, coffeepot in hand, ready to pour into Harry's waiting cup. He lowered the morning paper just enough to grunt an acknowledgement then raised it covering his face to avoid any amount of conversation. Undaunted, I painted a smile on my lips. "So, Harry, about my plans for your retirement party, have you changed your mind?" I'd hoped my honey-laced voice might soften him after last night's heated discussion.

"No." The answer was forceful enough to blow a hole through the paper, tossing my sugar-coated words back down my throat. Harry poked his head around the corner of the news. "Honest to God Kate, what part of I-don't-want-another-party didn't you understand?"

"Oh Harry, surely you deserve more than the one the bank threw. That was nothing but—"

"Don't start that again," he interrupted. "That farewell celebration was plenty enough for me." His voice took on that irritating, arrogant air. "Besides," he huffed, "I've never liked being the center of attention. You ought to know that by now."

"What I do know is that as much as you protest, you'll love it in the end … especially if you know your old banker cronies would be invited," I countered.

"This discussion is ended, Kate. I've had my say. No party. Final answer." He resumed his position, propping up the paper higher to avoid any more disruptions.

I rose and karate chopped the business section with one hand into a perfect 'V', and laid down my well-worn worded gauntlet. "It's not over, Harry Creighton."

Ego slightly bruised, I rose and pushed my chair against the table hard enough to spill a few drops of his coffee on the rest of his precious news. Harry responded with an unpleasant word and smoothed out the crumpled paper. I picked up my mug and walked my frustration outdoors, muttering unkindly. Romeo, our dog of indefinite breeds, plodded along behind. I plunked myself down on the patio chaise, while he investigated the yard.

Why was this party so important to me? Was it something I wanted to do for him, or had it simply come down to a challenge of winning the battle between two iron-clad wills? I shook my head. No, he deserved more than the meager recognition the bank gave him.

Harry may've played his final hand this morning, but I had a trick or two left. I was so sure of my success the invitations were already in the mail. I reckoned that between our four children and my friend Candace, we'd have him indoctrinated, medicated, sedated, and beat into submission by the time the RSVP's arrived.

The sprinklers turned on just as Romeo lifted his leg on the hydrangea bush. He jumped back and loped to the other end of the yard to finish his business. The sight broke my sour mood. I was about ready to shoo him away from the rose bushes when I heard voices coming from the Whitetowers' yard next door.

*Strange, I thought they weren't due back from their trip until the middle of August.* The Whitetowers divided their time between teaching at the University and digging up ancient artifacts during summer break. Lydia had verbally declined the invitation to Harry's party prior to their leaving.

As I headed toward the fence to greet them, I realized the voices did not have their distinct British accents. Curious, I crouched by the laurel bush to listen. It sounded like three men having a heated conversation. Nothing they'd said made any sense. Then I realized these people were speaking a foreign language. I wasn't close enough to figure out if it was European or Middle Eastern. Definitely not Asian.

Just then, Romeo ambled over next to me. He cocked his head to one side. A low growl rolled up his throat. The dog's unusual reaction to the mysterious voices caused a thorn of fear to prick the back of my neck. On instinct, I grabbed Romeo by the collar and ushered him back to the house.

I would've told Harry what was going on, but he'd just tell me to mind my own business. So I breezed through the kitchen, up the stairs to our bedroom and tiptoed onto the balcony to see if I could get a good look at the strangers. *Drat, it was too late.* They were gone. Maybe they'd heard me, or perhaps the dog's growl alerted them to continue their conversation elsewhere. Nevertheless, the incident drew a big question mark in what Harry called my overly inquisitive, meddling mind.

The next day, while Harry was having lunch with one of his banker cronies, Candace came over to discuss party preparations, and I casually mentioned the incident at the Whitetowers.

"Wow, Kate, can you imagine what a story that would be!" Candace bubbled. "I can just see the headlines 'Mystery Surrounds Small Suburban Neighborhood.'" She swept her arm across each imaginary word.

"Hold on, Candace, you're blowing this out of proportion." I knew where this was going.

"Really, Kate, there could be a great story in this." She paced about the room, one arm across her waist holding her elbow as she chewed on her thumbnail. "You know, you could make it that break-out novel you've been talking about writing ever since we met. Let's see, what could be a good name for it? How about 'The Mystery Behind the Fence,' or 'The Back Fence Caper.' Or maybe—"

"That's enough, Candace. There's probably nothing to this whole thing. If it wasn't for Romeo's unusual behavior, I wouldn't have given it another thought."

"But—"

"Come on now, we're getting off track. We've got a party to plan, remember?" Reeling Candace back into the moment was like trying to land a tuna with a trout pole. Finally, after considerable prodding, and after I assigned her the job of party manager, she changed direction, warming to her appointment. *She so does like titles.*

"I think we should have a string quartet play while guests mingle, drink champagne, and munch on *hors d'oeuvres*," said Candace. "Then let your son Kenny and his trio play while the caterers are serving the cake. His music will add zest to the party, even get people to dance. How does that sound?"

"Don't you think a quartet is a bit much?" I asked.

"I like it." She folded her arms, asserting her importance.

"Harry wouldn't go for it."

"Oh, pooh. We'll fill him up with drinks and he won't even know they're there. It'll be my treat."

I tried to refuse the offer but she wouldn't hear of it.

"No, no, Kate. I want to do this. I can certainly afford it."

"You know, Candace, you never fail to surprise me." I smiled, shaking my head.

"Yeah, I know." She smirked.

We worked steadily for the rest of the afternoon until I finally pushed my chair back and declared, "That's all for now. It's cocktail time."

"Whew, I thought we'd never stop," Candace laughed, waving her empty water glass. "This needs more zing in it."

"I'm sure glad Harry's out of the house. It's damn near impossible to plan anything with a retired husband interrupting every five minutes."

# Party Day

FOR THE NEXT few of weeks, nothing strange occurred next door. Harry had finally waved the white flag of surrender, with a caveat that he could bitch and moan at any time to anyone and at his own discretion. Most of the time, his complaining was aimed at me. After many years of marriage, I was used to it.

I busied myself with party plans and almost forgot the incident until the morning of the Harry's big day. I eased out of bed and slipped out onto the balcony. Wispy clouds moved aimlessly through the sky as pink rays announced the sun's appearance. The sweet scent of jasmine floated up from the flower bed. I inhaled deeply, taking in the morning air. My exhale stopped abruptly when a taxi pulled into the Whitetower's driveway. *Could it be them?* They weren't supposed to be home until the latter part of August.

Realizing I was not appropriately dressed for neighborly conversation, I crouched behind the chaise and peeked through the slats. Stanford Whitetower uncurled his tall, lanky frame and eased out of the taxi. He hurried to the opposite side of the cab and helped Lydia from her seat. She refused his support with a twist of her elbow. I couldn't make out their conversation, but judging by the body language, it appeared they were arguing all the way to the back door. The driver pulled suitcases and boxes from the trunk and placed them near the path. Stanford hurried back and retrieved a small box from the back seat.

While he was settling up with the cabbie, I got a cramp in my leg and accidently fell against the chaise, giving it a shove. The screeching sound echoed across the yard. Stanford's head jerked upward, surveying the surrounding area. *Crap! He's looking up here.* I scrunched lower. I gritted my teeth, waiting in pain for Stanford to finish his inspection. I desperately needed to shake out the cramp. After what seemed like forever, he turned and paid the driver, then headed toward his house.

When I attempted to uncoil from my hiding spot, I stumbled over the chaise. A litany of curse words streamed out of the bedroom, ending with Harry's shout, "What the hell's going on out there?"

"Shush! Lower your voice," I whispered, hobbling into the bedroom.

"What for? It's a free country." Harry's tone was anything but jovial.

"Ah…yes, but the Whitetowers just returned, and Stanford might've seen me." I sat on the easy chair, rubbing my leg.

"Oh, them again." Harry laid back against his pillow.

"Don't you think it's strange that they're back so soon?"

"Why should I care?" He yawned and rubbed the sleep from his eyes.

"You know, maybe if they decide to come to the party, I should tell them about the voices I heard a few weeks ago."

"What voices?" He shot me a questioning look.

"I heard some men talking in their backyard and didn't say anything to you about it because you'd tell me not to meddle," I snipped. "It's nothing really, except they spoke in a foreign language. I just thought it was a little weird, that's all."

I watched as Harry rolled over to his side, sat up, flung his feet on the floor and raised his body slowly into a vertical position. "You're right about one thing Kate. I would've definitely told you to leave well-enough alone. You don't want to be known as the neighborhood narc."

Ignoring his snide remark, I continued. "But isn't that being a responsible neighbor to let them know if I saw or heard something out of the ordinary … especially when they're away from home?"

"Don't waste your time on them."

"Well, since they're home, I could check to see if they'd want to come to your party."

"If it was me just getting back from a long trip, I certainly wouldn't want to spend the afternoon glad-handing a bunch of people I hardly know." He dropped down on the floor, preparing to do his daily sit-ups. "You know how I feel about the Whitetowers. It sure wouldn't hurt my feelings any if they didn't show up."

"Yeah, I know." This early morning bickering was beginning to give me a headache. I hoped Harry would concentrate on his exercise routine and leave it alone. But I was wrong.

Turning over to begin push-ups, he paused. "Since you brought up the Whitetowers, is there anyone else coming that I have no interest in seeing?"

"Oh for God's sake, Harry, you make it sound like I opened the phone book and picked names at random just to irritate you."

"Well?"

I stared at him in amazement. "You saw the guest list." His last comment threw me over the top. I limped toward him. He left little space for me to skirt around his workout area. I hesitated, the thought to kick him in the butt rose to mind as I started to step over his prone body. But the moment passed.

It was time to put a period to the end of the argument. I transferred my irritation to making the bed. I tossed the covers aside and pulled, fanned, and tucked in the sheet and blanket. I moved from one side to the other, straightening the comforter, fluffing up the pillows, and chucking them against the headboard. I glared at Harry who paid absolutely no attention to me. Through with his floor routine, he rose and did a few stretches.

"If you're done exercising, hurry up and shower. The people from the rental company will be coming with the tables and chairs at 10 a.m. sharp."

Harry opened his mouth to argue, but I slapped him on the ass and pushed him toward the bathroom.

"Oh, just go," I said. *What a beautiful start to the day this is.*

Shrugging into my bathrobe, I stomped barefoot downstairs, kicking the dog's chewy toy on my way to the kitchen. A good strong cup of coffee was in the forefront of my mind. Maybe that would ease the throbbing pain now entrenched in my head. I needed to find Harry a distraction this morning, mostly to keep him off my back.

Romeo greeted me wagging his bushy tail. I ruffled the dog's ears. "Romeo, all you need is a little attention and you're good to go. Gotta hang on a minute, pal; coffee for the missus, first." I put several scoops of French double roast into the coffee maker, poured in the water, and pressed the start button. Juliet, the stray white cat that followed Molly home from school a few years back, sauntered in, meowing her request for breakfast.

While the coffee brewed, I filled each pet's dish with food and clean water. Romeo chomped away at his kibbles and slopped up the icy drink. Juliet daintily picked away at hers.

I unlocked the doggie door and Romeo scampered out, leaving a trail of water slobbers. Juliet looked up from her dish and gave me a dogs-are-so-messy look, then finished her meal. I scanned Harry's 'to do' list that I'd started the night before, and penciled in "dog duty." *That should thrill him.* I smiled. But not kindly.

Coffee done I poured some in my mug and headed outside. I told myself I needed to give the backyard a final check, but what I really wanted was to see if there was any more movement coming from the Whitetowers.

A car noise lured me to the laurel fence. I listened closely. A door opened and loud music rolled out, along with a young female singing something like, 'Oh, baby, oh baby, yeah, yeah.' I recognized Shannon Simmon's voice from The Cat's Meow Sitting Service. The Whitetowers had left their cat Jasper at her shop while they were away. I heard Stanford's voice. The two exchanged a few words, then Shannon was back in her car and gone. *So much for intrigue.* Disappointed, I continued to survey the yard; dewy blades of grass tickled my toes. I followed the sweet scent of flowers to the pond. Water splashed over the rocks, cascading into to the pool below, nudging the water lilies. I counted the fish to make sure no uninvited animal had helped themselves to a late night snack.

Headache nearly gone, I ambled back to the house, ready to face my nemesis.

I entered the room and found Harry sitting at the kitchen table, slurping coffee and reading his "to do list."

"What's this for?" He waved the scrap of paper in front of me. "I thought my only assignment today was to show up at my party. How come I have to do a bunch of tasks?"

"Oh, good lord Harry, there isn't much for you to do. Besides, your day doesn't begin until 2 o'clock, no sooner." He was about to argue but I quickly added, "Look, I don't have time to go another round. Do the list. After that, do whatever you like."

As I moved to the sink to rinse out my cup, the phone rang on the counter. It was within his reach. I looked at Harry to answer, but he pointed to the items I had written out for him to do.

"Nope, not on my list."

"Smart ass," I sneered, reaching over his shoulder to pick up the phone.

"It's usually for you, anyway."

True enough. The caterer had a last minute question. It probably was a good thing Harry didn't answer it. Even though I planned the gala, he footed the bill, and any time he was reminded of the cost, I wound up getting an earful.

"Hey, what about some breakfast?"

I reached into the bread drawer, retrieved a couple of bagels, sliced one and popped it in the toaster. I placed a knife, a container of cream cheese, and a napkin by his elbow and kissed him on the top of his head. "I think you can figure out the rest." Before he could complain, I pulled a yogurt from the fridge, grabbed a spoon and headed up the stairs to change into sweats.

For the next few hours, Harry and I moved about the house, carefully avoiding one another, only tossing a few non-confrontational comments back and forth from time to time.

Neither needed another clash of the Creightons before the party.

Candace called to reconfirm arrival time, and oldest daughter Meg offered to send the twins over to entertain their grandfather. They loved listening to Harry recount his days as an Air Force pilot just as much as he loved telling them. What my daughter was really doing was giving me a breather. She knew her father well.

I checked the backyard one more time. The tables and chairs were in place. I marked off the last item on my "to do" list. Good. I had enough time for a leisurely bath. The thought was interrupted by the front door bell. *Now what?* I rushed to open the door and was greeted by the three neighborhood Findley children with Romeo in tow.

"Hi, Mrs. Creighton," said Haley, the oldest. "Mama was worried that you couldn't find Romeo and told us to bring him home."

"Oh my, the gate must've been left open and he snuck out. Thank you guys for bringing him." I ushered the dog in with a gentle pat on his behind.

"Um, Mrs. Creighton, there's something else," said Mac, the middle child.

"What is it, dear?"

"Um, do you see that big black car in front of the Whitetower house?"

I stepped onto the porch and glanced around the post. The car was actually a black limousine. *This is interesting.* "Yes, I do now." My remark was casual.

"Well, Romeo was sniffing at the car and then he...ah, um, he—"

"He peed on one of the tires," finished Charlie, the youngest of the three. "Then, the man standing by the car started yelling at him. He was talking funny. I didn't understand what he was saying, but he sounded mean. So, we called to Romeo, and he came over to our house. We wanted to wait until the man left, but, mama said to bring him home right away."

"Well, thanks again, kids. I really appreciate it. Now, I—"

"Ah, Mrs. Creighton, will the twins be at the party?" Haley twisted a curl that had fallen out of her ponytail.

"Haley likes Brian," Mac teased.

"I do not!" She shut him up with a dirty look, her face turning a pretty pink.

"Uh, huh," he chuckled.

Haley punched her brother in the arm. "I'll get you for this, Mac. I'm telling mom when we get home." Composing herself, she sighed, "Honestly, Mrs. Creighton, boys can be so immature."

"I agree," I smiled at Haley. "And, yes, the boys'll be here…but, kids, I've really got to get ready for the party. Thanks again for bringing Romeo home. Now, scoot along. I'll see you all later."

As the children raced toward the curb, I called out, "Be careful crossing the street, and don't forget to look both ways." They yelled and waved. I kept an eye on them until they were safely on the other side.

As soon as they were out of sight, I scrunched down behind the large rhododendron adjacent to the porch and peered through the branches. A man emerged from the Whitetower house, heading toward the limo. Even from a distance, he looked huge. His jacket molded to his body. His blond hair was cut short, military style. *Was he the driver or a bodyguard?* A much shorter man followed him. Dressed in a shiny silvery-gray suit, he moved with self-assurance, exuding wealth and power. The sun reflected off the top of his bald head like one of those garden globes so popular a few years ago.

I leaned farther into the shrub to get a better look. A small branch cracked. *Yikes?* I pulled back a bit and froze in place. No one turned my way. Before the bald man disappeared into the car, my cell phone beeped. Startled by the sound I almost fell headfirst into the bush. I reached into my pants pocket and saw a text message from Molly. Nothing important. I could answer her later.

I started to stuff the phone away when it dawned on me that I could take pictures with it. I fired off a few shots just as

Stanford rushed out of the house and down the brick pathway, waving his arms in the air. He exchanged a few words with the bald man then waited at the sidewalk while the bodyguard scoped the surroundings, casting an eye in my direction. Apparently satisfied that all was clear, he slid into the front passenger-side of the limo. Stanford waited until they were gone before going back inside.

I waited a minute, letting all I saw sink in, then I peeled my feet off the cement and backed into the house. *Damn, I wish I knew what the Whitetowers were up to.*

This mystery was steadily increasing, and my curiosity was growing along with it. But for now, I had to temper the imagination. Party first, the neighbors later. At least I had pictures to show Harry. Maybe then he might believe my suspicions for once.

Before I could march into Harry's office clutching the concrete evidence on my phone, I heard a car pull into our driveway. Children's happy voices wafted through the kitchen window. The twins bounded in with their dad bringing up the rear.

"Where's Poppa?" they asked in unison.

"Hey, what about, Hi Gram, How are you?"

"Oh, right. Hi Gram," they mumbled their hellos.

I cornered them for hugs and kisses. They brushed their cheeks with the backs of their hands and squirmed out of my grip as fast as ten year-old boys could.

"Is Poppa in his office?" Brady asked.

"Where else?"

They dashed off, hollering out his name all the way down the hall.

"You're a Godsend, Jerry." I gave my son-in-law a smooch on the cheek. "Now, don't you go wiping it off like those two little imps did."

"No way," he laughed. "I never mind a kiss from a good-looking woman."

"My, my, you certainly know how to flatter a lady." I grabbed the sides of my baggy pants as if they were a skirt and curtsied.

15

"I have a few minutes if you need help with anything, otherwise I'll—"

"No, no. You go ahead. I need to get moving or this party's going to start without us."

A blur of white fur scampered ahead of me as I headed upstairs to the bedroom. Juliet jumped up on the bed, selected the perfect spot right in the center, stretched and then curled into a ball for her noonday nap.

"Got to find something to wear, Juliet," I announced while peering into the closet. What to choose was always a problem with me, because decisions were hard for me to make. Harry labeled me the great procrastinator. I could never be as organized as he—truth be told, never really tried. I *liked* doing things on the fly. I held up one dress after the other, posing in front of the full-length mirror, finally settling on a pale green chiffon. I twirled around to face the cat. "What do you think, Juliet?" She yawned and opened one eye, turned her backside to me, and resumed her nap. "That's your final answer?" I harrumphed. "So much for your fashion sense...I'm wearing it."

A slight breeze twisted the curtains on the balcony doors. As I straightened the panels, thoughts of the Whitetowers popped back into my mind. Regardless of what Harry thought about them, I was rather fond of Lydia, and especially their only child, Chauncey.

I peeked at the clock on the dresser. *Darn, no time for a leisurely soak in the Jacuzzi, guess it'll be a quick shower.*

Afterwards, having slathered lotion all over my body, I shimmied into a one-piece undergarment, pulling everything together, stomach, thighs, butt, etc. *Ah, the wonder of spandex.* The dress felt soft and silky on the parts of my skin that weren't bound in elastic. What a far cry from my usual T-shirt and stretch pants.

Make-up and hair done, I applied perfume on all essential places and slipped into silver heeled sandals. Taking a last glance in the mirror, I glided down the stairs, carrying the opal and diamond necklace Harry had given me for our 30th anniversary.

Harry emerged from his office sandwiched between the twins, engaged in jovial conversation. They stopped suddenly in front of me.

"Wow, Gram, you sure do look better than you did when we first came in," said Brady.

"Why thank you, sweetie. I'll take a compliment wherever I can."

"The boy's right. You look quite lovely, my dear." Harry's lips turned into a wide grin.

His flattering words delighted me, something I hadn't heard much from him lately. I returned his smile with a slight kiss on his cheek, careful not to leave a lipstick imprint.

"You look pretty good yourself." I admired the way his dark suntan emphasized the whiteness of his linen open-collared shirt. There were times when we weren't bickering that he could still turn me on. This was one of them.

I handed Harry the necklace, turned and pushed up my hair while he attached the two ends. He gently squeezed my shoulders. It was such a tender moment that I slipped it into my invisible box of precious memories.

The boys weren't used to their grandfather's display of affection. They rolled their eyes and made gagging noises, hands covering their mouths.

"That's enough boys," Harry said abruptly, then cleared his throat. "All right now, let's get this party going."

Our grandsons ran ahead while we walked arm-in-arm slowly out to the backyard. The boys had done their job of softening Harry up a bit. I offered up a silent prayer of thanks.

There was no missing Candace. She had arrived, dressed in a Hawaiian print, one-strapped silk sheath that clung to her well-proportioned five-foot-9-inch frame. A matching headband held her long honey-blonde hair in place. Her gigantic hoop earrings dangled back and forth as she bounced about the yard in alarmingly high-heeled sandals. I had once asked if she'd been a Las Vegas chorus girl. Her strong denial led me to believe that it might've been true.

I caught her eye and she gave me the OK sign. I watched her bustling about, checking the centerpieces at the tables and giving final instructions to the caterers. She enlisted a few young men, friends of our son Kenny, who appeared to be only too happy to help secure the canopy over the buffet table. Then, with a swift movement, she signaled the quartet to begin. Candace was in her element.

A contingent of Harry's colleagues was the first to come through the gate *Hooray for the banker boys!* Hand-shaking, back-patting, arm-punching, cheek-kissing (to the spouses), and words of congratulations coupled with a few pleasantries were exchanged throughout the next half-hour. Relatives and neighbors added to the mix of well-wishers.

Newly divorced Darryl Harrison, the bank's mortgage officer, swaggered in with his latest arm décor. The young blonde's low cut-fire-engine red dress seemed painted on to her sensuous body. It was a miracle she could walk two steps in that tight skirt without falling over. Most of the male guests nearly had whiplash, craning their necks to get a good look, Harry included.

"Congratulations, old man," Darryl said, patting him on the back while shaking hands. "I'd like you both to meet my friend, Brandi Babcock." Darryl turned to Brandi. "Harry and I've known each other for many years."

Brandi giggled a hello.

"Probably way before you were born," I mumbled while plastering a smile on my face.

Overhearing my terse comment, Harry jumped in, and playing the perfect host, took her hand and gushed, "It's a pleasure to meet you. Are you new to the area?"

"Yes." Brandi purred through her wide, red collagen lips. "I just moved here recently from Iowa."

"Oh, that's some distance away. Is Darryl getting you acclimated to this area?"

"Um, yes he is." Brandi laughed, twisting a strand of hair.

"So nice of you to come…Bambi is it?" I slipped a bit of sarcasm into my welcoming.

"That's Brandi," Darryl corrected.

"Oh, I'm so sorry." Harry glared at me. I softened a little. "So tell me, Darryl, where did you meet this, ah *young* lady?"

"Brandi is the receptionist in our accounting department." He gave Brandi a little squeeze. She tittered.

*Oh good lord, I can't take anymore.* Thankfully, Candace swung by seconds before more damaging words spewed out of my mouth. I quickly took hold of Brandi's arm and announced, "It's so warm today. I'm sure you two must be thirsty. Candace, will you show Darryl and his ah, guest to the bar?"

"My pleasure." She winked at me.

"Enjoy yourselves, now." Harry patted Darryl on the back and grinned widely at Brandi.

Taken in by Candace's striking appearance, Darryl immediately took his place beside her as they strode toward the buffet table, leaving Brandi doing double-time trying to keep up with them. *What a cad.*

"You sure were impressed with Darryl's arm candy," I remarked to Harry.

"Well, you said that I should be nice to our guests."

"Yes, but you didn't have to spend the whole time admiring her, ah, two attributes."

"I was not," he said in defense.

"Okay, then tell me, what color were her eyes?"

"Um, I…"

But, I couldn't wait for his answer. The Whitetowers had just entered the yard. I left him sputtering an explanation.

Paying little attention to my surroundings, I nearly collided with Adeline, wife of former bank CEO Ed McHenry. She held a glass of champagne in one hand, an unlit cigarette in the other, her eyes fixed on the ground.

"Oops, sorry, Adeline…didn't see you. Did you lose something?"

Her head jerked up at the sound of my voice. She teetered a bit, and then regained her balance. I wondered how many glasses of champagne she'd had. Or had she had some other libations before coming to the party?

"Oh…Kate…dear me, yes, I seemed to have lost my sunglasses."

"They're on top of your head, Adeline."

19

"Oh my." She grinned sheepishly, reaching up to touch them. "Thank you. Oh, I feel so foolish."

"It happens to all of us at one time or another." I tossed her a sympathetic smile and waited a moment to make sure she was all right before I took a step toward my meeting with the Whitetowers. "Adeline, if you'll excuse me, I have to—"

"Wait." She grabbed my arm. "I must talk to you." Her voice held a tone of anxiousness.

I hesitated. *No, I can't let her guilt me into lingering.* The Whitetowers were still at the gate. I signaled to them, releasing her hand from my arm.

"Adeline, my dear, I'd love to stay and visit with you, but some more guests have arrived, and I must go welcome them. Can we talk later?"

She gave a long sigh. "Well, all right, but you promise you won't forget, now?"

"I promise." I pressed my hand over my heart then sped off to meet the Whitetowers.

It didn't take but a minute to sense a distinct difference in the two, but I couldn't put my finger on it. Stanford's normal audacious persona seemed a little shaken. Maybe it was jet-lag, or perhaps his meeting with the bald man and his burly bodyguard from the limo. Usually impeccably dressed for any occasion, Stanford wore the same pale green silk shirt and wrinkled tan slacks from this morning. His silver-gray hair, normally combed to perfection, was ruffled as though he had been running nervous fingers through it.

His tall frame shadowed Lydia's petite one. Her slight figure seemed almost lost in her beige linen tunic shirt. It hung loosely over palazzo pants. Several strands of her trademark bun escaped from its tight grasp, trailing limply down the sides of her pale cheeks. Her sweet and sensitive face was pinched, and dark circles had formed under gray-blue eyes. Lydia, usually the more talkative one, barely uttered a greeting.

I hid my suspicions and greeted them warmly. "What a nice surprise. We didn't think you were going to be back this soon."

I looked back to where I'd left Harry, but he must've beaten a path back to his bank of cronies. Suddenly, Brian dashed up and pressed his body against my side, apparently trying to hide from Haley Findley who was heading our way in hot pursuit. "Brian, honey will you do me a favor? Go find grandpa and tell him that I want to see him right away."

"You bet, Gram." He sprinted off, passing Haley before she had a chance to stop him.

"Grandchildren can be such a big help at times." I smiled. They didn't. Their faces were like sculpted marble. *Good God, weren't they kids once?* "We, ah, apologize for being late," Lydia finally spoke. "As you know, we were supposed to be in Africa for most of the summer, but unfortunately our trip was cu—"

"Cut short," Stanford finished, giving his wife a cold stare.

Lydia returned it with one of her own. "Anyway, seeing that we came back on the same day of Harry's reception, we felt it only proper to at least drop in and offer our congratulations."

Brian resurfaced with Harry in tow. I grabbed Harry's arm and jovially announced, "The Whitetowers just returned from their trip and wanted to extend their best wishes. Wasn't that nice of them?" I grinned up at him while squeezing his arm, hoping to get some kind of response, vocal or facial. Lydia expressed a whispery response.

"Ah, yes congratulations, Creighton," Stanford pompously uttered. The two men shook hands.

Harry muttered a thank you.

"So...how was your trip?" I tried to ease the apparent stiffness between the two men. "Did you find any interesting artifacts? I'm sure it must be sad to discover such beautiful ancient pieces and not be able to bring at least one small memento home."

Stanford and Lydia exchanged questioning looks. Maybe I pushed a button. I hoped so.

Regaining his arrogant posture, Stanford puffed, "It's illegal to take ancient artifacts out of Egypt. Certainly *you* should know that."

"Ah yes, of course." I knew it was against Egyptian law, but I disliked his arrogant attitude. I held my tongue, almost biting it off. Cooling a little, I stretched my lips into a smile. "Travelling the world must be an exciting change for you two."

"Change?" Stanford's tone increased an octave.

"Oh, you know," I laughed nervously, "when you spend nine months trying to motivate a bunch of college kids, it's nice to get away and do something quite the opposite."

No response. I was digging myself a hole that kept getting deeper with each comment. "I only meant that it's nice to have something you can look forward to when the school year has ended. I'd think getting away for a few months, free from dealing with student issues and grading papers, would be great." I felt like I was treading water and about to sink.

"My dear Katherine," Stanford replied, using my given name, "you mustn't be so frivolous with your comments regarding education. Saying that it can be so tedious that one would have to, as you say, 'get away,' demeans students and academia combined."

I took a step back, eyes wide.

"It's true that Lydia and I enjoy unearthing ancient artifacts. However, you must understand that we are committed nine months out of the year, seeing to it that our young scholars get a good education. Their introduction to the world of learning shouldn't be taken lightly."

I bristled at his comment.

"See here, Whitetower," Harry said. "No one's taking anything lightly. Kate was simply being friendly. If you want a discussion on the importance of a good education, I'll kindly comply. Otherwise, let's end this now." He stood nose to nose with Stanford and stared him down.

Harry's directness deflated Stanford like the last balloon at a political convention. Lydia was completely nonplussed.

*Bravo, Harry. My knight had brushed the rust off his armor to defend me.* I could've kissed him right there. Instead, I turned my attention toward Lydia. "My dear, you look exceptionally tired. Have you been ill?"

Before she could answer, Stanford stepped back into his smarmy superiority shield and harrumphed, "Lydia is still recuperating from a fever she caught while on our trip. She really needs to be home resting. Isn't that right, my dear?" He grasped her arm, and attempted to lead her away from the conversation.

Disgusted with his arrogant attitude, I shamelessly deflected his movement by reaching out for Lydia's hand. Defying him, I countered. "*She* should know better than anyone *how* she feels, Stanford. Isn't that true, Lydia?"

Her puzzled eyes shifted from her husband then to me. "Ah, yes...I've been a bit..." She stumbled over her words. "You see, I came down with a bug of sorts when we were in Tunisia, oh...I mean Egypt."

I watched her nervously peck at the sleeve of her tunic. Was that slip-up on purpose?

Lydia abruptly changed course and echoed Stanford. "Yes, Stanford's right, we should be going. I'm suddenly feeling quite tired."

I didn't buy it. Something more than the fever was affecting Lydia.

"Remember my dear, we're expecting a call from our son Chauncey later this afternoon." Stanford snapped, retaking hold of Lydia's arm.

I spoke up quickly to delay their departure. "Oh, Chauncey! We're so fond of that boy. He's been like a part of our family, ever since we became neighbors." I elbowed Harry to nod agreement. "We've heard great things about him. Is he still in New York on that audition?"

"How did you hear that?" Stanford exclaimed, pulling Lydia out of my reach.

*Damn, I'm losing them again.*

"He and Molly have been exchanging emails." I quickly switched tactics. "Won't you stay a few minutes longer? You must be hungry after that long trip. I know that the airplanes hardly serve anything other than peanuts or pretzels these days."

"Actually we fly first class," Stanford flung the comment right back at me.

That did it. I wanted to shove that man's words down his pompous throat or up his tightly pinched butt. Harry sensed I was revving up my ugly words. I was ready to fly into a fit until he wrapped his arm around my waist to keep me grounded. So I barely squeezed out, "Do tell."

Stanford finally broke the stiffening silence and cleared his throat. "Yes, well then, when Lydia's rested enough, she'll give you a detailed account of Chauncey's progress." His haughtiness returned. "Now, if you'll please excuse us, we must leave." Stanford ushered his wife out of the yard.

"Glad that's over," said Harry, mopping his brow with his well-used handkerchief.

"Thanks for helping me. I never thought that Stanford would take such offense to a little joking."

"I didn't like the way he was trying to put you down. I really wanted to smack him one. "

"Stand in line."

"I think we both need a drink." Harry signaled to a server carrying a beverage tray. He took two flutes of champagne and handed one to me. We clicked glasses.

"To us." The cool liquid slid effortlessly down my throat. "I think I'll meander about and check in on the rest of our guests. Want to come along?"

"Nah, I'll pass." Harry kissed me on the forehead, and then he drifted off to the security of his banker buddies.

Before I had a chance to move, Candace rushed up in a flurry of excitement.

"Is everything okay?" I asked.

"Just peachy." She fidgeted with her earring.

I purposely paused, knowing she had seen me talking to Lydia and Stanford. She was dying to know what transpired.

"So, what's up with the Whitetowers?" Candace finally asked.

I shook my head. "I couldn't get much information out of them, although their reactions suggested some kind of hidden agenda."

"Like what?" Candace's eyes lit up like two headlights on high beam.

"I'm not sure. Lydia started to say that she had caught a bug in Tunisia, then quickly corrected it, and said Egypt. I thought it sounded like a deliberate slip."

"Bet she contracted some rare disease while they were in the jungle."

"Desert, Candace. They were digging somewhere near the pyramids."

"Jungle, desert, whatever. It's still in Africa. Go on."

"Stanford said it was a fever, but I think it was something else, something more—"

"Sinister, maybe?"

"I don't know. It was obvious that they wanted to get away from me. I tried to engage them in light conversation which was a complete disaster. I won't go into all Stanford said, but he reacted like an arrogant, jackass."

"How rude."

"You should've seen Harry rise up in my defense."

"Well good for the old boy. What else happened?"

"Things went south when I told them I'd heard good things about their son through Molly. Guess they didn't realize he has a life outside of their realm."

"Probably not."

"At that point, Stanford pulled Lydia away from me with the excuse that she needed to get her rest, and off they went. If I wasn't so curious, I'd write them off."

"Glad you didn't," offered Candace. "Anyway, I want to know if you mentioned the limo parked in front of their house."

She took me by surprise. "How'd you know about that?"

"Lois Findley told me. She said her kids wanted to get a closer look at a really long car, but when a man yelled at Romeo, they got scared and called him away. She told the kids to take him back to you."

25

"Yes, they told me what happened. After they left, I hid behind the rhododendron and took some pictures with my cell phone."

"Really?" Candace's excitement escalated.

"I was so nervous that I'd get caught, I just kept clicking away. I'd be surprised if I got any good shots. Stanford was talking to a bald man, but I couldn't see his face. I might've gotten a good one of the other guy...probably Baldy's big bodyguard."

"Aha, just as I thought. There *is* a mystery afoot." She rubbed her hands together.

"Now, don't go sticking your nose into anything just yet," I cautioned. "I've barely scratched the surface."

"I *just* knew there were strange things going on in that house. I'm dying to see those pictures."

"You will later, but now there's something else I need you to do."

"At your service." She saluted me.

"It's Adeline."

Candace's face fell. "Oh shucks, I thought it had something to do with the Whitetowers."

"Sorry about that. However, this might turn out to be more interesting than you think."

"Okay, what is it then?" She sounded a little less perturbed.

"I literally bumped into Adeline on my way to meet Lydia and Stanford." I related the incident, then added, "Her actions were disturbing. She wasn't the usual self-confident person we're all used to seeing, especially at social functions. She begged me to stay and talk, but I kind of brushed her off. Either there's something bothering her or it was just the champagne talking."

"That *is* strange. As I recall, she's a one-drink woman." Candace replaced her earlier disappointment with renewed interest. "What do you want me to do?"

"Check on her once in a while, and make sure she has something to eat. Maybe see if you can find out what's up with her, but be careful. You don't want to—"

"Don't worry, Kate, I'm the queen of tact."

"Since when?" I scoffed as Candace scurried off to track down Adeline.

I drifted around the yard, speaking to guests and filling the air with pleasant conversation. As I approached the patio, the string quartet had finished playing, and Kenny's group was setting up.

"Hey, Mom." Kenny waved. "Hope you like the playlist. Candace scanned it and made some suggestions."

"Ooh, that scares me a little," I shuddered.

"Relax, Mom, she knows what you like, and I'm sure the guests will like it too."

"You're probably right," I sighed. "Go wow them."

No sooner had they started playing than a few couples moved onto the patio to dance. I watched their faces as they passed by me, lost in the magic of the music. Kenny winked at me. He was right, about both, the music and Candace's choices. I wondered if Harry could handle a whirl around the dance floor. *Fat chance of that happening, but maybe with a few more drinks I can persuade him.* I scanned the area. Of course, I should've known where he'd be. His banker friends had him comfortably corralled like a prized bull. No way could I snare Harry away from that group.

Gail, Harry Jr.s' wife, sidled up to me. She tossed her ash blonde head toward the banker group "See that? Like father, like son. Do those guys ever get tired of talking money and stocks and more money?" she sighed.

"Keeps them out of mischief." I laughed, bending a little to kiss her cheek. "But if I were you, I'd march over there and drag him onto the dance floor. He's too young to get so wrapped up in all that bank stuff. He needs to relax more and have a little fun now and then."

"How about you going with me?" Gail slid her arm through mine. "Surely we could get the two Harry's to commit to at least one dance."

"Bud is still young enough to be drawn away from the group. His dad? Well, I'm afraid what little whimsy he had in his earlier years has pretty much dried up." We chatted amiably for a few more minutes, then I shooed her off toward the *bulls* and the *bears* of the party. "Good luck," I shouted.

A moment later I literally ran smack dab into Adeline. Her sunglasses had slid onto her forehead. Her cheeks had that alcoholic-rosy glow.

"Aha! Just the person I was looking for," Adeline whispered close to my ear. "I must talk to you."

I took a step back; the combination of spirits and stale tobacco on her breath were overwhelming. Either she slipped away from Candace's watch, or she was slyer than I thought.

"What's on your mind, Adeline?"

"Come, we need to have a confidential chat about our retired husbands."

Taking hold of my arm with one hand and clutching a half-full glass of champagne in the other, Adeline steered me down the brick path toward the edge of the pond. She kept maneuvering the strap of her purse upward on her shoulder while making sure that no champagne spilled out of her glass.

"When did you start smoking again?" I asked.

"Not important." She brushed the question aside with a wave of her glass. "I must caution you about them."

"Them?"

"Our husbands, Kate." She took a drag from her cigarette. "Oh you know, they'll be home with you all the time…morning…noon…and night." Adeline paused to take a good swallow of champagne. She wiped her mouth with her handkerchief smearing what was left of her lipstick onto her chin.

"What are you getting at?" I tried to signal to her about the smudge, but she just gave me a lopsided smile and continued.

Adeline gave my hand a patronizing pat. Her words began to slur. "Oh, my dear, don' you see? It'll be one long, long bittersweet *honeymoon.*" She swayed a little, emphasizing the last word.

"I don't know what you mean." The phrase intrigued me, though I wasn't sure if it was meaningful, or just the booze talking. *I've never seen her like this.*

Adeline placed one hand on her hip, urging her purse strap up on her shoulder while attempting to strike an authoritative pose. She faltered a bit. I was ready to reach out, but she steadied herself.

"Our husbands were too busy being bankers. Never cared a f...fig about how well we ran the household, and without their help, the old coots." The last few words were mumbled as she rocked forward, sloshing the remains of her champagne directly at me.

"Oops! Oh, oh, I'm so sorry. Did I get any on you?" She started to wipe imaginary drops off my gown with a wadded handkerchief she'd plucked from her purse.

"No, no, I'm okay." I was relieved to see that there was no more alcohol left in the glass to pass through her lips. Unfortunately, she spied a server wandering nearby with a full beverage tray and motioned to her before I could wave the girl away. Adeline, with the rapidity of a magician, dropped her cigarette into the empty glass, grabbed a full one, and resumed talking as if nothing had happened.

"Now your Harry — bless his heart — wasn't a teensy bit interested in how *you* ran things at home, right Kate?"

I was too focused on Adeline's inebriated condition to realize she had asked a question. I needed to find Ed, and fast.

Agitated that she didn't get a quick response, Adeline pointed a finger at my chest, and repeated her last words, much louder. "RIGHT, KATE?"

"Oh, yes, yes, right." I snapped to attention.

Taking a good swallow from the fresh glass, Adeline continued, "Well, let's see now, where was I? Oh, yes after he has accli...accli..."

"Acclimated?"

Adeline hiccupped, put her hand to her mouth, and apologized. "That's the word. Thank you. Now then, after Ed—"

"You mean Harry." I helped.

"Oh, Harry, Yesh, Harry. Blessh his heart, good ol' Harry." Then she smiled at me, completely forgetting she had

29

just spoken. Her train of thought was sliding way off its track, and I couldn't help her. "Um, what was I talking about?"

"Something about Harry," I offered. *Where was Ed?*

After a brief moment, Adeline sailed back to the present and wagged her finger at me. "I'll tell you what ole Harry'll do. He'll pick on jus' about everything you do, how you do it, and THEN," she shouted, "he'll tell you how he can do it, and way much better'n you can, too." Adeline positioned herself directly in front of me. "Mark my words, my dear, he'll begin to mic...micro...micro-manage you. And you won't like it one teensy little bit." She teetered back then forward. "Good ol' Harry'll be looking over your shoulder watching every *shingle* move you make, and that will agri...agri... bug the hell out of you." At that comment, Adeline leaned forward, her body heading directly for the pond.

I quickly grabbed her arm. The force of gravity would've won out if Ed hadn't appeared and helped reel his wife onto solid ground. He put his arm around Adeline, gently removing the glass from her hand and handing it to me.

"Thanks, Ed." *Whew, that was a close one.* One more minute and she would've been floating with the fish, wearing a water lily hat.

"Come on, Addie, time to leave." Ed slowly maneuvered her toward the exit.

"Not yet, Edward," she answered, squirming free from his grasp. "You've interrupted a very important conver...conver talk with my good dear frien', Kate." She attempted a huffy voice. "And, besides, I haven't finished my drink." She spotted a glass in my hand, but not one in hers. She turned too quickly toward Ed, lost her balance, and bumped against him, nearly sending both into the water.

I kept my mouth tightly closed. I knew that it wasn't a laughing matter, but I couldn't help picturing what it would've looked like, the two drifting about among the startled Koi. I managed to regain my composure enough to help Ed steady Adeline.

"The party was great, Kate," said Ed. "Tell Harry I'll touch base with him later. Sorry about this." He nodded toward his wife.

"Is there a problem?" I whispered to Ed. "I'm worried about her."

"No, no. She'll be fine once I get her home." His tone seemed rather edgy.

"Oh, okay." I didn't press him any further. I gave Adeline a gentle hug. "Thanks for the advice."

Ed raised a questioning eyebrow. I shook my head.

"We'll talk again soon," I called out to her as they walked away.

Adeline leaned heavily on Ed's arm as he guided her toward the gate. I could hear her mumbling, "I know I had a drink, Ed. Wash happened to my drink? Did you take my drink?"

Adeline's entire conversation unsettled me. There must be something deeper bothering her. I must get in touch with her soon.

Candace caught me as I returned to the patio. "I just saw the McHenrys' leaving. What happened?"

"You're asking *me* what happened! You were supposed to keep a watch on her."

"Well, I did...I was," she answered. "She kinda fell off my radar." Candace cowered, lowering her head.

"How so?"

"Everything was going along pretty well. We chatted a bit while I helped Adeline fix a plate of food. She shooed me off to tend to other guests." Candace crossed one hand over her heart, pledging her allegiance to me. "Honestly Kate, I was only gone for maybe five minutes, and when I returned to the table, Adeline was gone, poof!" She threw her hands in the air. "I'm sorry. It just happened."

I touched her arm. "It's okay. I don't think you could've stopped her. She was on some kind of mission to drown out what was troubling her. She kept talking about retirement and it being a bittersweet honeymoon."

31

"Hmm. The Whitetowers and the McHenrys," said Candace, excitement lighting up her eyes. "Looks like we've got two cases to solve."

"Let's just stick with one for now okay," I said, curbing her enthusiasm. "By-the-way what's with this 'we' stuff?"

"You know you can't do it all alone."

"Who said?"

"Me. I did," Candace murmured. "Please, Kate, let me help. I'll do whatever you tell me to do."

"Of course you will." I laughed. "But right now, I think the caterers are looking for you."

"Sure they are," Candace smirked then followed my finger to where they were standing. "Oops, you're right. Guess they just can't make a move without me...but was that a yes to my question?"

"Go on now," I gave her a nudge. "We'll talk about it later."

Her infectious laugh trailed as she hurried away. Candace was a truly unique person. At times, her overly-enthusiastic nature caused some friction between us, and she had some crazy ideas, but once you were her friend, she was loyal to the core. I really couldn't ask for more.

# Post Party Wrap-Up

THE AFTERNOON SUN was playing hide and seek between the tall fir trees when the last of the guests showed signs of departing. Harry had mellowed into a benevolent host, thanking them and giving appropriate hugs and kisses as guests left. Several rounds of drinks had obliterated his earlier negative attitude, for which I was most grateful.

The caterers began picking up the remaining food and service items. I was thankful not to be a part of the cleanup crew. I watched Candace enlist Kenny and his friends into stacking chairs and folding tables to be picked up tomorrow.

Our children and their spouses dragged a bevy of tired grandchildren to their cars. Harry and I waved goodbye to them as they pulled out of the driveway.

"I'm sorry that Molly had to miss the party." I took hold of Harry's arm. "She would've gotten a kick out of the day, especially some of the more entertaining parts."

Harry nodded. We wandered back to the patio. I plopped down on one of the chaises and called to Candace to come join us. She gave one last look around, making sure everything was back in its original order, dashed into the house to get her purse and headed our way.

"How does that woman have so much energy left?" Harry wondered.

Candace dropped her purse on the table, eased into the empty cushioned chaise next to me, kicked off her sandals, and wiggled her toes between the cool soft blades of grass.

"So, did you enjoy your job, Madame Party Manager?" asked Harry.

"You bet. Every minute of it. But right now, my feet are killing me."

"Hell, with those sky-high heels, I shouldn't wonder." Harry handed her one of the water bottles he'd brought out from a cooler near the barbecue.

"Ah, nice." Candace took a long swig. "Thanks, I needed that. So, tell me, Oh Great Guest of Honor, did *you* have a good time at your party?"

"Yes, I did…after a fashion." Harry winked at me.

"I thought Kate did a fantastic job, didn't you?"

Before he could answer, she fired one question after another like shots from a semi-automatic. "Wasn't the food great? Wasn't Kenny fabulous on the piano? Oh wouldn't Molly have loved it?" Bombarding him with questions was Candace's way of getting him to leave so we could talk privately.

Harry raised his hands in mock surrender. "Whoa, give a guy a chance will ya?" He sighed. "And the answer to your questions, Candace, yes, all was great."

There was a long silence. We stared at him, waiting.

"Hmm…oh, I guess that's my cue to get out of your hair so you two can gossip."

"Harry, darling, we don't gossip, we discuss," Candace answered.

He rolled his eyes. "Well, if you'll both excuse me, I'm going in to take a well-deserved nap. It's been such a long *taxing* day," he sighed, dramatically. Giving Candace a hug and brushing a kiss across my lips, he retreated into the house.

"That's my man." I laughed.

"At last," Candace said. "Now, about those pictures…let's see what you've got."

"Okay." I picked the cell off the table and fiddled with it until I found the photos. We huddled together as I slowly scrolled through each one.

"Stop, roll back a couple," Candace demanded. "Here, that one." She pointed to the bald man getting into the limo. She stared at the picture for a moment, and then dismissed the thought. "Ah, it's probably nothing. I thought he looked like someone I once knew…but…" she wondered out loud. "But, if it was, he'd be way out of his territory."

"How so?"

"He never did business in the Northwest. Although…"

"What is it?"

34

Candace toyed with her long gold snake-chain necklace. "Why does your past always comes back to bite you in the ass?"

"What *are* you talking about?"

She inhaled deeply and exhaled a name, "Gino Busoni."

"Who?" My curiosity raised along with my eyebrows.

"He's someone I knew when I lived in Vegas." Candace took another gulp from the bottle. "It's a long story, Kate. No use going into it now; besides, you've got to be worn out after all this—"

"I'm not *that* tired." I interrupted, gripping her arm. "Don't think I'm going to let you go, not with that opening line. I'll chain you to the chair if I have to."

We stared at one another.

"Not until you tell me that I can help or not."

"Oh, of course you can. There never was any doubt." I smiled.

"I should've known all along," she grinned. "Okay, here it goes."

I relaxed back into the soft cushion and waited for her to begin.

"I first met Mr. Busoni at the club … where I was working."

"Aha, you were a showgirl, I knew it."

"Don't get ahead of yourself, girlfriend. There's lots of other jobs in a club besides being a chorus girl, you know," she said defiantly. "Now, hush up and listen."

I gestured by zipping my lips and signaled for her to continue.

"That's better," she said in a stern, motherly tone. "Now, I didn't know anything about him, except that he was pretty well-heeled. When I, ah, got involved with his son, Nicky, that's when I found out what his family did for a living."

I raised my hand. I couldn't help it. "What kind of business was it?"

"I'm getting to that; be patient. Geez you're worse than a kid."

"Sorry, Candace, but you've got to understand, I've known you for what, better than ten years, and I'm just now hearing this story."

"Yeah, I know. It's something I never wanted to talk about." She pulled off her headband and ran her fingers through her hair, as if she were combing out the past. "Mr. Busoni, Gino, was a collector of ancient artifacts. I hardly knew then what that word meant, except that it had to do with old stuff. I was so into Nicky, I didn't care what his dad did, so long as we could be together. That's all that really mattered to me." Candace's voice wavered. Her eyes gave away the feelings she had conjured up.

I reached out to comfort her.

She patted my hand and smiled. "I'm okay." She continued, "One day I overheard Nicky on the phone talking to his dad about an expensive painting that disappeared from a gallery in Hawaii. He told his dad that everything worked out as planned. I didn't think anything of it at the time, but then I remembered that a few days earlier, Nicky told me that he had to do some business in Maui. I asked him if he heard about the missing piece when he was over there. Nicky figured I'd heard the conversation and got real mad. He grabbed hold of my arm, and told me that if I knew what was good for me, I should quit listening in when he's on the phone."

"Was that a threat?"

"Well, I knew he had a bad temper, but that was the first time he'd aimed it at me. It got me wondering. What was really going on? So, I poked around and asked some questions. Kate, I can't believe I was so dumb. Everyone I worked with knew about the Busonis, and just figured I did, too. Guess I was blinded by love. And still, I couldn't break it off with him."

"Were they dealing in stolen goods?"

Candace nodded.

I popped up to a sitting position, nearly falling out of my chair. "I know I'm stretching this, but do you suppose the Whitetowers are smuggling ancient artifacts into this country to sell to private parties?"

36

"And dealing with Gino Busoni?" Candace asked. "It's totally possible. Oh, I just knew there was something strange about them. I'd pictured the Whitetowers as covert operatives, not dealers in illegal contraband." She rubbed her hands together. "Wow, what intrigue!"

"Hold on, let's not jump to conclusions. We don't have enough information to work with." I tried to calm the excitement building inside me. "If I could get Lydia alone without Stanford monitoring her every word, maybe I might get some kind of clue as to what they were really doing besides digging up artifacts for the Egyptian government."

"Ooh, I want to be there when you talk to her."

"I'd wait. Lydia might spook with the two of us asking questions. I think I could do better talking to her one-on-one."

"Darn. I suppose so. But will you let me know as soon as you do?"

"Sure, of course."

Candace checked her watch. "Wow, it's getting late. What a day this has been. It's high time I head for home."

"Thanks again for all your help, Candace. You did a great job keeping the guests in line and amused, among other things."

"Well," she beamed, "you know how I love to party." Candace started to leave, then paused. "Oh, I almost forgot. Sully told me he's counting on you to come to the theater first thing in the morning. You're supposed to finish the fall newsletter for the next production and get it to the printers before the end of the week."

"Crap," I muttered. "I forgot. Daniel Sullivan is so anal."

"All righty then, see you at the theater sometime tomorrow."

We gave each other air-pecks. As she started walking toward the gate, I realized Candace hadn't finished her story. "Wait a minute," I called after her, "what about this Nicky fellow?"

"Another time," she responded as she ambled out of the yard, swinging her five-inch high-heeled sandals in one hand and hauling her gigantic purse in the other.

# Romeo, Where for Art Thou?

I SETTLED BACK into the chaise and let the quiet envelop me. Juliet wandered onto the patio. Spying the perfect spot for a nap, she lay claim to my lap. "Well, little one, where were you hiding all day?"

She made several turns from one side to the other then settled in and waited expectantly for the back of her ears to be scratched, a nightly ritual Molly had started. I rubbed the cat's soft fur. She purred contentedly.

I closed my eyes and let the day's events meander through my mind. What was up with Adeline? Was there more to the story than a retired husband constantly underfoot? And, how about the Whitetowers? Eccentric, yes, but Stanford's attitude and Lydia's supposed fever upped the ante too…strange.

I must've dosed, off because the noise from the sprinklers jarred me into the present. The cat spooked, flew off my lap, and dashed to the family room sliding door.

The sun had finally dipped behind the trees, leaving the yard suspended in dusk. I managed to peel myself off the chaise and put the empty water bottles in a box by the cooler. I picked up my cell phone and walked toward an impatient Juliet who meowed loudly, waiting for my assistance. I barely pushed aside the screen before she squeezed through and darted ahead without so much as a thank you. *Cats.*

A loud snore welcomed me as I entered the room. Harry was stretched out on the sofa, his head resting on a pillow, arms folded across his chest. Setting the phone on the coffee table, I eased onto one of the cushions and, not too gently, nudged him. He woke with a start and sat up so quickly, I fell onto the carpet.

"For chrissakes, you scared the crap out of me!" He rubbed the sleep from his eyes. "What are you doing down there?" he growled.

"Looking for any stragglers from the party," I snipped. "What do you think I'm doing? You dumped me to the floor when you sat up."

"What time is it?"

"Time for you to wake up." Managing to maneuver between table and couch, I rose slowly to my feet, and turned on the lamp.

"Ooh, that's too bright." Harry covered his eyes with one arm.

"You'll get used to it." I checked to see if I had rug burn on my knee.

"Why are you being so insensitive?"

"Insensitive? If I was, I'd have tilted the lampshade and let the light shine directly into your eyes."

"Yeah, you would."

"Sorry Harry, guess I'm just tired. It's been quite a day." I yawned. "Did you happen to see Romeo before you fell asleep?"

He shook his head. "He's probably lying somewhere in a comfortable spot… uninterrupted."

"I don't think he's inside." I remarked, avoiding his snarky answer. "Bet he wandered out of the yard sometime during the party." I picked up my cell phone, and started toward the front door. "I'm going to look for him. See you later."

Normally, I wouldn't be too concerned about Romeo. He was our neighborhood's favorite animal, known to all as the Ambassador of Hayden Park Drive. But after the incident with the limo this morning, strangers may not feel the same about him. I vowed to keep a better watch.

A black Cadillac Escalade crept slowly away from the Whitetowers' curb as I stepped out onto the porch. When it was completely out of sight, I called his name, "Romeo…come!" Nothing. My stomach did a flip flop. I tried again, this time using a well-worn phrase, "Romeo, oh…wherefore art thou…you big mutt?"

A female response came from two houses down. "He's yonder in the Findley's back yard."

"Good answer," I yelled, relieved to hear the voice of Rachel Davenport, who lived on the other side of the Whitetowers. She was watering her begonias on her front porch when I approached.

"I can't help it, Kate, I love it when you quote Shakespeare to hail your dog," she laughed. "I saw his tail-wagging rear-end follow the kids into the back yard a few minutes ago. I'm pretty sure he's still there."

"Thanks, Rachel."

"Romeo's got charisma with everyone," she said. "I don't believe there's one neighbor on the block that hasn't succumbed to his doggish charms."

"I agree."

"By the way, did you see that limo parked in front of the Whitetowers, today?" Rachel asked.

"Yes, I did. I wonder what that was all about." I decided to exercise caution and not say anymore. "Maybe we'll find out eventually, but now I'd best get my wayward pet before he becomes a member of the Findley household."

"See you later, neighbor," Rachel said as she resumed her watering task.

I crossed the street to the Findley's. Their backyard lights were ablaze, and happy noises poured out from beyond the fence. I quietly opened the gate and crept around the corner of the house. What I saw took me by surprise. There in the middle of the three children sat Romeo, dressed in a black cape with a wizard's hat plopped on his head, secured by a bit of elastic under his thick, hairy neck.

I marched into the yard. "What's going on here?" I attempted a stern voice, but the sight was so hilarious, a giggle bubbled up, then another, until I collapsed onto the nearest patio chair doubled over into uncontrollable laughter. The excessive noise brought Lois Findley out of the kitchen.

"Oh my goodness, I didn't expect this!" She covered her mouth, holding back a big grin. "I do apologize, Kate. When the children told me that they were going to play Harry Potter, I never realized Romeo would have a part in it."

"And a big one, too. No need to apologize, Lois. That was the best laugh I've had all day."

She shook her head. "I never know what these kids of mine will do next. Can you stay awhile? I've got lemonade, and I think there might be a brownie or two left if my rascals haven't eaten them all."

"No thanks. I've already done enough damage to my body today." I turned to the children, "Say, I hope you guys didn't give Romeo any brownies."

"Oh no, Mrs. Creighton," said Haley. "We know chocolate isn't good for dogs. Mama gave us some doggie treats for him."

"But Lois, you don't have a dog!"

"What can I say? The kids love playing with him, and when I give them a treat, it's only fair that Romeo gets one, too."

"Now I know why he loves to come over here." I glanced at Romeo, the picture of innocence. *Is that a doggie smile on his face?* "By the way, the kids were curious about the limo parked in front of the Whitetowers. Know anything about that?" asked Lois.

"Not much. Just what they told me," I answered, pointing to the kids.

Looking up at the darkened sky, I turned to the children. "Hey guys, it's time for the Wizard to change back into just plain ole' Romeo…but, before you take the cape and hat off, I want to get a picture of you all." I shot a couple with my cell. "Great…I'll email you a copy."

"Cool," said Mac. "Hey, could Romeo come back tomorrow?"

"That might be arranged, if it's all right with your mom."

"Puleese?" They chorused, all eyes beseeching their mom.

"We'll see," Lois replied. "Now, you kids need to get ready for bed too."

"Take care, Findley family." With a wave of my hand, and the wag of Romeo's tail, we exited their yard.

When we reached the Whitetowers' house, a funny feeling came over me. I looked up at their picture window and caught sight of Jasper sprawled on the back of a chair watching us with eyes half open. This is ridiculous, I thought, rubbing the goose bumps off my arms. I'm used to his stare. *Get over it, Kate.* Romeo was more interested in sniffing along the curb where the limo had been parked. He re-marked the area. "Good going Romeo. Take that, Mr. Big Shot Limo man ... don't mess with *my* dog." I grinned the rest of the way home.

Silence greeted us at the door. The lamp in the family room was on, but the sofa was abandoned. I guessed Harry'd already gone to bed. I set my sights on doing the same, but not until I made sure that no window was left open, and all doors were locked. Romeo did a few turns on his large pillow before finding the perfect spot to curl up for the night. I prepared the coffee for the morning's breakfast, my last task for the day.

Wearily, I headed up the stairs and peeked into Molly's bedroom to see Juliet nestled atop her bed. I tiptoed into ours, grabbed my pajamas, and changed in the bathroom so as not to disturb Harry.

I had just slipped into my side of the bed when he turned over to face me. "Oh, did I wake you?"

"No, I was lying here thinking about the day. I have to admit it was a swell party."

"I'm glad you had a good time, Harry," I yawned. "Tell me again tomorrow after the alcohol has worn off."

"No, really Kate, I mean it. And I gotta say, you were the best looking gal there."

"Really? Better looking than Brandi?"

*"Much* better."

"That's nice." I cupped his face in my hand, gave him a goodnight kiss, and started to turn over when Harry slid his arm under my back and pulled me closer to him.

"Uh, Harry, don't you think it's a little late for anything other than sleep?"

"It's never too late, my dear," his voice was low and sexy.

Harry looked longingly into my eyes. The next kiss was so passionate it nearly set off a hot flash.

"Oh my, Harry," I whispered, half out of breath. "But don't you think..?" I tried to pull away.

"Oh, but I do think." He began kissing my eyes...I tried to resist...behind my ear and on my shoulder... shivers coursed down my back...the crevice of my neck...I was beginning to melt.

"Harry, I..."

"What," he whispered, unbuttoning my pajama top.

"Oh nuts." I caved.

# Monday, Monday

I AWOKE THE next morning feeling quite rested. I peeked at my slumbering husband and smiled. I hadn't realized he still had that much passion left in him…but no way would I let him know his ardent attention produced one of the most peaceful sleeps I'd had in weeks. *I'm not that dumb!* Gazing about the sun-drenched room, I stretched and then slipped silently out of bed. I started toward the bathroom, but the sound of squealing tires changed my direction. Rushing toward the balcony doors, I managed to catch sight of a taxi pulling away from my neighbors' driveway. I remembered that the Whitetowers had said something about waiting for Chauncey to call. *Could it be him home for a visit?*

Thinking of him brought back memories of years past. I remember Kenny bursting through the door one day, excited about the new neighbor who moved in next door. From the third grade through high school, they became inseparable. Chauncey spent so much time at our house, I considered him one of the family, sometimes setting an extra plate at the table whether he was there or not. He seemed to enjoy the dynamics of a house full of kids rather than the solidarity of being the only child alone in a house with parents too occupied with their lives to take much interest. So I believed.

If Chauncey is here, I could talk to him about his parents' odd behavior. I pondered that idea as I hurried downstairs to the kitchen. I kept telling Candace that patience was the key to any solution, but even my curiosity had a tough time keeping that key from turning the lock prematurely. Nevertheless, something besides the coffee was brewing at the neighbors, and I wasn't about to let it go without a taste.

The timer set on the coffee pot had worked for a change. I poured a fresh cup and moseyed outside to the patio. Harry wandered out a little while later. He plopped down on the opposite chair, mug in hand, and acknowledged my presence with a quick nod. I smiled.

45

He motioned in the direction of the rented furniture. "So, when are the people coming to pick up that stuff?" His voice was flat and slightly irritated.

"Soon." *Well, so much for last night's expression of love and appreciation. What a grump.* "Welcome to Monday, Harry."

"Yeah."

We sat in silence for a few minutes until I looked at him. "I can't help thinking about the Whitetowers, Lydia, especially."

"I sure as hell hope you're not planning to get involved with those people." Harry gave me an ominous look.

My eyes shifted away. "I just want to help, that's all."

"You know what happens when you stick your nose where it doesn't belong," he cautioned. "You always seem to get me involved somehow."

"Not all the time, Harry."

"Can you name one when you haven't?"

When I didn't answer, he surmised that he'd been correct and sat back in his chair sporting a huge grin. It wasn't worth arguing the issue.

"So, what are you up to, today?" he asked. "Nothing that includes me, I hope."

"Actually, I have to go to the theater. Sully needs me to finish the fall newsletter."

"Great! Then I'll have the day to myself."

"Have at it, kiddo." I rose, picked up my cup, planted a kiss on his forehead, and walked into the house.

***

As I sauntered down the theater aisle, a few hours later than expected, I heard, "Well, I see you've finally made it." Daniel Sullivan was pacing the stage as he looked at his watch. *Now it starts.*

"Patience, Sully, you know I always get the newsletter out in time."

"Harrumph!" His facial expression matched his grouchiness.

46

"Don't harrumph me, Daniel Sullivan." I marched upon the stage and got directly in his face. "Where else can you get such expert help for so little pay?"

"Point taken," he pulled back, averting his eyes.

I don't usually attack him, but I wanted him to know that I refused to be treated like one of his little minions.

Sully stared at his clipboard for a moment, apparently at a loss for words. Then he tossed the altercation aside and continued on as if nothing had happened. "Now then, there's no need to waste precious time. Everything you need is on your desk."

"You're so thoughtful."

"Yes, yes. Now off with you." He dismissed me with a dramatic wave of his hand.

The man could be a pain in the neck, but I had to give him credit for being a good director. He had a knack of sniffing out potential in young talent, like the Whitetowers' son, Chauncey. Sully's keen eye and directing ability, plus Candace's financial backing, kept the theater in the black.

However, when it came to anything on the business side of the organization, he was pretty much hopeless. I looked at the various sticky notes with his barely readable scrawl plastered on several pieces of paper on my desk, heaved a sigh, and began to assemble them into some order.

My concentration was interrupted by the sound of Candace's cheerful voice hailing Sully. I listened as sweetness and charm dripped from his lips, like honey sliding slowly down the side of an open jar. It was certainly not how I was greeted. But when a person was the theater's largest benefactor, a director needed to be a good schmoozer, and Sully was one of the best.

"Yes, my darling," he continued. "She's in the back working away at one thing or another. Come, let me take you to her. No, no, you won't be a bother."

I raised an eyebrow at that last remark. *Not a bother, he said.* As Sully ushered Candace into my office, he gushed, "Now, please my dear, let me get you something…coffee, tea?"

"Well, maybe some iced tea, and one or two of those wonderful cookies you get from the bakery across the street?" She batted her eyes at him.

"Coming right up."

"Thank you, Sully. You are too kind to me." She gave him a gracious smile as he backed out of the office.

"Money talks, I see. You two play beautifully off one another."

"But of course," Candace purred.

She tossed her purse on the coffee table and plunked down on the well-worn couch that had been used in many of the theater's plays. In fact most of the furnishings in my tiny office made their debut on the stage at one time or another.

"I can't get the Whitetowers off my mind. Did anything else happen after I left?" She asked.

"Not really, just another car leaving their place last night, a black Cadillac Escalade. Oh, and I saw a taxi pull away from their driveway this morning. I didn't see anyone, although it could've been Chauncey coming home."

Her eyes sparkled. "Ooh, something shady's going on...I can feel it." Candace paused while one of Sully's minions brought in a tray and set it on the table.

"That was quick." I looked over the array. "At least Sully had the decency to include me."

Candace filled two iced glasses. "*We* need to come up with a plan."

"Yes, that would be a good start." I reached for the drink she handed to me.

She picked up a cookie and nibbled on it for a moment. "I just thought of something...yum, these are so good."

"I'm afraid to ask. Toss me a cookie and let's hear it."

"If it was Chauncey this morning, why couldn't you throw him a little welcome home from New York party?" Candace took a sip of her iced tea.

"I could do what?" I glared at her. Incredulous was the first word that came to mind.

"Now, here me out, Kate, if you did, his parents would have to attend as well. So, when they're at your house, I'd just slip over to their place and poke around. See if I can find anything that looks suspicious." Candace leaned back against the sofa quite pleased with her idea. "What do you think?"

"What do I think?" I almost jumped out of my chair. "I think you're crazy!" I began ticking off reasons with my fingers. "First, you could be arrested for breaking and entering. Second, who in their right mind would want to throw another party so soon after an event like Harry's party?"

"Well ..."

"Third, you haven't the foggiest idea what suspicious would look like if it bit you on the nose."

Candace slumped deep into the cushions; her eagerness crumbled like the bits of cookie that dropped on her lap. "I guess I didn't quite have that figured out." Defeat marched across her face.

"Guess not." I tempered my voice. "Look, even if I did have a party and the Whitetowers came, don't you think they'd lock their house before leaving, especially if they had anything to hide?"

"I suppose they would," Candace mumbled.

"I really appreciate that you want to help, but I think I should try to talk to Lydia first, before you get involved. Best we take it one step at a time." I hoped that would appease her.

"All right, you win." Candace sighed. She peeked at her Rolex. "Oh goodness, I must be going. I've a nail appointment in ten minutes, and if I'm late, Arial will have a fit." She rose from the couch, grabbed her leather Hermes bag, slung it over her shoulder, picked up another cookie, and headed for the door.

I jumped up and caught her arm. "Candace, I'm sorry. I hope you understand."

"See ya later 'gator." Candace nodded waving her cookie as she walked out the door.

It was well after four o'clock when I finally closed down my computer. I'd spent more time than anticipated, no thanks to Sully's additions. I pulled my purse out of the bottom drawer and headed for the parking lot and a hot car. I rolled

49

down all the windows and drove home, enjoying the breeze through my hair clearing all thoughts of the day's events, especially Candace's crazy idea.

The mailman was leaving our box as I pulled into the driveway. I retrieved what amounted to mostly an assortment of advertisements and bills. Standing by the garbage can, I thumbed through the envelopes, tossing unwanted junk into the can and almost missed a letter that was wedged between the hearing aids and mattress flyers. It was addressed to the Whitetowers. *What luck ... I now have the perfect excuse.*

Rushing into the kitchen, I dropped everything but the letter and headed back out the door, but stopped short of going into their backyard. Stanford and Lydia were arguing. I stood behind a tall laurel hedge debating whether to interrupt. Instead, my curiosity took over and I listened.

"Where are you going now? You just got back." Lydia's voice sounded agitated.

"I told you, I need to find a better place to put it. It isn't safe to keep it here," Stanford answered.

"What if they come back while you're gone? What should I tell them?"

"Lydia, you know what to do." He sounded irritated.

"Stanford, I'm a bit worried. I'm sure some of the neighbors have seen all these strange cars coming and going in front of our house."

"So what? It's none of their damned business. Besides, there's nothing to worry about."

"I want this to be over." Her voice rose.

"Hush! Keep your voice down, Lydia. We'd better go inside before someone hears us. It's time for you to take your next pill."

"I'm so tired of taking those bloody pills. Stanford, please, you're hurting my arm."

I stood still as a statue, barely breathing, waiting until I heard their back door close. Then I quietly scurried back home. Leaning against the kitchen wall, I took a minute to slow my fast-beating heart. It was then that I noticed that my hand was clutching the letter. It would have to be ironed before I could deliver it. I placed the envelope on the table and smoothed out some of the creases. Then I examined it closely. "Oh!" I gasped. It was addressed only to Lydia. My eyes scanned to the return address, but I couldn't read it. Then I noticed the postmark, Tunisia. *Aha! I thought they were in Egypt the whole time. Candace was right. Something strange is going on. But what?*

I held the envelope up to the light to see if I could read anything inside and didn't hear Harry enter the kitchen. At the sound of his voice I jumped.

"Whatcha got there, a bill you don't want me to see?" he wisecracked.

"No, smartass, it's a letter for the Whitetowers. It got mixed in with our mail."

"Looks like it got caught in the mail sorter."

"That's my fault. I went over to return it, but stopped when I heard Stanford and Lydia in their backyard, arguing."

"What does that have to do with a crumpled letter?"

"Nothing ... exactly." My ambiguous response gave me away.

Harry leaned against the kitchen counter, arms crossed. "Oh, I suppose you stayed and eavesdropped on their conversation."

"No. Uh, yes, but I didn't mean to. I was afraid to make any noise for fear they'd hear me. I was so nervous that I didn't realize what I was doing to their mail."

"Uh huh." He nodded, but his face indicated doubt in my explanation.

"That's the truth, Harry, believe it or not." I slapped the envelope on the table and huffed past him to the sink to wash my hands. "You just might change your attitude after I tell you what they were saying."

"Okay, let's have it." Harry sighed, easing into a chair.

"Seeing the bored expression on your face, I'll just give you the condensed version: they admitted they're hiding something, and it has to do in part with the strange cars appearing at their house."

"Is that all?"

"Of course not, but if I told you the whole conversation, you'd say that I'm reading more into it. And, I'm not ... so there." I stepped over his outstretched legs to pick up the letter. Fingering it, I said, "I just have to figure out how I'm going to return it."

"How about saving yourself some embarrassment. Put the damn thing in their mailbox and forget about it."

*Always the logical one ... the man has absolutely no sense of adventure.* "No way, Harry. This is just what I was waiting for. Can't you see? It's the perfect excuse to talk to Lydia." I paced about the floor, wondering about the best way to do it. "Being that it's addressed to her, should I have her come over here, or should I do what I was going to and return the letter in person?"

"Kate, I wouldn't ..."

A knock at the kitchen door stopped him in mid-sentence.

I nearly jumped out of my skin. "Harry," I whispered, "Do you think someone heard us?"

"Hey, we've got nothing to hide. Just answer the door."

"I. Can't. Move. You...you get it."

"Oh for Pete's sake, all right." Annoyed, he headed for the door.

I set the letter on the counter, nervously toyed with the tea kettle, laid a towel over the oven handle, and picked up the letter again. I held it to my chest, shut my eyes, and prayed. My heart was beating so loud it nearly blotted out Harry's booming voice welcoming the 'door knocker.' "C'mon in, she's in the kitchen."

*Oh my God ... don't panic ...look busy ... smile ... inhale ...no exhale ...here they come.*

"Hi, Mrs. C."

"Chauncey! What a pleasant surprise." My adrenaline had hit the max.

A hot flash caught me off guard. I started to fan myself then realized I was using Lydia's letter. I quickly shoved it into my pants pocket. "Oh dear, it's been unusually warm this summer," I babbled on, unable to stop. "Would you like a glass of iced tea? Here, sit down. When did you get in?" I gestured to a chair at the kitchen table.

"This morning, and yes, iced tea sounds great." A smile crossed his lips as he slid into one of the kitchen chairs.

"How about you, Harry?" I tossed out the question at the same time, sending him a silent message to leave so I could talk to Chauncey alone without his interference.

He raised a disapproving eyebrow. "No thanks, I've got some things to finish up in the office. Nice seeing you, young man," he mumbled on his way out of the room.

"Same here," Chauncey replied.

"You look great, Chauncey." My adrenaline level began to decline while I fixed the drinks. I brought them to the table, along with lemon and sugar. "Show business must agree with you." I smiled, taking a seat across from him.

"Yeah, I really love it. But it has its moments."

"How so?"

"Well," he paused, squeezing a slice of lemon into his glass, "I love the glitz and glamor, but you can't always tell what will click with the audience."

"I suppose that's true." I took a sip of tea. "Well, I'm glad you were able to stop by."

"Hey, I wouldn't miss seeing you. You're all like my second family."

"How long will you be in town?"

"Just a few days. I need to be in Las Vegas by the end of the week." He paused, intent on wiping the condensation off his glass with his thumbs. "I have some news to tell you."

"I'm all ears."

"I've changed my name to Chad, Chad White."

"Really?" I wondered how his folks would take the change, especially Stanford. Chauncey/Chad seemed to sense what I was thinking.

"Yes, the family was a little upset over it, especially Dad, since Chauncey was his father's name, but my agent felt that Chad would be the better choice. Shortening Whitetower was really a no brainer."

53

"You're probably right. And you know, the new name suits you."

"I knew you'd understand, Mrs. C. You always listened to me. My parents never really tried. They had their idea of what I should be. I know they were disappointed in my decision, but you were the one to tell me to listen to my heart."

"I...I well..." The compliment caught me off guard. I could feel my face heat up. *No not another hot flash!* I sputtered out a thank you then quickly added, "I'm sure Sully had a lot to do with your choice as well. He was the first person to see that you had potential."

Chad agreed. "You're right. I need to thank him. He had my back when it came to convincing my folks to let me go to a performing arts school rather than regular university."

There was a long pause in our conversation. I took a moment to refresh our drinks. This small diversion gave me an opportunity to figure a way to ask Chad if he noticed anything different about his parents without being nosy. But before I had a chance to speak, a loud commotion came from the driveway. Car doors opened and banged shut. Laughter bubbled up, tossing itself through the open kitchen window.

I turned to Chad. "Now I wonder who that could be."

He smiled knowingly.

"See ya later, guys." Molly called out to a screech of tires, and then breezed in, dust flying off every inch of her body. Her curly auburn hair was pulled into a ponytail that poked through an opening in the back of a well-worn baseball cap. Her well-used backpack was slung over one shoulder.

"Hi Mom I'm ho...! Chad! What a surprise. My God, you look absolutely fabulous! When did you get here?" She dropped her bag and rushed to give him a big hug and kiss.

"Whoa, there, Molly," I laughed. "Don't you think you should brush yourself off, or at least wash up before attacking your neighbor? And how did you know he changed his name?"

"We text mom, remember?" She grinned.

Chad picked her up and twirled her around. "How's my favorite humanitarian?"

"Great. We've just finished the last house. I'm done with Habitat for the rest of the summer, what there's left of it. We built over twenty homes and one church." She wiggled out of his arms and gave me the same greeting.

"I'm glad you finally remembered me," I said.

"Ooh, iced tea." She spied the drinks on the table. "I sure could go for a cold one right now." Molly took a glass from the cabinet, added ice and poured in the cold beverage. She took a big swallow, drained the remainder into her glass, and plopped into a chair next to Chad.

"I gotta say you really do look terrific. You must be working out, right? I don't remember those muscles," Molly chuckled. "Hey, I thought you were going straight to Vegas?"

"I didn't realize you two were such good texting pals," I said. *Or is it more than that?*

"This is really just a pit stop. I'm headed back day after tomorrow." Chad looked at his watch and stood up. "Hey, I need to get going. It's been great talking with you, Mrs. C. Just like old times." He flashed a big Hollywood smile.

I started to protest his leaving so soon, but he was already at the sink rinsing out his empty glass. *—And we didn't even get a chance to talk about Lydia.* "Will we see you before you leave again?" asked Molly.

"Bet on it!" He wiped an imaginary spot off Molly's dirty cheek to kiss, gave me a hug and sailed out the door.

"He is such a fine young man, and quite handsome, I might add."

Molly nodded. "He's got killer blue eyes."

*Does my daughter have more than just neighborly interest in her neighbor?* "Honey is—?"

"Mom, I'm dirty, exhausted and have been dreaming about immersing my aching body in the tub filled to the brim with soothing oils and tons of bubbles. Where's Dad? In the office I bet. Can we talk later?" Molly grabbed her bag, popped her head in to see Harry, and then headed for the stairs before I could finish my sentence.

There went two opportunities; ferreting out information from Chad about his parents, and grilling Molly about her interest in Chad. I shoved my hands into my pockets and felt the letter. *Crap! Now I need to come up with another way of getting it to Lydia.* Molly was a different story. I would get information out of her even if I had to lock my daughter in the bathroom and skim off all the bubbles in the tub. *Not a bad idea.* "Oh, Molly…" I called out as I climbed the stairs.

# Lydia Does a Tap Dance

THE NEXT MORNING, a wonderful aroma of fresh brewed coffee teased my nostrils as I lumbered downstairs into the kitchen. I was surprised to see Molly sitting at the table reading the paper. "I thought you'd be sleeping till noon, hon." I filled a mug and sat down opposite her.

"I'm just used to getting up at the crack after working with the Habitat people for the past six weeks," Molly replied through bites of a bagel smothered with cream cheese.

"I'm not complaining." I grinned. "It's nice to look at a happy face at the breakfast table for a change."

"I heard that," Harry said as he shuffled into the room. He aimed some coffee into his cup and squeezed in beside Molly, tousling her hair. He took a swig. "Hmm, tastes great. You make it, Mol?"

"Uh huh." She gave her dad a peck on the cheek, parted with the business section for him, and passed the rest to me. Pushing away from the table, she rose. "I've got to get ready. Chad asked if I wanted to go with him to see Sully at the theater this morning."

I raised my eyebrow and glanced at Harry, but he was too engrossed in the news to pay any attention to what was said.

"Now, Mom, don't read anything into it," she laughed. "Besides, it's been ages since I've seen Sully. I always liked him, the sweet old curmudgeon."

"I'm sure he'd enjoy the visit." I turned to Harry. "How about you?" I asked loud enough to bring him out of a newsprint trance. "Do you have any plans, today?"

"Yes, as a matter of fact, I was thinking about having lunch with McHenry."

"Good." I tempered my joy in knowing he'd be out of the house for a while. "Say, maybe you can find out what's bothering Adeline."

He shook his head. "No way, Kate, obsessing over Lydia is enough. Adding her to your list of people to worry about is pure nonsense."

"What's the matter with Chad's mom?" Molly interrupted, concern crossing her face.

I gave Harry a look that would set a match on fire. "Honey, there were a couple of incidents that happened at your dad's reception. We were told that Lydia had caught some bug while on their annual archeological expedition, and Adeline … well, she had a little bit too much to drink, that's all."

"Oh, okay. I'll have to ask Chad how his mom's feeling."

"So Kate, What's on your agenda?" Harry fired back. "Are you going to take care of that leftover matter from yesterday?"

I wanted to cram his 'leftover matter' down his arrogant throat. Instead, I answered sweetly, "Of course, dear." Molly gave me a questioning look. "It's nothing sweetie." I quickly added, "Now, if everyone has their day planned, let's get a move on."

Later that morning after the two had left, I called Candace to let her know about the new development in the Whitetower saga. The mere mention of the name was enough enticement for her to hurry over. While waiting for Candace, I pulled the letter out of my shorts pocket and pressed the creases out with my hand. I was studying the return address when she appeared at the kitchen door.

"Quick, tell me what's going on before I die of curiosity," she panted.

"Or your last breath. Candace, please sit. Relax. Have a cup of coffee. By the way, how did you get here so quickly? Were you sitting in my driveway?"

She dropped her bag on one chair and slipped into another. "Nah, but I was calling you from my car. What are you doing with the iron?"

I took the crumpled letter and ran it under her nose.

Candace grabbed the envelope and stared at the address. "What? Where? How did you get it?"

58

"It was buried in my yesterday's mail. I immediately went over to their house with every intention of giving it to them. Look at the return address."

"L V, PO Box 232, Sousse, Tunisia? I thought they were in Egypt," Candace said.

I gave Candace the Cliff Note version of the Whitetowers' conversation I overheard yesterday, and why I still had the letter.

"Oh, that's why it's so scrunchie."

"Yeah, I was going to iron it out before taking it to her."

"Not until you find out who wrote it and what it says, I hope." She held the envelope up to the light.

"I thought about it, but with Harry around, I couldn't chance it."

"But, he's *not* around now, right?" The sly glint in her eyes matched the sneaky grin on her lips. "Come on, Kate, what's a little peek going to hurt?"

I was having a tug of war with my conscience. Sure, I wanted to see inside, but I felt it wasn't right. "No doubt there's some law against tampering with other people's mail."

"So, who's gonna see us?" Candace asked, spying the tea kettle. "Look, I'll do it. We'll steam it open."

She hurried to the stove, turned on the gas and waited for the mist to rise out of the spout. Slowly she ran the envelope back and forth, loosening the glue.

"Be careful. Don't get the front side too damp."

"I know what I'm doing," she huffed, "It's not like I haven't done this before."

"Many times, I suppose."

Candace nodded. She took the letter away from the kettle and carefully peeled the seal open. "Voilá!" Pleased with her success, she handed the missive to me.

I removed the letter from the moist envelope. My hands shook, partly from nerves and the rest guilt. It was like peeking into someone's bedroom. Still, curiosity overruled.

"What's it say?" Candace must've read the confused look on my face.

"I don't know."

"What do you mean, you don't know?"

"It's in French."

"Great, now what'll we do?"

"I remember a few words from high school French, but that was a long time ago."

"Well, try," she urged.

"Let's see, it starts out…'*Ma Chere*, Lydia.' That's easy." I scanned down the page trying to see if I could recognize any words. "This is interesting."

"What? What?" Candace was on the edge of her seat. "Candace, it's…it's signed, '*Avec tout mon amour*, L.' With all my love, L. It doesn't sound like a letter from some casual acquaintance."

"It's got to be a love letter," Candace sighed, clutching a hand to her heart. "And in French…how romantic."

"Romantic, sure … but, I don't see what connection this 'L' person has with those strange people showing up at their house. That, and their argument yesterday. It doesn't make sense."

"Unfortunately, we don't know exactly what it says."

"True. But, if it is a love letter, 'L' took a big chance sending it directly to her house. Unless…" I tapped my lips with my forefinger.

"Stanford doesn't know French," Candace finished my thought. "Oh wow, how I love the intrigue."

"I figured you would." I tried to slip the note back into its envelope, but the paper was too damp. I held up the two pieces to show Candace. "I don't think I'd better iron it."

"Say, why don't we go out to the patio and let the letter sun-dry a little while we think about what we should do." Candace studied her reflection in the chrome toaster sitting on the counter. "It's kinda moist in here from all that steam, even my hair is beginning to frizz."

I wasn't quite sure if that was the right drying method, but it was worth a try. "Oh, all right. Here, take the letter while I get us a couple of bottles of water from the fridge."

Once outside, Candace set the envelope and note on the table, securing them with her sunglass case. We settled into

60

our chairs, enjoying the light breeze tempering the heat from the August sun.

I was about to speak when I heard the creek of the backyard gate opening. I turned. "Holy crap." I poked Candace. We exchanged guilty looks like two kids caught in the act of snatching a couple of cookies. I whispered, "Here she comes. Quick, hide the letter."

Candace grabbed it off the table and shoved it under her seat cushion.

"Lydia, what a nice surprise," I jumped up to greet her. "Here, let me pull up a chair. How are you feeling? Would you like something to drink?" My words were tripping over each other.

"Oh, I'm sorry. I didn't know you had company." Lydia started to retrace her steps.

"Nonsense, it's only Candace." I smiled, turning to my accomplice, who threw me a dirty look.

"Lydia, do join us." Candace oozed with charm. "You and Stanford ran out so fast at the reception, I didn't get a chance to talk with you about your trip. Where was it now, Tu…Egypt?"

"Please stay," I butted in, hoping Lydia didn't hear Candace's non-accidental slip-of-tongue. "We'd love to hear about your trip."

Lydia sat stick-straight on the chair instead of easing her back onto the soft cushion. She fidgeted with a strand of hair that had escaped from the tightly wound braid hanging down her back. Her eyes darted toward the gate as if someone had been watching her movements.

The outline of her bony shoulders pressed against the soft material of her beige shirt. I couldn't decide if it was weariness or fear that played heavily upon her face. I opened the conversation.

"I hate to say this, Lydia, but you still look pale. That must've been some nasty bug you caught in Egypt."

"It wasn't in Egypt." She drew a deep breath, and then added, "Stanford thinks that's where it started, but I'm not certain." She rubbed her forehead. "These pills I've been

61

taking have gotten me so confused. Sometimes I don't know what's real or what isn't." She paused, gazing about the yard as if a bush or a single flower would help clear her mind.

"That's okay, Lydia. It doesn't matter where, only that you are on the road to—"

"No," she interrupted, "I remember now, it was in Tunisia … I'm sure of it."

Water spewed out of Candace's mouth, spraying down the front of her yellow print sundress. She coughed into her handkerchief, and then regained her composure. "I'm so sorry. Guess you just can't take a drink from a bottle and breathe at the same time."

Hoping that Candace's little scene wouldn't cause Lydia to lose her momentum, I urged her to continue talking. "I don't mean to be personal, and surely you don't have to tell us if you don't want to, but it seems there's more troubling you than this illness. Perhaps talking about it might help."

Lydia finally leaned against the cushion, placing her elbows on the arms of the chair. She closed her eyes, joined her hands together in prayer mode, and touched her lips to the tips of her fingers.

If there was any air left in the yard to breathe, Candace and I had inhaled it all, waiting for Lydia to either open up or tell us to butt out of her life. I was about ready to let her off the hook with an apology for interfering when she raised her head and began to speak.

"You're right, Kate. I am troubled … by many things. This expedition wasn't as beneficial as in years past. Maybe the excitement has worn thin."

"That seems kind of surprising. I'd think any find would keep you going back," said Candace. "I'd be giddy even if I found the sole of a child's sandal."

"Well, you'd think so," she admitted, "but I was ready for a change. Unfortunately, Stanford wasn't. Hamadi, our old friend, suggested we take a few days to relax before returning to the States. He even booked us into the Tunis Royal Thalassa Monastir Hotel in Tunisia."

"Now that's my kind of friend," Candace exclaimed, her eyes dancing with anticipation. "How exciting … laying by the pool, the sea air blowing away the dry desert sand from your bodies …"

"Candace, please!" I resisted the urge to tape her mouth shut with whatever was available.

Candace realized she was treading on thin ice, so she dialed back her dreamy tangent, returned to the present and concentrated on Lydia. "How dreadful to be ill in such a gorgeous place. What happened?"

"The first morning, I awoke with a fierce headache. Stanford paced about the room, a little annoyed that I was not up to par. He was anxious to visit one of the islands that Hamadi suggested, so he decided to go down to the front desk and inquire about tours, hoping that by the time he returned I would feel better."

"But, you didn't."

"No. As it was, Stanford went alone. Well, actually he went with Leo, a friend of Hamadi's, who just happened to be staying at the same hotel."

"What did you do while they were gone?" asked Candace.

Lydia played with a button on her shirt. "I thought an aspirin and some fresh air would help. I went down to the front desk and asked where I could get something for my headache. The concierge directed me to the combination gift shop and pharmacy. The hotel's resident doctor's office was next door. By the time I got to the store, I became dizzy and had to brace myself against the window to keep from falling. A man coming out of the pharmacy saw me stumble and caught me. I was inches from hitting the marble floor."

"Oh my," I said, "lucky for you he was there."

"Yes, it certainly was, and what's more, he happened to be the hotel doctor." Lydia explained. "I told him I was in search for some aspirin to ease the pain in my head. He helped me into his office and led me to an empty chair. His voice was soft and soothing. His dark brown eyes were warm and friendly. I immediately felt at ease. He spoke with a French accent." A small smile escaped her lips. *Ours too.*

That was the first time since her return that I'd seen something other than pained expressions on her face. This got my wheels turning.

"I told Dr. Dubois that my husband and I had arrived the day before from an archeological expedition in Egypt."

The initials on the letter were LV, so it couldn't possibly be from the doctor … unless. I stole a glance at Candace. She nodded, and raised an eyebrow.

"I explained that we'd taken several trips abroad and always made sure we were up-to-date with our immunizations," continued Lydia, unaware of the surprised looks on our faces. "I'd been far more tired than usual, but didn't think anything of it until that morning when I woke up with a painful headache. Dr. Dubois' kind face turned serious. He immediately insisted on checking me over. He took blood and urine samples. 'One can't be too careful when traveling to a different country,' he said."

"That's right," Candace agreed, fluttering her fingers in the air as one simpatico with another seasoned traveler. "I remember quite well, one time vacationing on the Riviera with my third husband, Winston, when with no warning, I came down with a dreadful case of…oh, ow!," she ended quickly, looking down at my hand tightly gripping her arm, then at me. She got the message.

"Please go on, Lydia," I urged, gently releasing the pressure on Candace.

"Dr. Dubois called in a prescription to the pharmacy, and then another to the front desk to have an attendant escort me to my room. He said he'd ring up later with the results, but I was to call him immediately if anything changed." She heaved a sigh, seeming to recapture the event. "You know, if it wasn't for LeVon's, quick action, I might have had a concussion, or worse!"

Candace and I stared wide-eyed at each other. She mouthed the letters LV. I pursed my lips and shook my head slightly, warning her to silence.

*Was the plot beginning to thicken … or boil over?*

Lydia swallowed and wet her lips with her tongue. "I wonder, could I have some water?" She asked. "My mouth gets so dry from taking those pills."

"Certainly, Lydia. Here take my bottle," I offered it to her. "I haven't opened it yet."

Lydia thanked me and took several swallows. She pulled a tissue from her pants' pocket and patted her lips. Her eyes roamed about the yard, finally resting on the gate. *Could she be getting ready to leave?* I had to keep her talking. "I presume the pills you're taking are the ones that the doctor prescribed."

"I think so. I'd been asleep most of that day, and when Stanford returned from his trip, I could barely raise my head above the pillows to tell him about seeing the doctor. He checked the pill bottle and immediately called Dr. Dubois. From that point on, I was in and out of consciousness for the next two days. I learned later that I did have a life-threatening infection, but luckily Dr. Dubois had caught it in its early stages." She took another sip of water, wiped the rim with a dry part of her tissue, and set the bottle on the table.

"So, I guess you didn't get the real rest that Hamadi suggested." I needed to keep Lydia on track.

"Well, that's true for me, but Stanford hadn't come to relax. So I found out later. Since Dr. Dubois was only a phone call away, he figured I'd be taken care of while he and Hamadi's friend, Leo, spent a day or two touring several of the islands. I was perfectly fine recuperating alone without him hovering over me." She waved aside a fly buzzing about her hair.

"I'm the same way." Candace, once again entwining her experiences with Lydia's. "Just leave me alone and I'll be fine."

"Oh really?" I raised one eyebrow. "You run your maid Anita ragged at the slightest sneeze."

"I do no such thing." She folded her arms across her chest and scrunched up her nose at me.

I ignored her and focused my attention back to Lydia. I noticed a smile brighten her face when she spoke about having the place to herself while Stanford was occupied elsewhere. I wondered if it was a special moment she secretly relived. Perhaps I could nudge it out somehow.

"Well, I guess if you had to get sick, you were certainly in a beautiful setting. Did Stanford and ah, Leo, have any interesting stories to tell you about the places they visited when they returned?"

"Oh, more than that." Her voice became animated. "On the day I was finally well enough to get out of bed, Stanford and Leo rushed into the hotel room, talking excitedly about an ancient artifact they acquired from one of the merchants on the island of Della Rosa. They weren't quite sure how old, but by the looks of it, Stanford guessed it to be about 15th century, no doubt belonging to royalty."

I stole a peek at Candace. *Now we're getting somewhere.*

"Stanford explained that a cousin of this merchant had found it in a cave near an old rundown farm. It had been wrapped in burlap and buried in a shallow hole."

"I can't stand it," Candace cried out. "What was it? What did it look like? How old? How big?" She fired off one query after another.

I had to calm her down before she pummeled Lydia with her battery of question marks. "I'm sorry, she gets carried away," I apologized to Lydia while aiming a keep-your-mouth-shut look at Candace, who responded by pressing her lips tightly together.

"That's all right, Kate." She smiled at Candace. "I was full of questions too before Stanford removed the burlap to behold a beautiful ornate gold chalice with a dome-shaped lid."

"I just knew it." Candace grasped the arms of her chair.

As Lydia began to describe it in detail, her eyes held a faraway look and her voice softened to almost a whisper. "Rows of diamonds, rubies, and emeralds lined the rim. Gold ropes hemmed the gems then wound around the stem and circled the base. There was a gold finial on top of the cover."

"I. Am. In. Awe." Candace flopped back on the cushion.

"I felt the same way. I was so completely captivated. It almost sent me into a relapse."

"Oh, I can just imagine," she gasped.

While Candace was busy salivating over the description of the artifact with Lydia, some things that she said didn't sit quite right with me. I was concerned about the word 'acquired' that Lydia had used when talking about Stanford's find. It had an illegal ring to it. Then there was Hamadi's friend, Leo. I wondered how he conveniently happened to be at the same hotel and available to take Lydia's place while she was laid up. Also, this Dr. Dubois. What was the real connection between this man and Lydia? I noticed her voice had changed from yesterday's confrontation with Stanford on the patio. There, she had taken a more confident stand with him. Today, she seemed sedate. But the big question that constantly nagged me was, what were they intending to do with the chalice, and why were strange men in strange cars showing up at their house?

I interrupted the love-fest over gold, gems, and whatnot. "Lydia, you said the cup might've belonged to royalty. Did you find any markings?"

Just as she was about to answer, the sound of Molly's voice pierced the air, preceding her as she rushed out the family room sliding door and onto the patio.

"Hey, Mom, there you are. Oh, I didn't know you had company. Hi, Mrs. Whitetower, how are you feeling, today? Chad told me that you'd been ill."

"I'm doing a little better. Thank you for asking, Molly dear." She clasped Molly's outstretched hand.

"Mrs. Whitetower was just telling us about her latest trip." I hoped that Molly's entrance hadn't brought an end to our conversation.

"Ahem," Candace, tugged at Molly's pant leg. "Don't I even get a hello?"

"Sorry, 'Aunty' Candace." She bent down to give her a big hug. "You know I'd never ignore you."

"Of course you wouldn't," Candace huffed, pretending offense to Molly's snub while giving me a little wink.

"You know I wouldn't." Molly laughed. "Mom, I just wanted to let you know that I won't be home for dinner. Chad and I are meeting a few old friends for happy hour at Bailey's before he leaves for Los Angeles tomorrow."

"Tomorrow? Oh my, I thought Chauncey was staying until the end of the week." The announcement flustered Lydia, who reverted to his old name.

"He was, but his agent called while we were visiting Sully. He has an audition set for two o'clock tomorrow afternoon, so he'll be taking an early morning flight. It's a pilot for a musical sit-com. He's really excited about it. I think I'm more excited."

"But ... but? I've hardly had any time to spend with him." Overwhelmed by the news, Lydia rose from her chair, nearly knocking it over. "Oh dear, I must leave right now. Forgive me for running off, but I'm sure you understand, Kate."

Reluctantly, I stood and laid my hand on her arm. "Of course, Lydia, I do ... family first." I smiled. "We've enjoyed hearing about your trip. It sounds so intriguing. I hope we can get together soon. We're anxious to hear the rest. Right, Candace?"

"Yes." Candace jumped in, almost pleading. "How about tomorrow?"

Lydia let the question hang in the air. "Thank you both for listening. It was nice seeing you too, Molly." Lydia walked briskly to the gate, opened it, and vanished quickly out of sight.

"Oh, oh, I feel like I've interrupted some serious conversation." Molly took the chair Lydia had just occupied.

"Yes you did, and we were just getting to the good part." Candace pouted slightly.

"I'd really like to hear about it, unless you don't want me to know what it is."

"Maybe later, honey," I put in.

Molly popped up off the chair. "Okay then. Uh, Candace, there's some paper or something that fell out of your seat cushion. I'll get—"

"Oops, never mind," Candace grabbed the letter and folded it in her hands.

"Oh, Aunty Candace, was that a letter from one of your many admirers?" Molly asked coyly.

"Never you mind, missy; now run along. Get ready for your date and leave us to our business."

"It's not a date. Besides I have plenty of time."

I shook my head slightly, giving her the not-now-later look.

"Okay, okay, I can take a hint. See y'all later." She waved her hand behind her head as she walked toward the family room door.

When I was sure that Molly was out of earshot, I wiped my damp forehead with a limp tissue I drug out of my pocket. "That was close."

"Well, hopefully Molly thought her guess was right. Besides, that wasn't too far-fetched. I have had an admirer or two send me a letter from time to time." She brushed the envelope across her lips.

I flashed a side-eyed glance at her. "Unfortunately, Lydia left us with many unanswered questions. I thought we were on the brink of finding out what was really troubling her."

"Gee, I wished we'd gotten more information."

"You know, if you'd kept quiet and not interrupted Lydia's story-telling to compare notes with your trips, maybe we would've made better headway."

"Why is it always my fault?"

When I didn't answer, she busied herself by screwing the cap on her bottle of water. "Well, not always," she offered, not quite ready to accept total responsibility.

We were silent for a while. I pondered this whole letter thing. Why were we so bent on finding out who sent the letter and what was in it? Was it merely curiosity or did it have something to do with the mystery that surrounded the Whitetowers?

Candace broke into my reverie. "So, this letter is from the nice French doctor." She fanned herself with Lydia's envelope, then waved it at me.

"We don't know that for sure. It could be from that Leo person, even though we don't know his last name." I chewed on my lower lip, thinking about something we should've done yesterday. "You know what? We should get the letter translated."

"How?"

"There are ways, my friend. Let's go into the office and fire up the computer."

"Could we get a little something stronger than water to drink, first? It must be after five o'clock somewhere in the world." Candace gave the choking sound of a person wandering in a desert, looking for an oasis, or a camel with a bota bag hooked on its hump.

"Good idea. I'll make us a couple of Margaritas."

"Now you're talking."

Back in the kitchen, I pulled out the premix, dumped some into the blender, added crushed ice, then the tequila, gave it a couple of whirrs, and poured the contents into two glasses.

I waited for Candace to hoist her huge purse over one shoulder. "Don't look at me like that. You know I can't go anywhere without my bag; my life's in there."

"Along with some others," I quipped. "Here take your drink." I grabbed a bag of chips and we were off to Harry's office.

"Ah, the sanctuary. I'm surprised Harry lets you in here without his presence."

"As long as we're very careful, he won't know we've graced his area."

"How come you don't have a place of your own?"

"I'm waiting for Molly to move out, and then I'll convert her room into my very own office-retreat-whatever. But enough of that ... let's have the letter."

I took the crumpled paper from Candace and flattened it out on Harry's scanner. Some of the words were blurred, but I ran it through anyway and saved it. *So far, so good.* I opened it and tried to highlight the writing. "Oh crap, this won't work."

"Why not?"

"For one thing, this letter was written with a fountain pen. I'm not sure the translator would be able to read it." I slumped in the chair, defeated. "It would take too long to translate it word for word by hand. What we really need is someone who knows French."

I stared at a spider slowly crawling across the top of the monitor. "I'm thinking maybe it's not worth the trouble, what do you say?"

"Well..." Candace mumbled something.

I looked over my shoulder and found her head nearly buried inside her purse. "Got a Frenchman somewhere in there?"

She popped her head up. "Ha, ha, very funny. I was looking for my cell phone to call my hair dresser."

My temper flared. "This isn't the time to make a hair appointment, Candace."

"Of course not, silly. If my Antoine can't translate the letter, maybe one of his relatives could." She flashed a self-satisfied smile.

"Smugness doesn't become you."

Candace blew me off with a flit of her fingers and made the call, but it went to Antoine's cell. She left a fairly detailed message. "Now be patient, Kate, it may be a while ... possibly not until this evening. The man is *terribly* busy. After all, he is *the* best in these parts."

"Yes, I'm sure he is. If you say so." I glanced at the clock on the wall. "Look, Harry'll be home soon," I said, slipping the letter into its envelope and sliding it under a stack on my desk, ready to go out into the mail.

"Don't you think that Harry might see it?" Candace frowned.

"Nah, he never pays any attention to my stuff. My business doesn't matter to him."

We tidied up the office, brushing some of the chip residue into the wastebasket and retreated to the kitchen. I refreshed our drinks while Candace slid into a chair still holding the bag. "Got any dip?"

We spent the rest of the afternoon hashing over Lydia's story when Harry strolled in. He brushed my cheek with a kiss and acknowledged Candace's presence with a friendly nod.

71

"You know, being retired has some really good advantages." He leaned against the door frame, hands in his pockets. An easy-going smile creased his lips.

"Like having a four hour, two-Martini lunch?" I eyed him suspiciously.

"Yes, we had a couple of drinks but we didn't spend the whole time at the restaurant. Ed wanted to look at the new Tesla. That's quite a car." Pointing to the Margarita glasses he retorted, "Might this be the stove calling the kettle black?"

*I'll give him that.* "Touché."

He eased into a chair across from Candace. Since he seemed to be in a mellow mood, I jumped at the chance to quiz him about his conversation with Ed regarding Adeline's strange actions at the reception. "So tell us about your lunch date."

"Yeah, what's going on with those two?" Candace nonchalantly tossed the question out while fiddling with a deck of cards at the far end of the table.

"Ladies, please, our time is better spent discussing important things. We talked about business, sports, the country, things of that sort, not gossiping." He winked at me.

"You can't fool me, Harry Creighton. You know something." I punched him lightly on the arm.

"Oh, all right." He plopped down next to Candace. "Actually, I didn't have to bring the subject up. Ed apologized for Adeline's behavior. He said that he was just as surprised as we were."

"And?"

"Details, Harry," Candace urged.

"Well, I asked him how Adeline was doing now, and he mentioned something about her being stressed or depressed." He scratched his head. "Can't remember which it was, though."

"That's it? Didn't you ask the why question?" I should've known Harry wouldn't push any farther into a discussion he thought might be too personal.

"Ooh, never send a man to sniff out good gossip from another man." Candace casually shuffled the cards.

"At least I did ask," he countered.

"We'll give you that." Candace and I exchanged little smirks.

"Good…I'm off the hook then?" When no one answered, Harry started quizzing us about our day. "So, what kind of mischief did you two get into?"

"None!" we chorused.

"I'll believe that when I see the Blazers win another NBA championship," he hooted.

"Have a Margarita, Harry," I offered.

Candace threw a chip at him. "How about a game of poker?"

***

The next day around mid-morning, Harry and I staggered into the kitchen, slumped into chairs, and stared into two cups of steaming coffee. A bottle of aspirin and a pitcher of ice water replaced the table's usual centerpiece.

"Good morning, family," Molly's cheerful voice greeted us.

The sound thumped through my ears like a set of bongo drums.

"It's a damn crime to be so happy in the morning," Harry moaned.

"Come on you two, what happened to those happy carefree people I saw last night?"

"That was a mirage," I managed to answer.

"It's a good thing Chad and I came just in time to drive Candace home."

"Uh huh." I offered a shaky thumbs up with the hand that wasn't holding my head.

"Was there some kind of celebration going on that I didn't know about?"

"Nothing special. When your dad got home, Candace suggested we play cards, had a few Margaritas, Later, I threw together a plate of nacho stuff, and…" My stomach lurched at the thought of food, and those damn drums beating louder against my forehead. "Sorry, no more dialogue. Just let me die in the quietness."

73

Harry lifted his head and glared at me with one red eye. "You cheated at poker."

"I did not, it was Candace's fault. She kept dealing the cards the wrong way."

At the mention of her name, I heard a scratching at the screen door, and a deep gravelly voice crackled, "Let me in, I think I left my head in there."

Molly unlatched the screen. Candace slowly stepped into the kitchen, dragging her large purse on the floor. Gigantic sunglasses covered most of her face.

I managed to squint at her. "You look like a poster for Ray Bans."

She ignored my comment and maneuvered her body into a chair.

"Here, have an aspirin." Harry shoved the bottle at her.

Molly poured Candace a cup of coffee and set it in front of her along with a glass of water.

"Thanks for taking me home, Molly ... it was you, wasn't it?"

Molly nodded.

"Does anyone remember what happened last night?" asked Candace.

Groans, moans, and then silence.

"Well, I can't tell you what went on earlier in the day, but I certainly know what I saw when we came in last night," said Molly. A grin creased her lips.

I looked at her, not wanting to, but needing to hear what she had to say. Then I could measure the amount of embarrassment we'd all have to endure.

"OK, What about us?" Harry's tone was a bit cautious.

"You two were pretty tame, although you were arguing over who won playing Texas Hold'em by trying to count the pretzel sticks and lost count when Mom kept snagging one of yours to eat."

*Well, that wasn't too bad.* Then I remembered that Chad witnessed it all. I just hoped Candace or I hadn't mention Lydia's visit yesterday.

Molly laughed. "That's not all. Candace was trying to make plane reservations to France on the TV remote."

"No wonder no one answered when I punched in the numbers," she remarked.

Molly eyed each of us. "I bet you guys didn't have anything to eat besides snacks. No wonder you all were so bent out of shape." Her voice was in mother-lecture-mode.

"Guess you're right." Ooh, the mention of food again sent my stomach into gymnastic somersaults.

Molly tried hard, but looking at our pasty gray faces sent her into spasms of laughter. "Guess I've done enough lecturing."

More moans issued from her hungover audience.

"Okay then, with that that said, I've got to get ready to meet some friends at the Mall. Anything you want me to do while I'm out?"

"No…wait, yes," said Harry, perking up a bit. "If you're going by the post office, I've got a couple of things on my desk that need to be mailed."

"No problem. Dad. Mom? Candace? Anything?"

"I could use a new head," Candace muttered; her sunglasses still plastered to her face.

"Sorry, don't know of any place that sells those. You'll have to be content with the one you've got."

We were still attached to our chairs when Molly returned a half-hour later. She was carrying Harry's envelopes and my mail. I couldn't see Candace's eyes, but the tiny gasp erupting from her mouth matched the panic rising in my stomach.

"M…my letters?" I stammered. The quiver in my voice caused Harry to raise both brows over his bloodshot eyes.

"Sure, I figured that since I was going to the post office, why not mail yours as well." She shot me a strange look. "I hope that's okay."

"Huh? Oh, that's so sweet of you, Molly, but they're not finished. I'll take care of them later" I rose a bit wobbly and took them out of her hand. "Now you go on and have a good time with your friends." I gave her a little peck on the cheek and waved her on her way.

I slowly weaved my way toward the counter. "Anyone for more coffee?"

"Ah, not yet, Kate, I need to get rid of what I've already consumed." Candace slipped out of her chair. She flipped her sunglasses on top of her head then suddenly slammed her hand over her eyes and squinted at the light through her fingers. "Man, that's bright." She stumbled down the hall to the bathroom.

I busied about clearing the table, picked up the letters and setting them on the far end of the counter. I flipped through them but didn't see Lydia's letter. "Would you like a piece of toast or a bagel, Harry?"

He was slumped over his coffee. "Is it my imagination or were you really acting kind of weird when Molly brought your letters to mail along with mine?"

"Um…" I frantically wiped the counter while searching for a good answer and silently praying for Candace to hurry in and back me up.

"I'm waiting."

"I'm thinking."

"The longer you stall, the more I can tell that you and your side-kick are up to something."

"Now why would you think that?" I rubbed the front of the toaster so hard I could see my reflection clearly in it. Furrows of guilt rolled across my forehead. *That was a mistake.*

"That's not hard to figure out, my dear. When you two get together, there's always something afoot and afoul."

Before I could answer, Candace strode into the kitchen, a little livelier and loudly humming the French National Anthem. She cocked her head slightly upward toward Harry's office. I saw the look on Harry's face, and playing along with his confusion, I shrugged my shoulders to let him know I couldn't always explain her actions.

Moving behind Harry, Candace thumped the back of his head before plopping down next to him. "I heard you telling Kate that we were up to something." She poked him with the stem of her sunglasses. "Honestly, Harry, your accusations are going to give me a guilty complex."

"As if anyone ever could," he muttered into his cup.

"We always have everyone's best interest at heart."

"And, you expect me to buy that?"

"Well, yes, it sounded good to me." Candace shot me a wink.

Harry ran his fingers through his hair. "I can't win with you two." He stood up and shoved his chair against the table, rocking the aspirin bottle. "I'll get a bite to eat after I shower."

The minute Harry left the kitchen, I huddled with Candace. "Did something happen on your way to the bathroom?"

"Yup." Grinning like a kid with a face smeared with chocolate, she continued, "Just on a whim, I peeked into Harry's office. Lydia's letter was still on your desk, partly under your desk calendar. " She pulled the mangled envelope out of her purse and placed it on the table. "Am I good or what?"

"Whew! Glad you found it," I said, fanning myself with a napkin. "As soon as we hear from your hairdresser we can proceed with Plan A and get it translated."

Candace's face suddenly changed from hero to fallen soldier. I turned and followed her look. Harry was standing in the doorway.

*Oh crap, busted again.* "Uh, Harry, I thought you were going to take a shower."

"That's where I was headed, until I found out that we were out of soap," he frowned at me.

Candace tried to put her purse on top of the letter before Harry passed her, but she wasn't quick enough.

"What's this still doing here?" He pointed to the creased envelope. "I thought you were going to put it in their mailbox. Wanna tell me why it's still here in our house?"

"I was going to, but I didn't get a chance. Besides, we think that Lydia's in some kind of trouble."

"That's funny. What makes you think that she is? Did she tell you she was?"

"Well, not in so many words, but when she was here yesterday, she—"

"She was here?" Harry's face reddened.

"Let me explain." Candace jumped in.

*Nooo Candace!* I silently screamed.

"You see, we got the envelope too damp after steaming it open, so decided to take the letter outside to dry in the sun. That's when Lydia suddenly appeared at the gate."

"I can't believe I'm hearing this," he said. "You realize there is a law against tampering with other people's mail."

"She wanted to talk about their trip, her illness, and some ancient artifact." I picked up Candace's account as fast as I could to temper his pending fury.

"But you didn't give her the letter," Harry scolded.

"Don't you see, we couldn't show it to her in the shape it was in … especially after Candace sat on it." I hoped he'd understand our reasoning. By the sour expression on his face, Harry wasn't buying any of it.

"You ladies just won't quit meddling. You're digging yourselves into a hole. And when you can't get out, you'll be looking to me for help." He lectured us like we were two kids caught smoking in back of the school gym. "Well, I'm putting an end to all of this nonsense." He marched to the door.

"Where are you going with the letter?" Thoughts raced through my mind, none of them good.

"I'm going to do what you should've done yesterday. I'm going out to their mailbox."

"Not with that towel wrapped around your waist!" I gasped.

"No, I'll get an old rain coat" Harry disappeared into the utility room. We watched him scurry out to the curb, put the letter into the Whitetowers' mailbox, and return.

"Mission accomplished. See how easy that was?" He huffed. "Now about that soap."

I pulled a bar from the pantry and chucked it at him. "Here, enjoy your shower."

"Indeed, I will." He sauntered off, head held high, out of the kitchen and down the hall.

"That went well," sighed Candace.

"Never mind him. While he's in the shower, would you run out and get it."

"Me?"

"Yeah, you're the one who's all dressed."

"Oh all right, I'll g..." Candace's cell phone buzzed. She dug into her purse.

"Hurry! Answer it." I urged. "Maybe it's Plan A on the phone."

With a nod, Candace confirmed it was her hairdresser, Antoine. While they were in animated conversation, I grabbed a jacket off the hook in the mudroom and snuck out the front door to Lydia's mailbox to swipe the letter back.

No sooner had my feet hit the sidewalk when the dreaded big black limo snaked slowly past my house, circled, and pulled up curbside in front of the Whitetowers. I did an about face, turning so fast one slipper stayed rooted to the ground. I couldn't chance stopping to pick it up, so I made like Cinderella and kind of half-skipped, half-hopped back home, slumped into a chair, and reached for my glass of water.

When Candace finished her call, I explained, between gasps what happened. "Unfortunately, I didn't get anywhere near the mailbox. But—" I noticed the gloomy look on Candace's face. "What's the matter? Can't Antoine translate the letter?"

"Uh, uh." Her voice quavered. "It seems that *my* Antoine is not really French at all ... and, and that's not the half of it, Kate. It isn't even his real name. Ah me, what a disaster!" She threw herself onto one of the kitchen chairs and laid her head on the table.

I almost choked on the little bit of water I had left in my glass. "Huh? What do you mean, not his real name?"

She raised her head and leaned it on one arm. "It's ... Marvin Yancoski, from Jersey City," she mumbled. "Oh Kate, you can't imagine how humiliated I am. After all the raving

I've done to everyone about my wonderful French hairdresser, he turned out to be a ...a ..."

"Fraud." Crossing my arms on the table, I rested my chin on my hands and muttered, "Embarrassing things happen to all of us at one time or another. You don't have to tell anyone. You'll get over it."

"I don't know if I can," she whimpered, taking a handkerchief from her bag. She dabbed carefully at her eyes to avoid smearing her mascara.

It never ceased to amaze me how she could be so hung over and still have the ability to apply full face makeup before leaving the house.

"That's enough, Candace. What say we chalk it up to another blind alley?" I sat up and leaned against the back of the chair. "I hate to admit it but, maybe Harry was right. We should forget about the letter."

Even though I said it out loud, I wasn't quite ready to let it go. I shook out of the jacket and placed it back in the mudroom before Harry noticed. I flipped off the remaining slipper and paced about the kitchen, barefooted, my sweaty feet making sucking noises.

"Wait a minute, Kate. Let's not give up yet." Candace suddenly pulled herself from the pit of her despair. "I've got another idea."

"Go on." I hoped I wouldn't regret hearing it.

"Let's say we get the letter, take it to Lydia, apologize, and explain why it was so messed up."

"Are you serious? Admit that we've had her letter for two days? "

"No, silly, we won't tell her that part, just the bit about finding it mangled and mixed in with your mail."

"Then what?"

"If it was from her *lover*," she emphasized by putting her fingers in quotes, "she might be happy we intercepted it before Stanford saw it."

"That's a possibility, but do you have any suggestions on how to get it out of the mailbox? The limo driver probably saw me. I'd be foolish to try it again. And worst of all, what if Harry catches one of us in the act?"

Candace scratched the back of her neck, thought a moment, and then popped up from the table. "No problem...I've got the answer. Get me a used envelope, ad, anything. I'll take it to their mailbox and pretend to put it in, but make the switch. Then I'll take Lydia's letter home and wait for you to call and give the all clear."

"But what if the driver sees you?"

"I don't think my actions would make him suspicious. The driver is supposed to stay by the car, and I'd be long gone before he could say anything to his boss. I do know a thing about chauffeurs," she said, displaying great confidence. "I've had one a time or two in my time."

I raised an eyebrow.

"Er, ah, no, it's not what you think."

"I didn't say anything." I pled innocence, although, she couldn't stop me from wondering just a little.

"Now all you need to do is make peace with Harry."

"Easy for you to say. I don't think he's in a mood to listen to any more of my excuses."

"Oh, Kate, you've been married to him for how long? You ought to know what to do by now." Candace winked, picked up her monstrous bag, and plopped the sunglasses over her eyes.

I found a mattress sale ad for her to use for the switch. "Before I deal with Harry, I'll watch from the dining room window. Just be careful, and if there's any problem, hightail it back here. Got it?"

She nodded.

Before Candace was ready to turn the knob, I asked, "While you're out there, would you mind picking up my slipper?"

"Sure thing."

For once, everything went according to plan. Candace gave me the okay sign, hopped into her car, and waved my slipper at me as she pulled out of the driveway.

Now it was my turn to execute Part Two of Plan A, seduce Harry. I hurried up the stairs, into our bedroom, and tossed my robe and pajamas onto the chair. I could hear water running. *Good, Harry's still in the shower.* I tiptoed into the bathroom, opened the shower door, and slipped in behind him. "Want me to wash your back?" I said in my most seductive voice.

"Huh? Okaay."

He drew out the last word. *Good, I caught him off-guard.*

I grabbed the soap out of his hand before it dropped to the floor and began to lather his backside. Reaching around his waist, I pressed closer to him, working on his chest in a circular motion, inching my way down to the point of no return. "How's that?" I murmured in his ear.

"F-f-fine," he stuttered.

*Men, they can be so predictable when it comes to unexpected sex.*

After a too successful execution of Plan A, Part Two, I couldn't get Harry out of the house for the rest of the afternoon. I phoned Candace about my situation and explained that we'd just have to hold off one more day to deliver the letter to Lydia. Meanwhile, I had to make sure that Harry didn't have any inkling of the real reason behind my shower seduction.

Later that afternoon, Harry and I were drinking iced tea out on the patio when Molly pushed the screen door aside and called loudly out to us.

"So we see."

"And hear," added Harry, muffling his ears with his hands.

"Have a good time?" I asked.

She held up a couple of large bags. "Yep. It's been ages since I shopped like this. I'm going up to my room and decide what I'll keep and what to take back."

"Sounds like something Candace would do."

"Yeah, it does," Molly laughed. "See you later." She disappeared as quickly as she'd arrived.

82

We were silent for a while. Harry took a swallow from his tea, pointed his glass toward the neighbors, and asked, "Not that I'm interested, but I can't help wondering what is it about this whole Whitetower thing that's got you and Candace so curious?"

I was hoping he wouldn't ask. But, since his mood had mellowed considerably, I began to tell him about Lydia's visit yesterday, carefully leaving out any incriminating parts. "All-in-all, most of what Lydia told us centered on her illness, and an ancient artifact they found in Tunisia." I paused, pushing the ice around in the glass with my forefinger.

"Was that all?"

"That's most of it. Lydia was going to say more, but then Molly burst into the backyard with news that Chad had to cut his visit short. When Lydia heard that, she almost flew out of her chair and rushed off. End of story."

"Well, all I can say is, I'm damned glad I put that letter in their mailbox. Let them deal with their problems," he replied, satisfied that he had single handedly remedied the situation.

*Oh, if he only knew.*

# Hey, Na-ne-na, The Limo's Back!

THE NEXT MORNING I slipped into my old sweats and trudged down to the kitchen. Harry swung past me, patting me on the behind. He called it a show of affection. I called it a dumbass irritation. But I threw him a smile as I padded out the front door to pick up the paper. I hoped the paper kid had slung it onto the porch and not in the bushes. It sat half-way up the walkway. *Close enough.* I took a moment to inhale the morning air then stopped short, almost choking on the exhale when I saw the same limo parked in front of the Whitetowers. Two men had exited the car and were walking up the pathway to their house.

I glued myself to one of the porch columns, waiting and watching. What felt like an hour was only a few minutes. When the men returned to the car, I watched the same burly fellow open the rear door for the man with the bald head. After carefully surveying the surrounding area, I unpeeled myself from the post and scampered down the few yards to pick up the paper and back to the porch without being seen. He turned my way just as I stood up. *Oh crap, act normal pretend it's no big deal. Stay calm Kate, don't panic.* My feet felt like two bricks of concrete as I tried desperately to move them toward the steps. Before I could reach for the doorknob, he was at my stairs.

*Geez, he's even bigger than I thought. Must be at least six-foot-five. Look at that thick neck, and those biceps!* They were straining at the seams of his jacket.

"Ca..can I help you?" My lips quivered as I forced my mouth into a smile.

"Yeah," said Biceps. "Your neighbors ... the White-towers." He flicked his head toward their house. "Seen 'em around lately?" His gruff voice matched his chiseled face.

"Er...no, I haven't." I hugged the paper to keep my heart from leaping out of my chest and crashing into his belt buckle. "D…do you want me to tell them that you stopped by?" *What a lame question.*

"Yeah, tell 'em Mr. B, don't like to be stiffed."

"Stiffed?"

"When somebody makes an appointment with Mr. B, they'd better keep it. You got it?"

I nodded. "D…does Mr. B. have a la…last name?"

His ferocious attitude was so scary it nearly sucked the air out of my body.

"They know who he is." He started to go, paused a moment, turned and said, "Tell 'em he'll be comin' back … *real soon.*" Biceps swaggered back to the limo.

I couldn't move. My feet were stuck to the porch floor. As I watched the limo crawl past my house, a shiver snaked up my spine. I could almost feel old Baldy in the back seat staring at me through the darkened car window.

Biceps' threatening message should have been a clue for me to take Harry's advice … again. However, I was certain that Lydia was in some kind of trouble. What kind? I didn't know. Of course, the letter alone was a mystery in itself. I didn't think that Candace and I would rest until we found out what was in it, and what connection it had with the artifact.

*But will Harry understand.* The entire incident replayed inside my head as I moved slowly back into the house. I felt like I'd been dropped into a scene from a bad B movie. I slid into a chair and heaved a big sigh. I could still hear my heartbeat thumping in my ears.

Harry was pouring coffee with his back to me. I tried to compose myself. "Sure took you long enough." He grumbled in his mug as he walked back to his chair. "Did the paper get hooked up in the shrubs again? I'm going to have a talk with that paperboy. That's the … Kate, what is it? What's the matter? Are you all right?" Genuine concern erased the annoyance of his earlier tone. "You look like you've seen a ghost."

I guess the frightening meeting at the porch hadn't quite worn off my face.

"What happened?" He put his cup on the table and reached across the table taking hold of my hand.

"It's the Whitetowers. I truly believe they're in some kind of trouble."

"Are you still on that track?" He pulled away slightly. "I thought I had convinced you to stay out of their business."

"Well, I can't, Harry." I knew I was dipping a toe into troubled waters by going against his advice. "Do you remember when I told you about the limo parked in front of their house on the day of your party?"

"Not really." His concern was beginning to ebb. He picked up the newspaper and searched for the business section.

"Just listen, will you?" The shrillness in my voice made him spit out the gulp of coffee he just took. "It was out there again, yesterday, and again this morning."

"How do you know it was the same one?" he asked in a condescending voice.

"I know it was, Mr. Prosecuting Attorney, because I saw them."

Harry dropped his interrogation routine, and changed to cautionary interest. "Them who?"

I paused, trying to decide how much to reveal. "They were the same people, Baldy and his thick-necked bodyguard with the big biceps. They were coming from the Whitetowers' house and getting into the limo when the bodyguard saw me. Before I could put my hand on the doorknob, Biceps was on our porch. He asked me in a very unmannerly tone if I'd seen the Whitetowers."

"You didn't call him 'Biceps' to his face?" His eyes widened.

"No, Harry. I'm not that crazy."

"Then what did you tell him?" Harry shifted into alert mode, giving me his full attention.

"I played dumb and asked if he wanted me to leave them a message. He told—no warned me—that Mr. 'B' didn't like to be stiffed, and to tell the Whitetowers that they would be back real soon, with emphasis on the *real soon*." His words made me shiver again. "God, Harry, the meanness in that brute's voice scared the holy hell out of me."

"Well, *that* should tell you something," he declared. "You need to butt out of their affairs right now before you get into more trouble, especially with those-gangster type people you've described." His tone was gruff, but I could see concern peeking out from behind his sternness.

I wanted to protest, but thought better of it. Instead, I tried another angle. "I suppose you're right, Harry, but if you were in trouble, wouldn't you want some kind of help from a neighbor?"

"Depends on what the trouble is and who the neighbor would be. I don't think I'd ask Stanford Whitetower for any assistance."

"I wish you were more on board with helping them," I sniffed.

Harry lowered the paper. "Apparently, the mob intimidation didn't scare you enough to stop getting yourself involved with their problems."

"But Harry—"

"Count me out." He picked up the paper and continued reading.

Harry's tone of voice was my cue to end the Whitetower conversation. *For now.* I busied about getting breakfast, grabbing bowls, spoons, milk, and setting them beside the cereal boxes, next to a dish of blueberries. "Bon appétit, Harry."

He muttered an unintelligible comment as I sat down across from him.

Tugging the comics out from under his elbow, I set about eating and reading. He rattled the paper loudly to drown out the noise of my spoon hitting against the cereal bowl. Next, I slurped the remaining milk in the bottom. I did it purposely to irritate him. I could feel his scowl burrowing a hole straight through 'Peanuts.'

I waggled my spoon at him. "Ah, come on, Harry, lighten up. Have some breakfast. Blueberries are good for your disposition." I attempted a bit of levity, hoping to warm the chill in the air.

"Where'd you hear that?" He wasn't amused.

"I don't know, must've read it in one of your health magazines." *Well that didn't go over well.*

Before he had a chance to refute my unproven claim, I rose, put my dishes in the dishwasher and left Harry to sulk in his cereal. We definitely needed some space.

Later that morning, while straightening up the family room, I heard the kitchen screen door bang, and a mumbled greeting from Harry. I called out, "I'm in the family room."

Candace breezed in. With a swish, she flung her notorious handbag onto the sofa and plopped down next to it.

"That was fast. I just texted you."

"Hey, you knew I'd break all records to get here, especially when you had important info to share, and did not want to talk on the phone. Okay, I'm here. Let's have it. I'm all ears." She leaned forward, ready to catch every word that slipped from my lips.

For the second time that morning, I related the incident. "I tell you Candace, after Biceps intimidated me with those final words, I couldn't get inside the house fast enough."

"*Biceps,* what a cute name," Candace chuckled.

"Haven't you been listening to anything I've said?" My shriek was loud enough to slam her back against the cushions.

"Whew! No need to shout. I heard every word." She paused giving me a minute to calm down. "I'm sure this Biceps person only wanted to scare you, nothing else."

"Well, Harry didn't take it so lightly."

"You told *him?*" Candace's mouth flew open in disbelief.

"What could I do? I was too shaken to act normal."

"I suppose he wants you to '*stop this nonsense.*'" she mimicked Harry.

"Candace, I've been so obsessed with Lydia's letter that I'm starting to wonder if Harry was right. If the Whitetowers are involved with thugs, maybe we should just give the letter to her and be done with it."

"Oh, no, we can't do that, Kate." Candace took hold arm and gently stroked it. "Look, I can see this is stre you out a bit. What you need is some relaxation therapy."

I took her hand and squeezed it with mine. "No, wl want is an idea, and I was hoping you might come up with something, crazy thinking on my part. But, relaxation therapy?"

"Yes, Hans, my yoga instructor, swears by it. I took you to one of his classes a while back, remember?"

"Ah, yes, good old Hans. Wait, he never taught that when I was there."

"It was a private lesson. Now, shush. Come, let's go outside into the fresh air."

She pulled me off the couch, dragged me to the patio, and sat me down on the chaise lounge. "Comfy?" she asked.

"Ye-es."

"Now, I want you to lean your head back, close your eyes, and let yourself go," Candace instructed. "Pretend we're at a swank spa resort in Hawaii, and—"

"We?" I sat upright. "I thought this exercise was for *me*."

"Well, of course it is, but as long as I'm doing this, I might as well go along with you. I could use a little stress relief, too. Now, lie back and close your eyes." She cozied herself on the chaise next to mine and began to speak softly.

"Biff and Brock, our twin blond, marvelously-built spa assistants, escort us to our lounge chairs. Towels are already arranged on them. We have a lovely view of the ocean and the waterfall that's cascading down into the pool. The trade winds are just strong enough to carry the blistering heat away from our bodies. Can you feel it? " she asked.

I nodded.

"The sweet tropical aroma of coconut invades your senses. Next, Biff takes the suntan oil from our table. Can you smell it?" She coos softly.

"Yes," I inhaled deeply.

"Biff motions for you to turn on your stomach. He opens the bottle, pours some in his hand applies it to your back. Brock does the same thing for me."

"Wait! Shouldn't he ask me first?"

"Hush, just enjoy. He massages the kinks out of your neck, shoulders, then onto the back of your legs," she purred.

"Careful there Biff, I'm a married woman."

"Honestly, Kate, you need to concentrate. It's just make-believe. Go with it."

"Sorry … but really, I'm a little curious. Do these, uh, spa boys really do this kind of thing at private resorts?"

Silence. I glanced at Candace. "Oh, I suppose it's happened to you."

"Um, well, yes sort of. But let's not go there right now." Candace sounded flustered, but continued. "Where was I? Ah yes, next, Raul—"

"Raul?"

"Quit interrupting," she ordered. "Yes, Raul. He's the wait person. He brings us a light lunch of two fruity iced beverages and plates of chicken and cucumber sandwiches; quartered, with the crusts cut off. Thin slices of kiwi surround—"

"Ew." I made a sour face. "I don't like kiwi."

She threw up her hands. "Okay, have what you want. Obviously you don't want to relax." Candace pouted, apparently frustrated at my outbursts.

I sat up. "Sweetie, I know you mean well. But when you bring Biff, Brock, and Raul into the picture, it's so hard to concentrate."

"I was only trying to help." Candace looked completely defeated.

"I know, I know, and I appreciate it, really I do."

Candace was quiet for a while. I thought she had given up. But then, she popped up and with a big smile on her face, asked, "Would strawberries do? I know you like them and they're part of the Kiwi family. Shall we try again?"

*What could I do?* I fell back into my original position. "Okay, tell me more about this Raul guy."

Candace continued talking for the next half-hour. Surprisingly, my body felt relaxed, as if I'd actually been transported to poolside at a luxury island hotel. I hoped I wouldn't accidently call out Biff's name while sleeping next to Harry that night. He did have soothing hands, though.

"Now, wasn't that a lovely virtual holiday, Kate?" Candace beamed, so pleased with herself.

"Yes, I have to agree. It was a wonderful relaxing trip." I moved my chaise to an upright position. "As a matter of fact, I'm convinced now that we should bow out of this silly adventure, give Lydia the letter and move on with our lives."

"I hate to give it up just yet," said Candace.

"It doesn't matter. It's really just curiosity that's driving us to find out what the letter says. Besides, if you remember, I do have a copy, so all we need to do is find a professor at the university who teaches French to translate it."

"Oh, uh right." Candace clutched the fire opal pendant on her gold chain. Her eyes darted from one side of the yard to the other. Then, as though a light bulb lit above her head, she leaned over to me and sporting a very confident grin, said, "It's so simple, Kate, we'll just—"

My cellphone buzzed. "Hold that thought." I looked at caller ID. "Oh. My. God. It's Lydia." We exchanged surprised glances.

"Answer it, quick!" she ordered.

I swiped the cell phone to connect. "Hi Lydia, Candace and I were...I can't understand...what is it? We'll be right over." I clicked the button, shot up off the chaise, and pulled Candace from hers. "Come on! Lydia's hysterical. She needs us." Whether that last statement was true or not, Lydia hadn't refused. We were at my gate when Candace suddenly did an about face and rushed back for her purse.

"Candace, for heaven's sake," I cried out.

"Lydia's letter."

"Oh, right." Her explanation wiped the frustration off my face.

Candace slung her bag over her shoulder and whooshed by me. I caught up with her in Lydia's driveway. We could hear muffled crying as we rushed up the pathway to her back door. I knocked first and then tried the handle. It opened. I called out to her as we entered the kitchen.

"Holy Mother of…" We stopped short, nearly falling over Lydia. She lay crumpled on the floor like a used napkin. Sobs sent her body into intermittent spasms.

"Oh dear, Lydia!" I crouched down on one knee and lightly touched her shoulder. "What happened? Did you fall? Did someone hurt you?" I looked for any sign of struggle.

She turned, grabbed my arm, and stammered with gasping breaths, "They…they're c…coming back, I'm sure of it. I don't know what to do."

"Here, we'll help you up." We managed to guide her into the family room and onto the sofa.

Candace grabbed an afghan and snuggled it around Lydia's shaking body. I sat beside her and spoke soothingly until her crying subsided. "Take some deep breaths and try to relax."

"Let me get you something to drink: water, tea, brandy, maybe?" asked Candace.

"Water please," she murmured, while taking a tissue from the box on the end table and blowing her nose. "Oh, Kate, I can't tell you how much I appreciate you and Candace being here."

"We're both concerned about you." I gave her an encouraging smile.

Candace returned with Lydia's drink in time to agree with me. "Whatever it is, I'm sure we can come up with something."

"Thank you," she whispered, taking the glass. She clutched it with both hands and stared into it for a moment before taking a sip.

"Now, whenever you're ready to talk, we're here to listen." Candace positioned herself on the couch sandwiching Lydia between us.

"Really I am a bit embarrassed. I'd felt a little faint and started to reach for the chair, lost my balance, and fell to the floor. I was so distraught and scared, I just lost it and started crying." Her voice faltered. "I…I shouldn't bring you into my problems, it just isn't fair of me."

"Why don't you start where you left off the other day," urged Candace. "I think you were talking about some nice doctor who—"

"Candace, I believe Lydia had passed that part." I tossed her a be-careful-what-you-say look. "I think it was regarding the artifact."

Lydia took a deep breath. "I wish we'd never brought it back. It's caused us nothing but trouble." Once again, tears welled up in her eyes. "I tried to talk Stanford out of it, but he and Leo kept assuring me that Hamadi had made the arrangements and all we had to do was pack it with our gear." She shook her head. "I was surprised it got through customs!"

"Hamadi probably took care of that." Candace nodded and whispered to me, "Paid somebody in customs, I bet."

My kernel of curiosity was now in popping mode. "Lydia, I've got to ask…does the bald man in the black limo have anything to do with all this, this…whatever this *thing* is?"

Lydia's eyes opened wide. "How did you—"

"I saw him twice, once on the day of Harry's reception and again this morning. It was purely accidental. Except this time, I was confronted by his hulky bodyguard."

"Oh dear," she murmured, drawing her fist to her mouth, fear spreading across her pale face.

"I had gone outside the front porch to pick up the morning paper when Biceps, the alleged body guard, spotted me. I tried to avoid him, but he was at my door before I had the chance to run inside. He asked if I knew where you and Stanford were. I told him I didn't know. He probably thought I was lying, and did his best to intimidate me."

"I just knew something like this would happen." Lydia bit her lower lip.

"His final words were to tell you both that they'd be back, and soon. It seems to me that your best bet would be to call the police and—"

"Oh, God, no!" Lydia grabbed my arm. "Please, no police."

The terror in her eyes scared me. Her fingers pressed into my flesh, causing me to flinch. "Okay, okay, we won't call them. Please calm down."

"Thank you."

"This sounds suspiciously like a Mafia-type handling…not like I know anything about that." Candace rose and started pacing the floor. "Was the baldheaded man supposed to be Hamadi's client?"

Lydia nodded.

"Okay, then why were you afraid to meet with him? And where the hell is Stanford? I can't believe he'd leave you alone if the deal wasn't done," Candace said.

"Hamadi called Stanford yesterday. He wants him to hold off with the sale. Stanford told me he had to make a quick trip to Las Vegas to meet with another prospective buyer. He was supposed to be back here this morning." Lydia drank some more water and then set the glass on the coffee table.

"Where is the artifact, now?" I asked.

"I don't know. Stanford was going to put it in a safe place and would let me know after he returned." Lydia played with a piece of loose thread on the afghan. "But now it's nearly noon, and he isn't home yet. I've tried his cell phone, but it just goes to voice mail." More tears began to trickle down her cheeks. "Kate, I was too scared to answer the door this morning. I didn't know what to tell those men. Now, if they're coming back and Stanford still hasn't returned, I don't …" More sobs muffled her words.

My heart broke for Lydia. *How could we help this woman?* "Lydia, you need to get out of this house before this Mr. Baldy comes back," I advised.

"But, where would I go?" Her body seemed to cave in at the perplexing question.

"I'd say stay with us, but I'm afraid Biceps would be watching the house and me." I paced about the room, contemplating where to sequester Lydia. For now, we just needed to get her out of the house.

"She can stay at my place," Candace suggested.

"Great idea." I tossed her a grateful smile. It was the perfect solution.

"Oh, I just couldn't …" Lydia gasped.

"Yes, it's settled. Now, throw some things in a suitcase. We've got to hurry." I was in order mode bustling about the kitchen straightening things back into some order.

"But, what will happen to Stanford if I'm not here?" Lydia whimpered.

"Let him deal with Mr. Baldy. It's his mess. He can jolly well get out of it all by himself," I answered. Candace nodded in agreement.

"We've got to be careful. Since my little conversation with Biceps, I'm probably on his radar. Candace, go back to my house and fill Harry in on what we're doing."

Lydia rushed into the kitchen. "I've got to find Jasper. I can't leave him alone."

"Where's the cat's carrier?"

"In the utility room."

"I'll get it. Go find your cat."

# Oh, What a Tangled Web We Weave

WHEN WE ENTERED the kitchen, Harry eyeballed me, puzzled by all the commotion. I started to explain when Lydia immediately touched his arm and murmured so softly that he had to bend down to hear her. "Oh Harry, I'm so sorry to have to drag you into all my problems."

"Oh, ah, no bother." He was so flustered by her apology that he stumbled back against the counter.

*Good job Lydia.*

I helped her ease into a chair at the kitchen table. She held the carrier tightly in her lap.

"Excuse me, ladies," Harry interrupted. "I'd like to speak to Kate alone for a moment." He took me not-so gently by the arm and ushered me into his office. He lowered his voice a decibel or two below a shrill pitch. "What in the hell is going on?"

I twisted out of his grasp and faced him head on. "Lydia's in trouble. She needs to be somewhere safe, and Candace offered her place. I thought she told you our plan."

"Yeah, she did. But she throws so many words at me, I have to sort through them all to figure out what she's really trying to say. It's so frustrating when she babbles like that." He rubbed the back of his neck.

"Candace gets flustered when she has to tell you something important," I answered. "It's called intimidation, Harry … by you."

"Okay, so what do you want me to do?"

"Would you take Romeo and canvass the area for any suspicious cars or a limo parked in and around the next couple blocks?" Before he could reply, I quickly added, "You'd be the logical one, because none of those people has actually seen you … at least not that I'm aware of."

"I should hope not," he huffed.

"Oh Harry, it won't take but a few minutes. Look at it this way, Romeo needs the walk and you could use the exercise.

Take your cell and call the second the coast is clear." I exuded as much confidence as I could to let him know I was in control of the situation. *Well sort of.*

"Don't push your luck." He wagged his finger at me. "I'll do it, but on the condition that when I get back, you tell me everything you know about this Whitetower business ... and start from the beginning."

"Deal," I sighed, relieved for the moment.

"What happened to the carefree days of retirement I was promised?" he muttered as we hurried back into the kitchen.

Juliet, who had followed behind, got a whiff of *strange cat in the room*, and started a hissing match with Jasper. Romeo, hearing the commotion, wandered in and immediately growled at the contents in Lydia's carrier.

"Oh God, we don't need any more confusion in this house." Harry's irritation was on the rise once again. "Come on, Romeo, the missus says we have to take a walk." The dog was at the door with his leash in his mouth as soon as the word "walk" hit his floppy ears.

Keeping a firm grip on Juliet, I outlined our latest plan to Candace and Lydia. "So, as soon as Harry lets us know all is okay, you two leave. Candace, give me a call when you're settled. If all goes accordingly, I should be at your place in an hour." I crossed my fingers and offered up a silent prayer.

We waited pretty much drenched in nervous perspiration until Harry finally called.

I passed the info to Candace. "All's quiet in the neighborhood. Quick, let's get Lydia and Jasper into the car." I picked up Lydia's bag and tossed it into the back seat. "Be careful, and drive safely. See you soon." I waved them off.

That part done, I still couldn't breathe easily until I honored my promise to Harry. How could I convince him why I needed to help Lydia—without getting into any more trouble—especially after I'd explained her rather perilous circumstances? There had been moments when I wondered if I really should be involved but it had gone too far, so I'd hoped Harry would understand. Head down and deep in thought, I wandered back into the kitchen, nearly colliding with Molly.

"Mornin' Mom." She yawned widely, rubbing the sleep out of her eyes. "Boy, for two people, you and Dad sure made a lot of racket."

"We weren't alone," I replied. "Candace, Mrs. Whitetower, and her cat were here, too. You missed them. They just left."

"All of them? Together?" Molly asked as she poured coffee into her favorite Mickey Mouse mug. She plopped down on the kitchen chair, curling one leg under her.

I thought about making up some crazy story, but telling the whole truth would be weird enough. So, I skirted the issue as best I could. "Actually, there's been some problem at the Whitetowers, so Candace offered Lydia her place to stay for a while."

"Say what?" Molly looked at me, eyes wide in disbelief.

"I'll explain it all as soon as your Dad gets back from walking Romeo."

A smile crossed Molly's lips. "Candace and Mrs. Whitetower? Somehow I can't imagine those two together. If ever there was an odd couple ..." Her sentence was interrupted by the appearance of a red-faced Harry being dragged into the kitchen by a thirsty dog. Harry could barely get the leash off before Romeo bounded for his water dish and started lapping away, only looking up once, letting the excess water stream down the sides of his mouth.

"Damn dog nearly pulled my arm out of the socket," he groaned, rubbing his shoulder.

"Oh, Dad, you've got more muscle than that," Molly laughed.

"When was the last time *you* took Romeo for a walk, little girl?" Harry ruffled her hair as he slid into a chair beside his daughter.

"Mom filled me in about Lydia staying with Candace for a few days."

Harry threw me a quizzical look.

98

Before his question dropped out of his mouth, I quickly responded, "I only told Molly the immediate situation, not the full story, Harry."

"Okay, go on. I'm all ears." He leaned against the back of the chair, arms folded across his chest.

"Boy, this's gotta be good," Molly declared, hiding a snicker behind her coffee mug.

My eyes darted from one of them to the other. I had to play my hand carefully. Without rambling, I highlighted the incidents. By the time I finished, Molly was wearing an 'oh wow' look.

"That was some story, Mom. It sounded like something out of a crime novel."

Harry sat for a long time stroking his chin, finally asking, "Do you think Lydia is really that innocent?"

"I never thought of it any other way. Her actions looked pretty authentic to me."

"But how do we know she wasn't playing you?"

"How do you figure?"

"Lydia's story has more holes in it than a piece of good Swiss cheese. First, what kind of a man would take off for Vegas, leaving his wife to deal with the kind of people you described? Are you willing to believe her story about having some strange illness and being too sick to realize there were illegal actions going on around her?"

"But, she could've been—"

"The Whitetowers are professional archeologists," he continued. "They know full well the penalty for smuggling a precious artifact out of the country. Why would they chance it? Come on Kate, Lydia has one or two academic credentials behind her name. She just can't be that naïve." He shook his head.

"You make a good point, Harry."

"Then, you'll drop this whole business and let the authorities handle it?"

"No. More than ever I've got to get Lydia to open up."

Harry was protesting when Molly threw in her two cents worth. "I agree with Mom, Dad. I'm really concerned about

99

Chad. He's got to be the innocent one here. I'm sure it would devastate him to find out that his parents are thieves." She turned to me. "I think you and Candace need to work on Mrs. Whitetower, and maybe mention what it would do to their son."

"Nice, Molly, I like your reasoning," I smiled.

Harry waved a finger at me. "You might be overstepping boundaries to a point where you wind up becoming the enemy of the very person you're trying to help. Think about that."

"I understand what you're saying, but I believe it's a chance worth taking."

Harry let out a defeated sigh. "Ah well, I don't much like it, but it looks like you're hell bent on butting in on her problems."

"Trust me on this, Harry." I moved toward him.

He held me at arm's length and nailed me with his eyes. "Look, if things start heating up, please, for God's sake, call the authorities. I don't care that Lydia said 'no police.' Just make damn sure you keep a watchful eye out for anything out of the ordinary."

"Don't worry, hon, I've got Candace as my wingman."

"You mean wing nut," he corrected. "And that's supposed to reassure me?" He grabbed a couple of aspirins from the bottle on the kitchen shelf and drew a full glass of water. He gave me a kiss on the forehead, and whispered, "Please be careful," before retreating to his study.

On the way to Candace's house, I thought about Harry's assessment of Lydia. His words began to nag at me. Was she the victim or one of the main characters? Her fear seemed genuine. Either that or she's been keeping a talent well-hidden from all of us.

I swung into Candace's driveway that encircled a fountain. Water poured out of a goblet held by a statue of a scantily clad boy. The two large flowerpots, newly planted with a mix of bright fall mums, stood sentry on either side of stairs leading to the massive front door. I couldn't help admiring the lovely grounds. I felt like I was stepping into a masterpiece of a landscape painting every time I visited.

Winston Carrington-Jones provided quite well in his will to Candace. Fortunately for her, there were no other heirs.

Candace's maid, Anita, ushered me into the sun room where Candace and Lydia were seated. Lydia looked more relaxed and even offered me a feeble smile.

A kernel of doubt had begun to fester inside me, shadowing my earlier concern for Lydia. It presented itself in my tone of voice to her. "I see that it didn't take you long to recover from that terrible ordeal this morning."

Lydia's eyes widened as she touched her hand to her throat.

Surprised at the sharpness, Candace attempted to smooth things. "Oh, it must be the serenity of my little abode that's helped you recover so quickly." She placed her hand on Lydia's and fired a stern look at me.

"You are so right, my dear." Lydia sighed and stifled a yawn behind her white-laced handkerchief. "This whole morning has simply exhausted me. Do you suppose I could lie down for a while?"

"Certainly, Lydia. I'll have Anita take you to your room."

"Thank you for your kindness, Candace." Patting her hand, Lydia rose and jutted her chin haughtily in my direction. "I'm sure to feel much better after a bit of rest."

As soon as Lydia left, Candace scowled at me. "What's up with you? Why the sudden change?"

"I'm having some doubts."

"Like?"

"Remember how I told Harry that if he'd walk Romeo around the neighborhood that I'd tell him what was going on with Lydia?"

"Yeah, that was a dumb thing to do."

"Maybe so, but after I gave a highlighted version of Stanford's attempt to sell the chalice to the highest bidder, he didn't buy Lydia's innocence in the whole scheme. He thought it was all and act on her part, pointing out a couple of pretty big holes in her story. He even backed it up with one or two examples to prove his point."

"Since when have you ever listened to Harry?"

"I do…sometimes. But this is serious, so listen."

Candace sat upright, folded her hands in her lap, and looked intently at me. "I'm all ears. Continue."

"So, according to Harry, he finds it hard to believe that Lydia is some kind of damsel in distress. He thinks she may even be an integral part of the whole scheme."

Candace leaned forward, dropping her 'Miss Manners' façade. "Something's beginning to make sense."

"What do you mean?"

"Shortly after we arrived, Lydia wandered about the main floor admiring my paintings and sculptures, asking questions like a museum curator. I don't think she figured me for an aficionado of the arts. All the same, I was thrilled with her compliments. But I didn't realize until now how quickly her earlier, ah, franticness evaporated. Hmmm, was that a real word?" she wondered.

I shrugged my shoulders. "Something seems strange. I think we should be careful and not take everything Lydia tells us at face value."

"Right." Candace gave me an opened mouth wink.

"Hah!" I smirked. "Okay, enough now. It's time to get down to business. We've only scratched the surface. Whoever wants the alleged chalice might go to great lengths to get their hands on it."

"What kind of lengths?" Candace squirmed in her chair.

"I hate to say it, but somebody might even kill for it."

"Yikes!" she grimaced. "Let's hope it doesn't come to that."

Candace rummaged around in her purse for Lydia's letter. "What should we do about this?" She waved it at me. "Maybe if we put a little pressure on her, we just might get at the truth."

"Not a bad idea."

Candace beamed. If she were wearing suspenders, she'd have her thumbs tucked under each one, chest out and strutting about the room like a proud peacock. "So, are we going to play good cop, bad cop? I want to be bad cop," she exclaimed, warming up to the thought.

"No." I was emphatic. "We will take things slowly and let her poke holes in her own story."

"How will we know?"

"By intuition, I guess. Hopefully, she'll trip up somewhere, so be on your toes. If there's any change from her original story, we'll need to drill into that hole until the truth comes gushing out."

"This is getting better and better." Candace rubbed her hands together excitedly. "Maybe we'll strike oil."

"Yes, but remember, we've got to take it slow. If we don't, it may become more dangerous for us than for Lydia."

\*\*\*

We mulled over the latest events for an hour until Candace sat back in her chair and declared, "Let's take a break and get some lunch. I'm starved, how about you?"

"I've been so involved in this Lydia situation, I even forgot to eat breakfast. What time is it?"

"Well after two o'clock. It's time to feed our stomachs as well as our minds."

"My, aren't you the sage advice giver."

"I'll take *that* as another compliment," she snickered.

"Don't get too smug," I replied, heading out the sunroom. "Rustle up something, and I'll go wake Lydia."

Candace's laughter followed me up the stairs. I was about to knock on the bedroom door when I heard Lydia talking. *Ah, she must be on her cell phone.* Quietly, I pressed an ear to the door.

The tone in Lydia's voice rose in a hushed but decidedly frustrated manner. "Yes, I'm all right. I'm staying with Candace, you know, Kate's friend. No, I haven't talked to Viorsky. I thought he was supposed to make the deal."

I gasped. There was a long pause. I quickly clamped my hand over my mouth.

Lydia spoke again. "I want this over before they get too curious, Stanford. I've already sensed a change in Kate's manner toward me since this morning. What? Yes, I gave a

103

stellar performance but she's no dummy. Remember, she had a confrontation with Gino's bodyguard."

Stomach in knots, I steadied myself against the wall, hardly able to take a breath.

Lydia continued hurriedly. "God no, Chad mustn't know any of this. Get out of his apartment before he gets back from Los Angeles. What? No. Man up Stanford. Just take care of it. I'll call you later."

I waited a few moments to calm the rapid heartbeat pulsing in my ears. I conjured up enough saliva to wet my lips before tapping lightly on the door. "Lydia, it … it's Kate. Are you awake?"

A muffled answer came from inside.

"We're about to have something to eat. Would you like to join us?"

"Oh, ah, yes…that would be nice, Kate. Just give me a few minutes to freshen up. I'll be down shortly."

I was amazed at how quickly Lydia's voice switched from authoritative to submissive. "Good, take your time. No rush," I responded light-heartedly, and then flew down the stairs into the kitchen and collapsed on one of the high-back stools surrounding the island work station. Between gulps of air, I filled Candace in on what I'd heard.

"Good Lord." Candace froze, holding the French knife, ready to take aim at a tomato. "Now what'll we do?"

"I don't know." I shook my head while biting my lower lip. "I can't believe … all this time she *was* playing us. Now I see why she didn't want the police involved."

"That's so true." Candace began slicing furiously.

A thought suddenly occurred to me. I jumped off the stool and reached for Candace's arm, stopping her in mid-cut. "That's it!" I shouted.

"Whoa there, Kate, you came pretty close to having red meat with your turkey sandwich. What is *it*?"

"The hole we were looking for. If Lydia wants our help, she needs to tell us everything. Otherwise we'll—"

"Call the cops," Candace's eyes lit up. "Yeah, we'll shine a bright light in her face and give her the third degree."

"God, Candace, you've been watching way too many cop programs. We need to be more discreet in our approach. We can't let her suspect we know anything, just yet."

"Okay, but—"

I saw Lydia approaching the kitchen, and I nudged Candace. "Shush, here she comes. Follow my lead."

"Good timing, Lydia. Candace is making delicious sandwiches. I hope you're hungry." I changed my tone of voice back to earlier caring mode.

"My *fabulous* turkey, avocado, lettuce, and tomato, with chive dressing on fresh croissants," Candace announced.

We busied ourselves setting out glasses and napkins. Candace placed each sandwich on a plate and had started to pour ice water from a crystal carafe, when I said, "You know, with everything that's happened this morning, I think we all deserve something more interesting than water." I winked at Candace. "Got anything else cool and refreshing hiding in the fridge?"

Taking the hint, Candace open the Sub Zero and rooted around inside. She pulled out a bottle of champagne and motioned for me to take flutes from the cabinet. "I always keep a bottle or two cooling in case of company dropping in unexpectedly." She grinned. "We can pretend we're in New York. It's after five there." She laughed while popping the cork and filling the glasses expertly, not spilling a drop.

Lydia started to refuse, but Candace overruled her. "Come on, now. It'll relax you. You're not going anywhere for a while."

I watched as Lydia devoured her sandwich and kept her occupied with idle conversation while Candace continued refilling her glass.

"My, I didn't realize I was so hungry," she said, taking the last bite of sandwich, followed by a swallow of champagne. "Thirsty, too."

When we had finished eating, I suggested we take our glasses and return to the sunroom. "We can relax and be more comfortable there."

"I'll bring another bottle." Candace added, plucking one from the refrigerator.

"This is so pleasant." Lydia smiled. She snuggled into one of the cushiony chairs. "I do feel so safe here."

"Good." As hoped, the effects of the alcohol had loosened her. Weighing my next words, I moved slowly back to our earlier conversation, "Now that you seem to be more comfortable, perhaps you can remember some more details about the chalice." Lydia's eye twitched slightly. *Maybe we gave her too much to drink.* "OK ... why don't you begin with your illness in Tunisia. Perhaps you could go into more detail about the doctor and this friend of Hamadi's, Leo, ah—"

"Viorsky," she finished. "Yes, well you see, it's hard for me to put together clearly what happened in the hotel room. I was really quite out of it, before the medication kicked in and my fever finally broke. Thankfully it wasn't too contagious." She finished with a nervous laugh.

The effects of the champagne began to slow her movements. She stared out the window, and let out a soft sigh.

Candace urged her on. "Was that when you finally realized that Stanford was brokering a deal with Hamadi and his friend to smuggle the chalice into the States?"

Lydia's eyes widened. "I wouldn't call it that. Hamadi told us that he had a...a legitimate buyer."

"But, Lydia, you of all people must've known the ramifications if you *had* smuggled an ancient artifact out of the country, or," I paused for effect, "was it only a replica that Hamadi wanted to pass off as the real deal to his buyer?"

"Of course it was real." Her eyes flared. "And, yes, I was aware of the penalty, Kate." Calming down somewhat, she continued a bit patronizingly. "You must understand, I was still under heavy medication and my guard was down. He was pretty persuasive."

"Who? Stanford? Leo? Hamadi? The doctor?" I applied a bit of pressure.

"Yeah, that doctor De, Du something." Candace wondered out loud. "Could his role in this scheme be more than pushing pills?" Before Lydia could answer, she pulled out the letter and waved it in front of her nose.

I watched the color drain from Lydia's face. "Where? How did you get it?" she gasped, clutching her throat.

"Never mind that." Candace had her interrogator hat on. "Could this be from your friendly doctor, inquiring about your ah, health?"

"You, you read it?" Lydia tried to grab it out of her hand.

Candace pulled it out of her reach. "Not entirely."

"We skimmed over it," I lied. We had to be convincing enough to get her to believe us. "Was this *amour* of yours in on the sale, or were the two of you cooking something on the side?"

"Yes, what about this Dr. Luuv?" Candace drawled out the last name.

Lydia ran a hand over her forehead, as though trying to dredge up an answer. She gazed from one of us to the other. "Please, I can't think. You're asking too many questions all at once."

"Look Lydia, you could be putting us in some real danger." It was time to apply more pressure on her to come clean. "You've got to realize we can't go on protecting you if you keep lying to us."

Suddenly aware that she had trapped herself, Lydia heaved a big sighed. "You're right. You've both been so kind to me. I can't go on deceiving you anymore. I'm so sorry." Apology was written across her face.

"Why don't you start at the beginning?" My tone was softer but guarded.

Lydia propped her elbow on the sofa's arm and rested her head in her hand. "My mouth is so dry. May I please have some water?"

"Here, have some more champagne." Candace took the bottle and drained it in her glass.

She was about to speak when Anita entered the room and rushed over to Candace, all a flutter. The interruption broke the tension that had been building.

"Excuse me ma'am." She nervously twisted her hands into a ball. "I'm terribly sorry to disturb you, but there's a phone call for you, and the caller says it's extremely important."

"Really Anita? I can't think of anyone so important that needs my attention." Candace grinned at us. "Tell the person that I can't be interrupted right now. Take a message, and I'll return the call later." She waved her off, but Anita stood rooted to the floor.

"Um, ma'am, I … I already told him that, but … but" she stammered, "he … he was quite insistent. Wouldn't give his name but made it very clear that he needed to talk to you right away."

"Oh, all right. It's okay, Anita. Now don't look so worried, I'm not upset with you." She smiled at her maid and then turned to me. "It's probably my gardener, Del. He's always phoning and whining about some kind of catastrophe that needs my attention."

"I thought you got rid of him." I raised an eyebrow.

"Guess I didn't do a very good job," she laughed. "I shouldn't be but a few minutes." Candace started to leave then stopped in front of Lydia, and commanded, "Don't you say one word until I get back." She walked quickly out of the room with Anita trailing behind, offering more apologies.

Lydia and I sat in silence, volleying a weak smile back and forth.

*How awkward. This is hardly the time for small talk. What do I say? Well now, doesn't Candace have a lovely home? Isn't this great weather? Read any good books lately? What about those Blazers? I hate they changed the Rose Center's name to MODA. What's up with that? God, hurry up Candace, I can't stand this.*

I began to fear that we might've lost the momentum, and it may've given Lydia an opportunity to rethink what she was going to tell us.

When Candace returned, I said, "*Finally, we can …*" The look on her face stopped me in mid-sentence. Her pleasant attitude was replaced by a very somber facial expression, one I'd rarely seen.

"Uh, Lydia, I need to talk to Kate for just a moment, please excuse us." She grabbed me by the arm, dragging me out of the room.

When we were out of earshot, I asked, "What's going on?"

Candace struggled for words, starting, then pausing. "I'm afraid that we … really I … but then you are part of it … so it's we …" she stammered.

"Spit it out!"

"We've got a major problem."

"I'm guessing that wasn't Del on the phone."

"Ah, yeah. Remember when I told you about my, involvement with Gino Busoni's son, Nicky?"

"The Las Vegas dealer in ancient artifacts, legal or otherwise?" I dared to ask.

"Yes."

The tone in Candace's answer was foreboding. Tiny fingers of dread crept up my back. I shivered.

"I can't explain everything right now, but the bad news is … the Busoni family are the first buyers that Stanford contacted. And," she drew a deep breath before continuing, "Gino knows I know."

"I don't understand. Who told Gino, Nicky?"

"Oh, no, not him. It was Joey Peanuts."

If she didn't look so worried, and I wasn't so afraid to hear the rest of the conversation, I would've laughed hysterically at the name. "Who's this Joey Peanuts?"

"It's actually Joey Pinole. He had a thing for unshelled peanuts and never went anywhere without a small bag stuffed inside his coat pocket. Thus the name. Anyway, he's one of Busoni's lieutenants who always had a soft spot for me. He calls once in a while to see how I'm doing. This time, though, he gave me a heads up. In his words, '*The Boss learnt you was associating wit a certain friend who's got her nose somewhere it don't belong.'"*

I could feel the color drain from my face. It had to be Biceps. He must've seen Candace at my house. "Wha…what else did he say?"

"He told me I should stay away from you until the transaction is completed, and I was to tell you that, '*If she knows what's good for her, she should do likewise.*'"

"That sounds pretty much like a threat all right," I said, biting my lower lip.

She nodded slowly, casting her eyes away from mine.

"I get the feeling there's more to the Nicky Busoni story that you haven't told me."

"Yes … you're right," she hesitated, her brows furrowed. "But, it'll take too long, and right now we've got to figure out what to do about Lydia."

"Not we, Candace, me," I stated firmly. "You've got to listen to this Joey guy and step out of this … this, whatever this thing is. I don't want you getting hurt. I'll deal with Lydia."

"No way. I won't let Gino Busoni ruin my life or scare away my good friend." She slapped her fist against the open palm of her hand. "We're doing this together."

"Boy, when you get that way, there's no changing your mind." I gnawed on my lower lip. "Just give me a minute to think."

"We need to hurry back to the sunroom before Lydia gets suspicious," she warned.

"Okay, there are two ways to go," I said. "We could cut Lydia loose and bow out of her mess. That would be the sane thing to do."

"Yeah, but what's the fun in that? What's the second?"

"We'll continue doing what we started, and play Lydia at her game, only this time we'll let her think that we totally buy into everything she tells us."

Candace didn't answer right away. She seemed to really be pondering my two suggestions. I almost hoped that she'd choose to drop this whole escapade. "It's not too late to bow out, Candace, really. Anyway, Harry'd probably dance a jig if I were to go home and tell him we were letting it go."

A little grin lifted the sides of her mouth. "I know, Kate, but, as much as I'd like to see Harry doing a victory dance, I um, I choose to continue. Yeah, we'll give her enough rope to hang herself." A tiny bubble of laughter escaped her mouth.

"That's right, Candace. But it'll be trickier if we go ahead with it. The first thing we've got to do is stay one step ahead of the mob, and Lydia, who we've recently found out to be a very convincing liar."

"But we can lie as well as the best of them," she said, holding her hand up for a high five to solidify our agreement.

Before I took a step toward the sunroom, Candace suddenly pulled me back. "What now?"

"The letter," she groaned. "I left it on the table when I went to answer the phone. Lydia's probably read it by now."

"Oh, it's just as well," I said, brushing the thought aside. "Even if we didn't get it translated, it wouldn't make any difference at this point. There's little need to make an issue out of it."

"Well, true, but I sure would've loved to confirm who it was from, and what he had to say," she muttered.

"I'm sure we will … eventually."

Upon entering the sunroom we caught Lydia slipping back into her chair. She could've either taken a furtive glance at the letter, or quite possibly had enough time to read and then replace it back on the table. We exchanged looks.

"My goodness, you took so long, I was beginning to worry," said Lydia

We took our seats across from her. Lydia's voice and manner gave no hint of any deception.

"I hope it wasn't anything critical." Her attempt at concern had a hint of insincerity in her voice.

"No, of course not. Everything's peachy," assured Candace.

"Oh, good. Now before I go on, I have a little confession to make."

"And what would that be?" I asked. *Liar, liar pants on fire.* "It's about the letter. While you were out, I just had to peek to see who it was from. After all, it is mine," she replied with a hint of indignity.

Candace and I suppressed a surprised gulp. Her boldness caught us off guard. Had she actually done just that, or did she have time to read it? We had to play it carefully. Should Lydia discover we didn't know French, we'd be dead in the water, and trying to get the real truth out of her would be next to impossible.

I rested my hand on Lydia's arm and responded contritely, as I handed the letter to her. "Certainly, Lydia, it is yours. We weren't planning to keep it from you. But … you see, the seal on the back of the envelope had come loose, and while I was stuffing the letter back in, I happened to notice something written about the chalice." *I can match her whopper for whopper.*

She let out a tiny chuckle. "But of course you found out that it was nothing more than a note from my dear friend, Louis Vanier, inquiring about our latest find."

"LeVon, Leo, now Louis? How many more men does she know with those initials?" Candace muttered under her breath.

Ignoring her comment, I pushed a little farther. "Really? That's all? I got the impression Louis expressed a little more than mere friendship." That tiny bit of information caused two spots to redden on Lydia's cheeks.

"Oh, you know those Frenchman, always in love with love." She fanned her face with her handkerchief. "He's forever joking about me running away with him."

"Hmm. From what I gathered, you were tempted more than a few times," Candace pushed harder. From the smug expression on her face, she was telling me that she could lie just as well as I could.

Lydia's eyes shifted from me to Candace and back. *Aha! Did the mouse catch the cat?*

Like a balloon losing all its air, she collapsed deeper into the chair cushions. The chess game had gone on long enough. We were breaking her down.

112

"Don't you think it's about time you told us exactly what's going on?"

"Yeah, give it up, Lydia," added Candace.

Lydia slowly raised her head, stared straight into our eyes and murmured, "Where do you want me to start?"

"Well …" I began to tick off the items on my fingers, one at a time. "There's Hamadi's proposition, the trip to Tunisia, the doctor, your illness, the artifact—"

"And the two buyers, Leo, and the French guy with the letter," Candace tossed in. "Pick one."

"Why don't you start by weeding out all the lies you've been mixing in with the truth." I held her gaze until she blinked. Lydia shifted in her chair, glanced at a painting behind my head, then down to her wedding band that she nervously fingered back and forth.

"Lydia!" I commanded her attention. My patience was wearing thin.

She jerked her head up. "Yes…yes, all right," she stammered. "It all started a day or two before we were scheduled to leave for Egypt. Stanford mentioned to Hamadi that this would be our last dig. He told him the hot desert sand had taken its toll on his health … mine, too, for that matter."

"Interesting … you've always led me to believe that the two of you would be doing this long after your retirement from the university," I said.

"Things change, Kate," she countered. "I'm sure you've been down that road once or twice in your life."

"Let's not get off track," Candace interrupted.

Lydia reached for her glass and finished off the remains of the champagne then picked up where she'd left off. "Seeing that Stanford was serious, Hamadi had a business proposition for us."

"What kind of business?" Candace asked, settling back in her chair, arms folded. "Most likely the monkey kind, I bet," she snickered.

"I'm coming to that," Lydia remarked curtly. "I guess you'd call it trafficking in illegal artifacts. Of course, *we* were quite surprised to find that our friend had been doing this for a number of years. "

"How did Hamadi get you to agree to move the artifact? Some kind of tidy commission, I bet," Candace scoffed.

"Well … yes, as a matter of fact money did become the deciding factor." Lydia let a small smile escape from her lips. "All we had to do was meet Hamadi's business partner at the Tunis Royal Thalassa Monastir hotel in Tunisia. He'd take care of the rest."

"Was his partner, Leo Viorsky?" I asked.

"Yes. Leo emailed a picture of the artifact to Hamadi, who forwarded it to his buyer in the States. We were to meet Leo at the hotel, and he'd make all the arrangements for us to transport it home."

"How come Leo couldn't take it?"

"According to Hamadi, Leo had other business to attend to, so he couldn't leave early enough, and the buyer was insistent that the piece be delivered in the agreed time."

"So, what about your, ah, high fever?" I made the significant finger quotes. "How real was that?"

"Real, actually. My illness was a plus because it gave us time to inspect the artifact. Please, let me explain." She leaned forward, her tone of voice confidential.

"There is something more to the chalice. At first we thought it was all one piece, until *I* found out otherwise." A hint of pride formed on her lips.

"Was it still covered with all those precious gems you described?" Candace's voice rose a pitch in expectation.

Lydia nodded and continued. "The craftsmanship appeared to be early 15th century, but the signature under the base had worn. Leo told us that the chalice was found on Della Rosa, a tiny island in the Mediterranean, a mile out from the Sicilian coast. There's an old legend that an Italian explorer, Antonio Ferrero discovered it and named it after his wife. It's not known for certain whether Ferrero found the chalice on the island, or if it was from Della's dowry. Anyway, the legend goes on to say that both his wife and child died in childbirth. He believed the chalice to be cursed and buried it on the other side of the island, far away from his family's grave."

"Oh," sighed Candace, "how romantic." Her eyes glowed *Dammit, Candace, stay focused.*

"It's only a legend." I frowned at her then laid a skeptical eye on Lydia. "If there is any truth to this, I think it's strange that centuries have gone by and no one has researched, or even looked for the chalice until now."

"Oh, I suppose many have tried. Apparently, Leo was at the right place at the right time. But, I'm just getting to the most exciting part," she hurried on. "Like I said, we thought it was one piece, until I felt something waxy between the base and the lid. I dug my nail into it, picked at a fine thread, and gently inched the strand out from around the rim. The lid became loose. I gave it a little tug and the top came off in my hand." Lydia's eyes glazed as if she was reliving the moment of discovery.

"The chalice was not empty. Inside the velvety lining, I pulled out a tiny red drawstring bag." She paused for more dramatic effect.

"Don't stop. Tell us. What was in the bag?" Candace exclaimed.

Any fool could see Lydia was dragging out the story hoping to reel us in. It felt like a dramatic interpretation of what really occurred. I realized she was staging this whole act, and Candace was buying it, one word after another. Irritated with both, I sprang from my chair, gritting my teeth. "Drop the dramatics and get to the point, Lydia. Just tell us what you found."

"I pulled open the drawstring, turned the bag upside down, and a brilliant cut pink diamond fell into the palm of my hand. I'd say it was about half the size of the Hope."

"Oh, wow!" Candace's eyes lit up like two shiny beacons guiding lost ships into the harbor.

"Huh?" *I wasn't expecting that.*

Candace grabbed hold of my arm and squealed, "Kate, can you imagine how exciting that must've been?"

Wincing from her outburst, I covered my hands over my ears. The noise sent vibrations throughout my body. "Candace, please." I signaled her to dial down her exuberance.

Whether it be truth or lie, I needed to play along and add to Candace's excitement. "My word, that was quite a find, Lydia," I declared.

She gave me a broad smile. *Hah! She thinks she has us.* "I wonder … did you tell Hamadi about the diamond?" I returned the smile, trying not to let pessimism tiptoe into my voice.

"Ah, no. We…um didn't tell him." Lydia stammered. She grabbed a napkin and waved it quickly in front of her face. She toyed with a small watch pendant hanging from a long sterling silver chain around her neck.

"What happened next?" asked Candace, finally recovering from diamond shock.

*Good Candace, keep the momentum flowing.*

Lydia took a few seconds to compose herself. Clutching the pendant to her breast, she uncoiled her slouched body and breathed deeply. Her confidence returning, she continued. "Things took a different turn. Stanford and Leo decided to keep the diamond apart from the original sale. They would go with the same plan and give Hamadi his half, minus our commission, of course."

"Where's the diamond now?" I asked.

"Stanford put it in a safety deposit box at the bank, and the key is safely locked in our home safe. He changes the code daily and records the number in a file in our computer. He changes the code almost daily"

"So Stanford's not beneath double-crossing a longtime friend?" remarked Candace.

"Sadly, no. After he set eyes on the diamond and saw its potential worth, I'm afraid friendship was the last thing on his mind." Lydia dabbed at a single tear welling up in the corner of her eye with her napkin fan. "I'll miss Hamadi. I was really quite fond of him, you know."

*No we don't know.* "I don't understand, Lydia. There's something missing. Didn't you tell us Stanford was contacting a second buyer interested in the chalice?" I pointed out, "Weren't you afraid that you'd be the one left to face one of the buyers by yourself? Isn't that why you were on the floor, in tears and near hysteria when we found you?"

"Uh...oh, yes, that's true." The answer came, hardly audible.

Lydia's moods moved from sad to calm to contrite in a few sentences. It was quite unsettling. I'd started to call her attention to this when she raised her hand to indicate she wasn't through.

"You see, at Harry's reception, I could tell that you were beginning to question our strange behavior. You're a very perceptive person, Kate. I played upon your sympathy with my illness. Again, please believe me, the fever was legitimate." Her pleading eyes shifted from me to Candace. "It was easy to pretend to be the frail, ill neighbor. I'd hoped it would throw you off track."

"Apparently it did, for a while." I stole a glance at Candace to read her expression. Her eyes signaled a mixture of frustration and disbelief. We were in sync.

"I assure you, Kate, it wasn't all play-acting. I couldn't face Gino Busoni's men alone knowing Stanford was working with another buyer. I gambled that you'd seen the limo parked out front and would be concerned enough to come when I called for help."

"Something's bothering me," Candace interrupted. "If the deal was supposed to be made in Las Vegas, and I presume the buyer was this Gino Busoni, how come he's here in Oregon? It's pretty far away from his territory."

It was Lydia's turn to raise surprised eyebrows. "How did you—"

"Never mind that," Candace interrupted, "Just know that we know."

That bit of news caught Lydia completely off-guard. I was afraid we'd blown our whole amateur investigation.

"Mr. Busoni had some other business up here and decided to meet at our house," she stumbled through a feeble explanation.

Lydia's statement wasn't lost on us, especially Candace, who was nervously fiddling with her gold charm bracelet.

"But, you said earlier that Stanford was in Las Vegas," I probed further.

Lydia squirmed in her seat. "I guess there was some miscommunication between Leo and Gino. I was told they were supposed to meet at Gino's estate in Henderson, Nevada."

"Wow, Lydia, this is too much." Exasperated, I gave her a sharp eye, rose, and walked briskly toward the glass French door. With arms folded, I abruptly turned to face her and erupted, "Your story gets more convoluted each time you tell it. How can you expect either of us to believe everything you told us just *now*, is the real truth?"

"You've got to believe me." Lydia jumped up and grasped my hand. "Stanford has never done anything like this. I'm afraid he may be putting too much trust in Leo."

I freed my hand from Lydia's and returned to the couch. "I'm confused, Lydia. You said that Leo and Stanford were in Vegas right now. Is that correct?" I asked.

"Yes, they're staying at our son's apartment. Chad's in Los Angeles auditioning for a part in a TV series."

"What do you think's going on?" Candace asked.

True tears began to puddle in her eyes. "I think Leo may be trying to double-cross all three of us," Lydia said, "But I have no proof."

*Sounds like a game of 'Who do you Trust.'* I was unsure of Lydia's latest appeal. "Something's still doesn't set right. Does Leo know where the diamond is?"

"No, not actually. Stanford only told Leo that he'd put it somewhere safe." Lydia grabbed a pillow and clutched it tightly to her chest.

"Well, if that's the case, your husband appears to be in the driver's seat," I said. "Surely Leo wouldn't want to foul up the deal unless he could put his hands on the stone." Lydia's

118

explanation didn't jibe with her earlier phone conversation with Stanford.

*What to do now? Do we play along with Lydia or tell her we've got her game and call the police?* My mind was running in circles. I vacillated which way to go. Finally, I turned to Lydia. "When do you think you'll hear from Stanford?"

"I'm supposed to call him later this afternoon." She released the pillow long enough to wipe the tears from her eyes with the soggy napkin wetted by her empty champagne glass.

"Well, with the exception of avoiding this Gino person breathing down your neck, there's not much we can do except wait for Stanford's call," said Candace.

The cell phone buzzing in my pocket startled me. "Oh, oh. It's probably Harry. I'll call him later." I pressed the ignore button.

I leaned toward Lydia, placed my hand on her arm, and in a placating voice said, "I think you should call Stanford. Tell him what happened at home, and that you are staying at Candace's place for a few days. I'm sure he'd be relieved to know you're safe."

Lydia's eyes brightened. "Yes, yes, you're right. I'll call him right away."

While she was occupied retrieving her cell phone from her pants pocket and sliding it open to call her husband, I mouthed to Candace, "She's still lying to us."

Candace gave me an understanding nod.

"Oh my…" Lydia exclaimed. A puzzled expression crossed her tear-stained face. "I've got a text message … from Stanford,"

"What does it say?" I asked.

"This is so strange," she looked at me. "It says, 'don't call— in a hurry—Chad likes book *Flash Drive*— will call soon.'"

"That sure sounds pretty cryptic. Do you know what any of it means?" asked Candace.

"I'm not sure, but I'm afraid Stanford may be in trouble." Her once-red cheeks faded to pale ash.

"Huh? How do you figure? Is *Flash Drive* some kind of code to mean he's in trouble? What do you know? Are you hi—"

"Lydia," I quickly interrupted Candace's battery of questions before she tipped our hand. "I think it's time we call in the police. Don't you?" I waited for her reaction.

"Oh, no, you mustn't." Lydia let out a fearful cry. "That'll surely bring the media. We can't have any publicity, especially with our connection to the university. The president would surely be appalled, not to mention the entire faculty. Some of them are our close friends." She wrung her hands. "And … Chad, what would our son think of his parents being involved in such unsavory business?" She dissolved into more tears.

*You should've thought of that in the first place.* "But what if Stanford's been kidnapped, or worse? Wouldn't you want the police to help?" I tried to reason with her.

Lydia slumped back in her chair, resting her head on the back cushion. She flung her arm across her forehead.

Watching her actions, I couldn't figure out if she was thinking about her humiliation, or what might be happening to Stanford, or merely giving us another dramatic performance.

*What does it take for this woman to come clean?*

Then, in a sudden flash, Lydia went from semi swoon to complete composure. She sat upright. "I hear what you're saying, Kate. But, we really don't know for certain if Stanford is truly in trouble. If the authorities get involved now, they may cause more problems."

"Come on now Lydia, that's the kind of stuff we see on those TV crime shows," I said dismissively.

"You may be right, Kate." Candace waved her hand in the air to get my attention. "However, Lydia *is* dealing with the Busonis, I'd opt out of calling the police for now but still keep all options open. That's my opinion." A tiny grin danced across her face.

Candace played her cards right. *Nice finessing. Well done.* I wandered about the sunroom, glanced out the window, and then stopped a moment to take a whiff of some pale pink tea roses atop a glass table. I had more questions, but I purposely extended the silence, wanting Lydia to think that she had control of the situation, until I pressed further.

"It seems that there's still a lot of things to consider," I began. "Did Stanford and Leo have a falling out? Did Leo decide to double-cross Stanford by telling Gino about the diamond? Did Hamadi find out what was going on and inform Gino?"

"Or," Candace cut in, "Did Hamadi get wind of it all and connive with Gino to have Stanford and Leo fitted for cement shoes?"

Lydia gasped at Candace's last remark. "It just doesn't make sense at all. Hamadi has been our friend for years."

"Oh really?" Candace responded. "Let me get this straight in my mind. There's two buyers for the chalice, but we don't know if it's been sold or not. A huge diamond is stashed away in a bank safety deposit box, and only Stanford changes the code to your home safe where the key is hidden. A strange text message appears on your phone." Her adrenaline seemed to rise with each item, until slapping her hands together, she burst out, "It looks like there is a mystery that means to be solved."

"Okay, calm down, Candace. Don't get ahead of yourself," I warned. But something she said struck me. "Wait a minute. Stanford has the new code, but even so, he's not the only one who knows where the diamond is being kept."

I faced Lydia square on, forcing her to look directly into my eyes. "Enough, of this game playing. You know exactly what Stanford was texting. Either you tell us the truth, or we'll have no alternative but to call the police. Let them untangle this mess. Better it be them than you facing up to those questionable shady buyers."

"I ... you're right. I'm so tired of all the subterfuge." Lydia murmured, shaking her head. "I'll admit that I do have some idea of what Stanford was trying to say in his text. But

Kate, I'm having difficulty deciphering it. You see, we decided early on that if he was to find himself in a precarious position, he'd send me a text instructing me to get the diamond from the safety deposit box and then meet him at a preset location. If this text means that he is in trouble, then I am, too."

"What do you mean?" I asked.

"Stanford's so paranoid, he's taken extra precautions for hiding the key. After he enters the new code into the computer he saves it to a thumb or flash drive, I think it's called. Yesterday, he changed the code before he left for Las Vegas."

"Where does he keep this thumb/flash drive?"

"It's in a secret compartment in the top side drawer of his desk."

"I suppose he has a key to the desk too." I could barely stand any more additions to this story.

She nodded. "But the drawer was unlocked and when I pulled it open, it was empty. I think he took it with him."

At that moment, the answer came to me. I slapped my hands together, startling both women. "Flash Drive, that's it. Don't you see, it's also the name of the book Stanford must've been referring to it in his text."

"Yes, you could be right, Kate. The book is some kind of electronic espionage thriller."

"That's a start," remarked Candace. "But I can't understand why Stanford would risk taking the thumb drive with him."

"I'm, um, not sure," Lydia faltered, but only for a moment. "Oh yes, Stanford must've been in such a hurry and probably forgot to put it back in the drawer before he left."

"Makes sense. But it could be that Stanford realized he'd forgotten to tell you the code, so he marked a page in the book with a code that only you would know," I replied. "Or, maybe he hid the device somewhere in Chad's apartment and left a clue in the book."

"That's it! I've got the answer!" Candace nearly jumped out of her chair.

*She is warming up to something. I'm almost afraid to ask.*
"The answer to what?"

"What we need to do. It's simple" More excitement was revealed in her voice the longer she talked. "This is what we'll do, Kate. The two of us will fly down to Vegas and search for the missing flash drive in Chad's apartment, then when we find it, will air-mail it to Lydia. Isn't that a smashing idea? What do you say?"

I took a moment to sort out everything that Lydia told us. She was such a prolific liar, why would we even care? Ah … but, whether we believed her or not, I was curious to find out just how far her lies would go, and a trip to Vegas would answer some questions. It'd even give Candace and me a little fun in the sun if nothing panned out. On the other hand, if a few of the things she told us were the truth, it might not hurt to check out Chad's apartment, satisfying our curiosity. Candace interrupted my silent soliloquy

"Ah, come on, Kate, look, it's no big deal. If we come up empty, then we'll just have to spend more time, shopping, seeing a show, lazing around the pool. Did I mention shopping?"

"Yes, twice."

"Ah, yes. I guess I did," Candace tossed me a sheepish grin.

The thought of spending a couple of days in a carefree atmosphere away from Lydia and her problems did seem tempting. "Well, it might be doable."

"Yes!" By the twinkle in her eyes, I could see she'd already had the plane tickets bought and our bags packed.

"Not so fast, my friend. First, I've got to get past the biggest roadblock."

"Harry?"

"Yeah. I've got to convince him we should be the ones, and not Lydia, to go to Las Vegas and search for a missing thumb/flash drive. Plus … and this is a big one, I have to downplay the possibility of being at the other end of a gun pointed at us by some very upset gangsters."

"Well, just tell him it was my idea to get you away from this Lydia stuff for a while," Candace suggested, winking at me. "Think he'd buy that?"

"Not unless you were the Pope."

Lydia, who had been sitting quietly listening to us volley words back and forth like a couple of pro ping pong players, piped up. "Shouldn't I be the one to go?"

"No!" We both exclaimed loudly.

"It's too risky for you to be anywhere else but here. Besides, you're still recuperating from that terrible fever. My house is the safest place for you right now," replied Candace. "I'll tell Anita you'll be staying here indefinitely. We'll let you know when or if we find something."

"Also, if you get any more messages from Stanford or Leo, let us know, but for heaven's sake, don't tell them what we're doing," I warned. "You've got to keep it a secret, promise?"

"Oh, of course," Lydia answered. "I won't say a word." She sealed her lips with a lock.

*If I could only believe that.*

"Candace, I'll dash on home, break the news to Harry, and phone you as soon as the air clears."

"Bring out the artillery, Kate. Knowing Harry, you'll need every weapon in your bag. "

I scooted off the sofa and grabbed my purse.

"Hey, a little sex wouldn't hurt either." Candace's voice followed me to the door.

"I've already done that … twice, remember?" I shouted back, as I ran down the steps to the car.

\*\*\*

It was late afternoon when I arrived home. Harry was in the family room, lounging in his recliner, sipping his favorite scotch. World News was on TV. I wasn't sure if that was his first or second drink, but was relieved that he appeared relaxed. I hoped my timing was right. Perhaps the liquor had lulled him temporarily into a more favorable disposition.

"Hi, Harry," I said cheerfully. I crossed to the side of his chair and bent down to give him a peck on the cheek. He acknowledged it with a mumbling grunt.

*Oh, oh, bad sign. Trouble brewing—most likely to the boiling point.* His tone was that of a husband thoroughly pissed with his wife. "So good of you to finally make it home."

"Now Harry, you know it took time to sort out everything with Lydia. She wove one lie into the next, until I finally came right out and accused her of not being totally honest."

"And, what were the results?" His voice was flat.

I needed more time to think of how best to answer. Eyeing his nearly empty glass, I asked, "I think I'll get a drink, first. You want a refill?"

Harry drained the amber liquid and held the tumbler out for me to take.

"Perhaps you'll have thought up a good answer by the time you return," he huffed, then turned his attention back to the TV.

*Smartass.* His sarcastic reply followed me toward the wet bar at one end of the family room. "Oh, looks like we need more ice. Be back in a jiffy," I called out brightly and hurried off to the kitchen.

While emptying the ice from the freezer into the bucket, I decided the best way to tell Harry would be brief and to the point, underplaying the possible danger involved in taking this trip. Back to the bar, I filled a martini glass with vodka and skewered a few olives to soak in the spirits. I poured an extra jigger of scotch into Harry's iced glass. After handing him his drink, I nestled in one corner of the sofa, facing him.

I stirred the olives in my glass then took one off the little harpoon and popped it into my mouth *Best f I begin by heaping praise on him.*

"You know Harry, you hit the nail square on the head about Lydia's story. It's been flimsy from the start."

He nodded, making a self-satisfied snort.

I gave him a rundown of all that happened in the last few hours. "Now, it appears that Stanford and Lydia are involved in an elaborate scheme with Hamadi's business associate, Leo Viorsky. And the latest is that Stanford and Leo are planning to cut Hamadi out of the sale of the diamond because he supposedly doesn't know it even existed."

Harry remained quiet, his face showing little emotion. When I got to the part about the strange text message Stanford sent Lydia, and what she claimed it might be, he sat upright in his chair. "Where are you going with this, Kate?" Concern mixed with anticipation swam across his face as he waited for my answer.

I took a big swallow of my drink. "Well ... Candace and I were sort of, maybe, possibly, thinking of taking a trip to Vegas to see if we could find the missing flash drive, or the book that is somewhere in Chad's apartment. No big deal, really."

"Ha, you've already planned it," he snapped. "So what happens if Chad isn't home? How are you going to get into his apartment to do your *little* search?" His face reddened. He abruptly stood up and pointed a finger at me with a warning. "Breaking and entering is against the law. Did you happen to think about that?"

*I hadn't.*

"That's a good question." I did a brain search. *Think quickly for a good answer.* "Um, oh, Lydia most likely has a key to her son's apartment."

He raised his left eyebrow and squinted his right eye at me. "Yeah, I suppose she would."

"Now Harry, what could it hurt...a little inspection of Chad's place, nothing more. We'd be in and out in no time at all."

"Are you two insane?" he shouted. "Maybe Candace is, but you have more sense than to put yourself in the middle of a scheme that could blow up in your face." He stormed around the room, tossing out one expletive after another. "I'd sure as hell hate to have to identify a couple of corpses." His voice hit an all-time high.

"God, Harry, don't get so dramatic. We'd only be gone a couple of days," I tried to calm him.

*Damn, maybe I should've taken Candace's sex suggestion after all.* He stopped suddenly in front of me. "Say, what's the matter with Lydia going instead of you two? It's her problem. Let her solve it."

I tried a little logical reasoning. "We thought it best that Lydia stay in hiding. Besides, we'd be able to approach the search objectively. We have nothing invested except to look for the flash drive."

"Nothing invested? Just your lives, that's all!" Harry started to go off on another tirade when Molly entered the family room.

"What's all the yelling about?" she called out over her father's ranting. "I could hear you clear out in the garage."

"Your father and I were having a little disagreement." I sent her a reassuring smile. "What were you doing out there?"

"You have no idea what your mother is planning to do," groused Harry, "and don't change the subject, Kate." He finally thumped back down in his chair.

"Aunty Candace and I are planning a little trip to Las Vegas to—"

"That's not all they're planning," interjected Harry.

"Does this have something to do with the Whitetowers?" asked Molly.

"What do you mean?" I asked cautiously.

"Come on, Mom. Ever since I disrupted your conversation with Candace and Mrs. Whitetower on the patio, it's obvious you haven't told me the whole story. So, you might as well tell me everything."

"Well, we've been quite concerned about her health," I said, playing with the olived swizzle stick.

Molly plopped down on the couch next to me, reached over, and pulled an olive off the stick from my martini glass. "That may be so." She spoke while chewing. "But if that was all there was to it, you and Candace wouldn't be constantly talking about her strange behavior."

Wiping her fingers on the side of her shorts, she plucked bits of Juliet's fur off the sofa pillow. "I've seen that mysterious black limo parked in front of their house, too, you know. And that racket going on this morning? We haven't had that kind of fuss since Kenny threatened to shave his head and become a Hare Krishna."

Harry hissed at me. "See, now you've got Molly twisted into this mess."

"Dad, I figured it out all by myself. Besides, Chad and I email frequently, and he's pretty worried about his folks."

"You don't know the whole story. They're not going to have a little fun in the sun." Harry quickly filled Molly in on what transpired a few hours ago. "So, don't you see how ridiculous it is for your mother and Candace to snoop around in Chad's apartment looking for a book or a flash drive that his mother needs? Lydia should just call Stanford and ask him for the code." He pleaded his case to his daughter. "They're begging for trouble, Molly. It's just illogical."

"Harry, Lydia doesn't want to involve Chad." I tried a little logic. He simply shook his head.

"Ah Dad, what could possibly happen in a couple of days?" Molly asked. "Besides, I know Chad won't mind, and he'll probably be back from LA by the time Mom and Candace leave for Vegas."

Harry's eyebrows elevated so high they almost hit his hairline.

"See, even your daughter thinks there's no problem." I mouthed a thank you to her.

"Yeah, take the advice of a child over one who knows so much better."

"Hey, I'm officially over twenty-one, remember?"

Though he was reluctant to give in, I saw signs of impending defeat tiptoeing across his face.

"I told your father we'd go to Chad's place, see if we could find the flash drive or the book and if we couldn't…well, we'd spend the rest of the time enjoying the weather."

"Probably shopping, too, if I know Candace," Molly threw out as she bounced over to the wet bar to make herself a drink.

"I should've known I couldn't win with the two of you ganging up on me," Harry complained, reaching for his scotch.

"Good, it's settled." I sank back into the sofa enjoying the last swallow of my martini.

*Now, that wasn't so bad.*

"How soon are you planning to leave?" Molly asked.

"As soon as possible. Why? Are you …? Oh right, the garage. You were getting your things ready to go back to school this week. And I was supposed to drive you down."

*So much for relaxing. Perhaps Harry could take her.*

"Ah, Harry?" I gave him one of my special help-me-out-looks.

He brandished his glass toward me. "Sorry, sweetheart. No can do. I promised Meg I'd help Jerry finish their new deck in time for the twins' birthday."

"Yeah, you're right."

He swiveled his chair back to the TV. "Between you and that crazy blonde friend of yours, I'm sure you'll come up with something."

With his snarky attitude and my dilemma with Molly, thoughts twisted in my head like a French braid. *Damn, he's not going to budge.* With a mixture of martyrdom and reluctance, I pulled myself slowly off the sofa. "All right then, I guess I'll just have to call Candace and tell her she'll have to babysit Lydia for a couple of days until I get back from taking Molly to school."

"Wait a minute, Mom. I've got the perfect solution." She slipped back into her same spot, drink in hand. "Why don't you guys drive me down to Southern Oregon? SOU is really close to the Medford airport. You can catch a plane there to Vegas. I'm sure Candace would like that better than playing nursemaid," she laughed.

"I love it. What a great idea." I gave Molly a big hug. "I'm sure she'd go for it."

I poked Harry on the shoulder. "How's that for a quick solution?" It was my turn to smirk.

129

"Oh, hell," Harry threw up his hands in defeat. "You never listen to me, anyway. You always do what you want, regardless of any good logical reasoning I give."

Molly and I gave each other a high five.

Dialing back his temper a notch, he made a request. "All I ask is that you be careful, Kate. When you're in Vegas, I don't want the two of you taking any foolish chances."

"We won't." I grabbed Molly's arm. "Come on, sweetie, we've got to hustle."

# Road Trip

THE NEXT DAY, all packed and in the car, Molly and I waved to Harry standing in the driveway, Romeo at his side. We motored off to pick up Candace. Upon arrival, we were met with four rather large suitcases placed on the porch next to the front door. When Anita answered the bell, I didn't wait to say hello, but marched up to Candace's bedroom, threw open the door, and shouted, "Four suitcases? Are you out of your mind? We'll only be gone a couple of days."

"But, Kate—"

"No, 'but Kate' Candace. I'm sorry. With all Molly's stuff, I hardly have room for even two of those *steamer trunks* you packed."

"Oh you exaggerate too much," countered Candace. "There're not *that* big."

I ran to the stairs, bent over the railing, and called down to Molly to help Anita bring up the luggage.

After negotiating a repack, despite Candace's pleading that everything in the suitcases was critical to maintaining her stature, we managed to fit everything into one compact bag and one carry-on.

"C'mon people, time's wasting. We need to get a move on." I ushered everyone downstairs to the car. We shoved things around to fit Candace's stuff into the back seat. It was a good thing Molly didn't take up much room.

Anita scurried to the front porch to wave us off. Lydia stood next to her, holding Jasper and gently stroking his furry neck. I caught a strange smile crossing her lips as we drove out of the driveway. It made me shiver.

The first few hours on the road were uneventful. Candace kept me occupied with idle chatter while Molly cuddled against the window, listening to music on her iPod and checking the email on her iPad. I was in thought mode and didn't here Candace until she nudged me.

"So what is it, Kate?"

"What's what?"

"That thingy we're supposed to be looking for, a thumb drive or flash drive?"

"Both. Some say flash others, thumb. Do you know what it does?"

"Not entirely. I'm not as computer savvy as you."

"You save your important documents on it so in case something happens to your computer, you still have the data you've stored."

"Sort of like a safety deposit box," she mused.

"Never thought of it that way, but why not?" I high fived her. "Good one."

Suddenly, Molly unplugged her ear buds and shouted, "I just got an email from Chad. He says he's close to being picked for a part in a new sitcom. Oh, and he said that Jimmie B will be playing in Vegas this weekend. Boy, I'd sure like to see him. "

Candace's non-stopped prattle suddenly ceased. The silence remained for the next few miles.

Because of the huge dark sunglasses shielding Candace's eyes, I couldn't tell if she'd nodded off, or was just daydreaming. "Hey, are you awake or did you finally run out of words?" I joked.

"Huh uh." Her voice was barely audible.

"I was only teasing." She didn't answer. Her sudden silence worried me. "Are you all right?"

She shook her head. "I was just thinking about something that happened a long time ago," she murmured, then turned to gaze out the window, avoiding any more conversation.

"Want to talk about it?"

"C'mon Aunty Candace, you've always had the best stories to tell about the olden days," Molly kidded.

Candace turned to me, her brow furrowed. "How come you never told me that Chad knew Jimmie B?" Her voice was almost accusatory.

"I didn't think it was important." I shrugged. "Chad sent Molly an email about a month ago, telling her that they had the same agent. That's all I know about him, except what

Molly told me. His band, *Bonasera,* recently came out with an album that's making the charts—her words—not mine." I flipped my head back toward my daughter.

"Not only that, he's one total hottie! That wavy black hair, those deep brown eyes, and those thick, black, curly lashes...sure sends those little tweenies into fits of total ecstasy."

"The older ones, too, I gather." I caught her expression in the rear view mirror. Molly squished up her nose at me. I nudged Candace playfully, but she didn't respond.

"Come on, I know we share a lot, but I didn't think it was a big thing to cause you to ... Candace, what is it?"

She removed her sunglasses. Puddles of water formed in her blue eyes.

Molly pushed her iPad aside and squeezed into the opening between the two front seats. "Do you know something about Jimmie B?" she asked, cautiously.

Candace barely nodded. "Kate ... Molly, you've got to swear that you'll tell no one of what I'm about to say."

"Pinky swear," said Molly, reaching out her little finger to Candace.

"I swear too," I said, joining mine with theirs.

"Jimmie B is ... he's my son." A gusher of tears spilled down her cheeks.

The surprise confession caused me to swerve, nearly throwing us into a ditch. Regaining control, I eyed a rest stop up ahead. "I think I'd better turn off here. We need a break."

Molly fell back in her seat. "I can't believe I'm in the same car with Jimmie B's mom."

I exited the highway and pulled into a parking space.

Molly fired one question after another until I held up my hand. "Molly, slow down. Let's give Candace a chance to tell her story."

I reached into the tissue box next to the armrest and handed several to Candace. "You told me once that you had lost a baby, but I thought he died in childbirth."

Candace dabbed at her eyes and blew her nose. Her voice was strained and solemn. "Molly, your mother knows this first part. I was once involved with a, well … a kind of man who came from a family with ties to the Las Vegas Mafia."

"Ooh, that gives me goose bumps," said Molly, rubbing her arms.

"I met him when I was working at a night club in Vegas. Nicky Busoni was the handsomest man I'd ever seen; tall, dark brown curly hair; eyes so black they could reach into your soul. We started dating. He bought me jewelry, fancy clothes, all the things a small town girl dreams of having." She looked at Molly. "You probably think that seems pretty lame in today's world. But that was the way it was back in those days. In my circle, Women's Lib didn't hit Vegas as fast as in other places."

"Oh my, it sounds so romantic. I'm fascinated," replied Molly.

"You won't be after I'm through with the story. Friends of mine who knew Nicky kept warning me about him, but love is blind and so was I. We got married, and a few months later, I was pregnant." Candace paused, and smiled briefly. "I'd never thought I could be any happier."

"What happened next?" asked Molly, curiosity pushing her higher in her seat.

Candace turned away from us and stared out the window. She shielded her eyes with her hand from the bright light of the afternoon sun. "Boy, I sure learned a lesson about blind love and living happily ever after. I thought we'd be getting a place of our own, but Nicky had it planned that we'd live in his parent's house. We'd have a wing all to ourselves, very private. His sizzling, sexy eyes melted away my complaints. A few days after settling in, I got a creepy feeling that I was being watched. When I mentioned it to Nicky, he said I was being silly."

"I imagine you found out different," I said.

"Oh, yes. His mother, Philomena Busoni, known to everyone as the Iron Lady, fixed her evil eye on me the minute we moved in. Nicky was her first born, and she was furious to think he would marry some low class Vegas nightclub floozy. When Mama Busoni found out I was pregnant, she put her evil plan in motion. She did her best to let Nicky know how excited she was about becoming a grandmother. But when I was alone with her, she showed another side." Candace stopped to take a sip from the bottle of water I handed her.

"Didn't you tell Nicky what his mother was doing?" I asked.

"I did." She nodded vehemently. "He even questioned his mother. But Philomena told him that I was being too emotional because of the pregnancy. She was clever, the old bat. I pleaded with Nicky to get us a place of our own, but he said it was ridiculous to move with the baby coming. Maybe later, he promised."

"After Jimmie was born, Mama Busoni made it a point to arrange for a personal maid to take care of my needs and a nanny for the baby. When I complained to Nicky that I barely got the chance to be alone with my son, he berated me for not appreciating his mother's generosity. There was nothing generous about it." She shook her head. A hint of bitterness crept into her voice. "The two women were really paid to take over my job of caring for our child. Philomena's plan was to drop little hints to Nicky that I wasn't showing enough interest in being a mother. She wanted to convince him that perhaps he had made a mistake in marrying me. That unbearable woman would go to any lengths to disgrace me. The sad thing is, her people would back her up regardless of the truth." Candace gnawed on her lip.

"Ooh, how dreadful." Molly shuddered.

"It gets worse. When Jimmie was six months old, Philomena found the perfect opportunity to destroy me. She waited until Nicky had to go out of town on family business for a few weeks. I won't go into any of the sordid details. All I can tell you is she took out all stops to discredit me, even accused me of having an affair with Sammy Sunseri, my personal body guard and one of Nicky's trusted friends. It was one lie after another. To her, I was nothing but a thief and a whore."

"That vicious bitch!" I cursed. "What did she want?"

"She wanted my son." Candace's voice cracked the minute she said the words. "I told her that Nicky loved me, and wouldn't believe anything she accused me of. Her lips twisted into a wicked smile. I knew then I was no match for a malicious pro." She slumped in her seat, the pain of her loss relived in her sad face.

"Philomena wanted me out of the house before Nicky returned. Her plan was to tell him that my post-partum depression had gotten worse, and arranged for me to go to a private clinic for help. She'd handle everything from stopping the vicious rumors being spread about me to showing deep concern for my well-being. I was not to have any calls or visitors. I couldn't believe this horrible woman could stoop so low to take a child away from his mother, but I was too young and too afraid to fight her."

"Did you actually go to the clinic?" wondered Molly.

"No, that was just her excuse for kicking me out of the house." Tears rolled down her cheeks.

"I can't believe she would do such a horrible thing." I said, handing her a fresh tissue.

"If I tried to fight her, she would claim that I had dishonored *The Family* by my conduct. Anyone that does that would have little chance of survival. Knowing what could happen if I fought back, I had no choice but to comply with her demands because …" she stammered, "because it wasn't only my life that was in jeopardy, but Sammy's too. I just couldn't … bear the guilt of that happening." Candace broke down into a shower of uncontrollable sobs.

The front seat was in an uncomfortable angle, but I wrapped my arms around her, holding her tight until the crying subsided

"They'd k … kill him too?" I stammered.

She nodded. "Make no mistake, they'd do just that."

"I'm so sorry. I wish I'd never brought up Jimmie B." Molly's eyes filled with tears.

With effort, Candace pulled herself together and gained control of her emotions. She turned to Molly. "It's not your fault, sweetie." She gently caressed my daughter's cheek. "It happened a long time ago, but I've learned to accept it."

"Did you leave that same day?" I asked.

"Yes. The sooner the better. The Iron Lady made quick work of me. I threw a few things in a suitcase under the watchful eye of the maid in case I should take something that belonged to the Busoni family. I grabbed Jimmie's baby picture from the dresser and stuffed some of the heirloom pieces of jewelry that Nicky had given me into my purse. The maid could tell the bitch whatever she wanted. I didn't care. When I was ready to go, Philomena ushered me into the library. Their attorneys had papers ready to sign. My hand shook and tear drops fell on the document. I could hardly see to write. Afterward, Sammy was ordered to drop me off at the bus station."

"Bus station?"

"Those were his instructions."

No one spoke for several minutes. It was a lot to digest.

Molly finally cut through the silence. "How did you find out that Jimmie had a band?"

"Sammy. He was my lifeline to my son. He felt I didn't deserve what the Iron Lady had done and sent me messages when he could. Sometimes a school picture of my boy would pop up in the mail."

"Didn't Jimmie wonder what happened to you?" I asked.

"Nicky told him that I walked out one day and never came back."

"That is so cruel!" Molly declared. "I'm sorry you had to relive that sad part of your life."

Candace heaved a sigh and relaxed back in the seat. "That's okay Molly. It kind of felt good to finally tell someone. Almost like going to confession."

"Oh my God," Molly suddenly exclaimed. "Then the Whitetowers are mixed up with gangsters, and they probably have no clue."

"They know, Molly, all too well," I said. But her comment had me thinking. Candace's story put a different slant on our trip.

*Maybe we're getting in too deep by going to Vegas. I'm no bonifide private eye, and neither is Candace. Once we find the flash drive, what happens next?*

My hands gripped the steering wheel. I had to ask myself again, *why are we helping Lydia?* "Maybe we should've let Lydia go instead. We could still back out. Drop Molly off at school and take our time driving home, maybe see a play or two in Ashland."

"Or," said Candace, "We could fly to Vegas and spend time relaxing around the pool, and do some serious shopping."

"We could." I wasn't quite convinced. Then I remembered looking out over the balcony the morning of Harry's reception, envying the Whitetowers' trips to Africa. I wanted to have a bit of excitement to spice up my life, and to be honest, helping a friend in need wasn't my main motive. It was the thrill of the adventure. And now, Candace's confession made it more important to go. If nothing else, just giving her the gift of seeing her son was more than enough reason to go through with this caper. I heaved a long sigh. "No, what's done is done, we're going." I checked my watch. "Time's running out. If we don't leave this rest area right now, we'll miss our plane."

I squared my shoulders and turned the key in the ignition. As I drove toward the exit I said confidently, "If we're careful, nothing should put us in any danger, right?" I glanced at Candace for encouragement.

She grinned and patted my arm.

Back on the highway, no one spoke for a few miles. There was a lot to think about.

Molly was the first to slice through the fog of silence. "Mom, I was thinking. I'd sure like to go to Vegas with you and Candace."

"Are you out of your mind, Molly?" I gasped, nearly driving off the road again.

"Why not? Look, school doesn't start for a few days, and I'd really like to help since—"

"What could you possibly do besides give us one more thing to worry about?"

Molly ignored my question. "I could text Chad that we'll be in Vegas tonight. His email said he'd be back to his apartment before noon tomorrow. I'm sure he'd keep me company while you two are doing your 'investigating.'" She finger quoted.

"I don't think—"

"Oh Mom, I need to have some fun. I spent my twenty-first birthday in Mexico this past summer building houses. I know, it was my choice, so don't give me the 'no-one-forced-you-to-go' lecture."

*How well she knew me.*

"I just think Vegas would be a great place to celebrate my, um, coming of age, don't you agree, Candace?" Molly placed her hands softly on the back of my neck, slowly massaging my shoulders as I drove the next few miles.

"Well yes, to the celebrating part," I countered. "But with this possible gangster business looming in the background, it may be too dangerous for you. Not only that, your father would kill me if he knew you were in Vegas with us."

"We don't have to tell him," Molly replied, finishing up with my back rub. She placed her hands on each of the front seats, eying each of us, waiting for an answer.

Not getting a quick enough response from me, she turned to Candace. "I'll even ask Chad if he could get us in to Jimmie B's show. Think of it, Candace, you'll be able to see him perform in person. Wouldn't that be great?" When she didn't reply, Molly hurried on. "Trust me, I won't tell Chad that Jimmie's your son. We pinky swore, remember?"

I caught sight of my daughter's imploring puppy-dog eyes in the rear view mirror. I glanced at Candace and saw the beginning of a smile surface upon her lips.

"She does make some good points." said Candace, glancing at me out of the corner of her eye. "What do you say, Kate? Think Molly pled her case well enough to go with us?"

"Okay," I reluctantly agreed. "I guess it'll be all right, but, Molly, promise me that you'll stay at the hotel or with Chad the whole time."

"I promise." She gleefully shoved her right hand over the front seats to collect high fives from both of us. "I'll send Chad an email right now." I heard her fingers dance upon the keypad, as she hummed one of Jimmie B's latest tune.

Traffic was light and we were able to make it to the apartment Molly shared with two other girls. She dropped her stuff, threw a few things into a carry on, and left a note for her roommates. We hustled to the airport with just enough time to buy another ticket, go through security and scurry to the gate before last call. It wasn't a direct flight, so the plane bumped into Reno for a one hour stop over and a plane change.

Molly was anxious to try one of the slot machines. "Don't expect to win here. Few people have much luck at airport terminals," I warned, as she put a dollar in the quarter machine. "You've got plenty of time to give this state your money."

No sooner had the words of wisdom left my mouth than the machine came to life, signaling she'd won fifty dollars. *So much for my counseling.* By the time she cashed in her winnings we were ready to board the next flight.

# What Happens in Vegas...

THE BRIGHT LIGHTS of Las Vegas lit up the night sky as the plane headed in for a landing.

"Talk about a place far removed from where *I* was this summer," uttered Molly. "I wonder how much their electricity bill is."

Candace playfully nudged her. "Don't worry, sweetie, they collect enough money from the tourists to more than cover the cost."

We followed the signs to the baggage area and collected our suitcases. The evening temperature was still quite warm, and we savored it after being in an air conditioned airplane. Taxis were lined up along the curb. Candace waved and within seconds one pulled up to us from the queue. The cabbie put our luggage in the trunk, asked where to, and we were off.

Molly hung her head out the cab's window, oohing and aahing as we passed from one huge hotel façade to another down the famous Strip. "Oh, my!" She was completely entranced by the dancing waters in front of the Bellagio.

"Wait until you see the inside." Candace motioned to the hotel behind the musical waves.

"You mean we're staying here?" Her jaw dropped in disbelief.

"Yup!" answered Candace. "This was Winn's and my favorite place to stay on the Strip."

"Everything is so ginormous," Molly whispered, as we entered the lobby.

"Oh sweetie, you ain't seen nutin' yet," Candace remarked as she approached the registration desk. The concierge greeted her warmly by name.

Molly grabbed my arm. "Did you see that? I. Am. In. Awe." Her eyes widened in wonderment.

"I'm just as impressed as you." We stood like two small-town tourists gawking at our surroundings. We admired Candace's calm poise. She definitely had command of the situation.

"Let's go." Candace motioned us to follow her and the bellhop to the elevators.

Molly kept a constant chatter during our ride up to the suite.

Once inside, the young male attendant placed our bags in the rooms that Candace assigned. A bottle of wine, a box of chocolates, a dish of assorted nuts, along with a bouquet of fresh flowers—compliments of the Bellagio—were decoratively displayed on the large glass coffee table.

Molly wandered about the suite, investigating every inch. From time to time, murmurs of delight escaped from her lips.

"I must say, Candace, you sure know how to live." I slipped out of my shoes and aimed my tired body at one end of an inviting comfy, cushy, sofa.

"Sometimes it pays to marry for money, and not for love. And he did have a lot of it, money that is."

"You mean you didn't love Winston?" I faked surprise.

"Winston Carrington-Jones was a very smart, shrewd man, but not foolish enough to think that I was in love with him. However, I really did have great respect and cared a great deal for Winn. He taught me a lot, especially how to enjoy the finer things."

"Sort of like Eliza Doolittle to 'Enry 'Iggins," suggested Molly, opening the small refrigerator to inspect its contents.

"Molly!" I started to berate her for her boldness, but Candace brushed the comment aside.

"Something like that." She laughed.

"How long were you two married?" Molly asked.

"Only five years. Winn was quite a bit older. He had a heart condition long before we met. I was up front about our relationship that I wasn't in love with him. We both knew that we'd only have a short time together and made the best of it. After the last episode with Eddie, I found a wonderful

companion in this marriage. I really was quite fond of him."
She toyed with a small glass bowl atop the coffee table.

"Wait a minute, back up the train. Did I hear you say Eddie?" It was my turn to offer up a surprise gasp.

Molly's eyes flew wide open. "I thought his name was Nicky. Who's Eddie?"

"Eddie Carbonetti, husband number two. Well it wasn't really a marriage since he sort of forgot to tell me he hadn't actually divorced his first wife."

"Oh Candace," I sighed. *What next?*

She just grinned and continued on with her story. "Thought I had money socked away somewhere."

I smirked. "You'd think you would've learned your lesson to steer clear of Italian men."

"Yeah, I should've, but darn, he was so handsome. Charisma oozed out of every pore. And oh the sex…man it was sure good."

"Candace!" I threw a threatening look at her, along with one of the side sofa pillows.

"For goodness sake, Kate, Molly's an adult. She probably knows more about sex than we ever did at her age."

Molly collapsed in a chair, laughing so hard she could hardly choke out, "Candace, I love you … and Mom, you should see your face."

"That's enough, you two." Slightly irritated at being the brunt of their teasing, I changed the subject. "Okay, let's unpack, freshen up, and get something to eat before we all turn into zombies." I inched out of my comfortable spot before my body decided to permanently mold itself in place for the duration.

"I'll call Olives and see if they're still serving dinner. Or we could order room service," Candace added.

"If we're voting, put me down for the latter," Molly said enthusiastically. "I've always wanted to do that. It seems so glamorous, having your food brought to your room … at least that's what it looked like in the movies."

"Glamorous or not, that's probably a good idea. We've had a pretty exciting day. Let's kick back this evening. Okay by you, Candace?" I asked.

"Fine by me. Let's do it." She took the dark brown leather hotel binder off the coffee table and thumbed through to the room service menu. We poured over the items and picked out our selections.

That done, I turned to Molly. "While Candace is calling in our order, why don't you call your father and let him know that you arrived at your apartment, then call Chad and tell him where we're staying."

"Any more assignments, Sarge?"

I laughed and shook my head. "Now off with you."

Molly saluted me, and with a grin, marched off to her room.

I turned to Candace. "What do you say we get out of these travel-weary clothes?"

"Let's do," she agreed.

While I was slipping into my sweats, Molly hollered that it was my turn to call Harry, which I did. Our conversation was short, just enough to tell him that we'd arrived and that we were staying at the Bellagio. "Yes, it's pretty posh, but Candace insisted, so I agreed, and I'm glad I did. We should stay here sometime, maybe for our anniversary." I yawned loudly. "Sorry, it's been a long day. Yes, we'll be careful. I'll let you know more after we've talk to Chad." I clicked off. That task done, I joined Candace in the living area.

We were snuggled in our original spots, sipping a glass of wine from the complementary bottle, when Molly returned. Her earlier jubilant manner was replaced by a very somber appearance. Still wearing the same clothes, she plunked down on a chair near me.

"Here, have a glass of wine," offered Candace. "Something tells me you might need it."

I quickly uncoiled from my relaxed position. A finger of dread tapped at the back of my neck. I watched Molly accept the glass from Candace.

"I spoke to Chad," she said.

144

"What's wrong? Did something happen to Chad?" My uneasiness was growing stronger.

"Chad's fine...although, he's still a little shaken after talking to the police."

"The police? Wh...why?" Dread now gripped my stomach.

"They … there was a dead man in his apartment."

"A what?" Candace choked on her drink.

I clutched at the lapel of my bathrobe. "Was it…?"

"No, Mom, it wasn't Chad's father. Mike knew what his dad looked like."

"I'm confused. Who's Mike?"

"He's Chad's friend."

"Molly, I think you'd better start from the beginning. What exactly did Chad say?"

She picked up her glass and took a good swallow of wine, steeling a moment to gather her thoughts. "Mike was keeping an eye on Chad's apartment while he was at his audition. This morning, he stopped by to check on things and found the front door unlocked. He didn't think too much of it and figured Chad had finished sooner than expected and taken an earlier flight back to Vegas. When Mike got inside, he found the place torn apart and a dead man sprawled on the living room floor. He immediately called 911, and then texted Chad."

The news struck us speechless. I finally found my voice and asked, "W…what happened next?"

"There was no identification on the body. Apparently, the man's neck had been broken. Chad hopped the next available plane out. By the time he arrived, the body had been taken to the morgue. Chad told the police he had no information to add, other than what Mike told them. The Las Vegas crime scene investigation unit is checking every inch of his apartment for clues, so Chad has to stay at Mike's place tonight. The police want him down at the station tomorrow to see if he can identify the body." She drained the rest of her wine.

"Wow! What a story!" Candace jumped up, bumping the coffee table, and nearly spilling the nuts. "It's almost like that

TV program. Kate, can you imagine, not only do we have to be like CSI and find where the flash drive is hidden, now we have to solve a murder."

"We're not sure that this has anything to do with the Whitetowers. It could be a rand—"

"No way. This is not a random act." Fear replaced her exuberance. "This type of viciousness is somehow connected to the Whitetowers. You see, the way this man was murdered has the Busoni family's handiwork written all over it. That's exactly how they handle things when someone crosses them.Though they usually leave the area pretty clean without much of a trace."

"But the apartment was ransacked," Molly interjected.

"That's the one difference that doesn't make any sense," said Candace, "unless they were interrupted and had to leave in a hurry."

I cringed at the mention of the Busoni name. "I'm not liking how this is going. I'm almost convinced now that it wasn't a smart idea to come here after all. Knowing what the Busonis are capable of scares the hell out of me." A shiver ran up my spine as I glanced at Candace's pale face. "How about you? With Winston gone, you have no protection from those animals. This could leave you wide open to—"

"I've already thought of it, Kate," Candace interrupted, pacing back and forth. "I'd rather take my chances. Right now, the opportunity to see my son trumps anything the Busonis could do to me."

This new wrinkle set me wondering. "God, Molly!" I turned to her. "Murder wasn't on my mind when we conceived of this plan. Maybe it's best if you fly back tomorrow."

"Mom, look, it was my idea to come here, not yours. Don't worry, I'll be all right, especially with Chad as my bodyguard of sorts."

"I know, I know. You're not a child anymore. But, you can't stop me from being concerned about you."

Candace picked up the wine bottle and began filling each of our glasses then curled up on the other end of the sofa and asked, "Is Chad at Mike's now?"

"Yes. I told him to come to the hotel tomorrow around 10 o'clock, if that's all right with everyone."

"That's fine, no problem."

A knock on the door startled us.

"Room Service," a male voice called out from the other side.

"Lord, we forgot all about food." Molly started to get up.

"No." Candace pushed her aside, racing to the door. She squinted through the peephole a long moment before opening it.

The attendant rolled the cart into the room and stood quietly by the table while Candace surveyed the display. She signed the tab and sent him off.

"That knock on the door rattled my nerves." I looked at Candace. "You don't suppose anyone knows we're here?"

She shook her head. "It seems unlikely … this soon."

Those last two words bothered me. If my suspicions were right, someone had been watching us from the moment we set foot on the ground. "Could you be a little more specific?"

Before she could answer, Molly interrupted with a groan. "Hey, I'm starved and the food is getting cold. We can eat and talk at the same time."

"You're right," said Candace. She quickly picked up her dish and took it to the table.

Molly's interruption had given Candace an opportunity to avoid answering my question. Reluctantly, I gave in and joined them, but I wasn't letting her off the hook. I'd be waiting later for an explanation.

For a few minutes, we split time between talking and devouring everything on our plates but the garnish.

"That really hit the spot," I said, draining the last of my coffee. I stared for a while at a tiny drop left in the bottom of the cup. "Uh, Candace, you never answered my question."

"What was that? I forgot." She mumbled into her coffee.

"About being watched. Is that a strong possibility?"

147

"Probably so."

"That wasn't quite the answer I was looking for. Weren't you usually with Winston on these trips?" My mind was in overdrive thinking of all the things that might happen, could happen.

Seeing the distressed look on my face, Candace tried to reassure me. "Kate, don't worry. We'll be all right. Believe me. I'm sure nothing's going to happen."

The long day caught up with me. I was too tired to argue. "Okay, but we should figure out how much to tell Chad what we know about his parents before we meet him tomorrow."

"I think we've done enough thinking for tonight. Let's sleep on it," yawned Candace.

"Don't you think we should wait to hear what Chad has to say before we do that?" Molly asked.

"That's true, honey, but we need to find out if he has any information about his parents' activities, or, if they have something to do with the dead man in his apartment."

"Oh, let's just wing it, Kate. We'll ask him a few questions and go from there."

"Mom's probably right, Candace. We should have some kind of plan."

Candace sat quietly across from us, arms crossed over her chest, deep in thought.

I knew I shouldn't ask her what was on her mind but… "Got anything more to add?"

That snapped her out of her reverie. Candace's lips curved into a wide grin. "Yes, yes, you bet I do. And it's just perfect."

"What is it?" The excited look in her eyes sent up a big warning signal.

"Kate, you and I need to find a way to break into Chad's apartment."

I winced. *Oh, Geez, It's worse than I thought.*

"You won't need to break in, Candace." Molly leaned back in her chair, rubbing her tired eyes. "The crime scene guys are probably through. If the tape is still up, just use Chad's key."

148

"Smart girl," I replied. *I knew that kid had a good head on her shoulders.* "Okay, before we get too ahead of ourselves, let's take Molly's idea and wait for Chad's input."

Molly yawned and nodded at the same time.

I glanced at my watch. "Good lord, it's after midnight. We need to get some sleep. Candace, if we do decide to go, will you see about getting us a rental car tomorrow?"

"I'll put it on my list," Candace answered.

"What list? You never make a list."

"Oh, Kate, I always have a lot of things to do when I'm in Vegas." She sauntered off to her bedroom with a wave of her hand. "'Night all."

I heaved a big sigh. It was settled. As far as I could tell, we'd made a plan without planning.

# The Morgue the Merrier

THE NEXT MORNING, Molly and I waited for Candace to finish dressing.

"Two bucks says she'll hold us up for a half an hour," I said. "Be ready to text Chad that we'll be late."

"You're on," laughed Molly.

"Hey, what's so funny?" asked Candace as she sprinted into the living area.

"Uh…er…ah," I stammered.

"Mom bet me you'd take forever to dress, and I'd have to tell Chad that we'd be late," she giggled.

"Hah, gotcha this time, Kate." Candace smirked, thumping me on the shoulder.

"That you did." I was quite surprised, but at the same time a little curious about her punctuality.

"Pay up, Mom."

"Don't worry, you know I'm good for it."

"Hurry up, and let's get going. We don't want to keep Chad waiting." Candace took the lead and headed out the door.

We rode silently down the elevator. Perhaps it was the anticipation of finding out what Chad had to say that kept us from speculating what the next step would be. That is, if there would be a next step.

Chad met us with big hugs as we exited into the lobby. Although his smile was warm, I could see worry and uneasiness in his dark blue eyes. *Probably didn't get much sleep.* Before I could say a word, Candace linked her arm into his.

"Come on, everyone, let's get out of this noisy area." She looked around then immediately propelled us toward the Pool Cafe. "It'll be a little quieter in there so we won't have to yell to be heard."

I noticed the anxious expression on Candace's face.

*Had she seen someone familiar in the midst of all the people weaving in and out of the lobby?*

When seated, Candace suggested Bloody Marys for all. After drinks were served and orders taken, the questioning began.

Chad repeated the same information he'd told Molly the night before. "I was at the morgue just before coming here," he explained. "Like I told the detective, I've no idea who the man is—was," He stirred the celery stick in his drink.

"Did you see anything unusual? A scar or a tattoo on his face?" I asked.

"No...uh, yeah, I think there was something like a birthmark near the left side of his temple."

"Was he fair-skinned or dark?"

"Not dark, sort of light tan. I couldn't tell the color of his hair because it was shaved." Chad gave me a puzzled look. "How come you're so interested in this man?"

"Just wondered." I shrugged. "Did you make contact with your father while he was here?"

"I saw him twice, and both times I noticed something different about him. He seemed to be on a continuous adrenaline rush, talking fast, fidgeting with anything he had in his hands. That's definitely not like him."

"So, he didn't stay at your place at all?"

"Not overnight. He stopped by the evening before I left for LA. That's the last time I saw him."

"Did anyone besides Mike have a key to your apartment?"

"No. Well, Dad did." He hesitated then asked, "Why all the questions, Mrs. C?"

"Before I answer, Chad, I need to know how much you know about an ancient artifact that your parents brought back from Tunisia,"

"Not much. Something about a vase or chalice."

"Do you know what they were going to do with it?"

"I think Dad was supposed to meet someone here in town." He picked up his glass then stopped in mid-sip. "Do you think there's any connection between that person, and the dead guy in my place?"

"We don't know for sure," Candace said, pointing her half-eaten celery stalk at him. "But, there's a possibility your parents may be in a lot of trouble."

Chad sat up stick-straight, his face tightened. "You'd better tell me everything you know."

Candace and I exchanged looks and nodded. After quizzing Chad, it was apparent we knew more about his parents' activities than he did. I took a deep breath. "I'll start. Candace and Molly can add anything I've missed." It only took a few minutes to bring him up-to-date.

"We need to find the most recent combination to your parent's safe. So, that's why we're here," said Candace.

"But what we didn't count on was finding a man murdered in your apartment," added Molly.

"Whoa, this is a hell of a lot to swallow." Chad slumped in his chair.

"I know, but I hope you understand that we're trying to help," I said in my most comforting voice.

I put my drink on the table and reached for his hand. "You can't imagine how this has mushroomed since the first day I saw the black limo in front of your house."

"I know what you're trying to do, Mrs. C, and I appreciate it. In fact, I'll call Mom and ask if there's anything I can do to help."

"I'm sure she'd like to hear from you." I tried to sound encouraging, but I wasn't convinced there was any more he could do. At any rate, it'll validate what we are trying to do for Lydia.

Chad punched in his mother's cell number, stood and mouthed that he'd be right back.

He returned within a few minutes. "Guess there wasn't anything else I could do to help." He rubbed the back of his neck. "But how can I not be? It's my apartment where the crime took place." Frustration played upon his face.

"Sounds like your mom doesn't want you involved," Molly assumed.

Chad suddenly thrust his irritation at her. "I don't understand why you came here if you knew that this trip could wind up being dangerous." He shook his head in disapproval.

Molly touched his arm. "It didn't seem that risky when we left Oregon. Mom and Candace didn't want me to come, Chad, but I insisted. It was my idea. Outside of all this, I wanted to see Jimmie B. I also had to promise not to wander too far from the hotel assuring them that you would take care of me." She grinned.

"That goes without question." He laid his other hand over Molly's reassuringly. His annoyance at her subsided. "So, what happens next?"

"We need to find out who the dead guy is," I said. "I have a feeling that Lydia might know, but all we have to go on is a man with a shaved head and a birthmark." A thought struck me. "The M.E. probably took a picture of him, and if there was no identification on him, the police may've sent it to the newspaper. Let's check the local paper."

"I've a better plan," Molly piped up. "I'll go back to the morgue with Chad."

"To do what?"

"To get a picture of the body."

"Not on your life," I cried. "I don't want you mixed up any more in this than you already are. Besides, your dad would have my head if he ever found out."

"He won't Mom. It shouldn't be dangerous—a little spooky maybe—but Chad could phone the coroner's office and tell them he wanted to take a second look at the body. I don't think that's an unusual request."

"I'm sure you're right." Candace's head bobbed up and down in agreement.

"I'll pretend I'm a Criminal Justice college major, visiting my friend. While I'm distracting the medical examiner with a bunch of questions, Chad'll take a picture with his cell and send it to his mom. She'll be able to tell almost instantly if she knows who he was."

Totally impressed with her quickness, Candace asked, "Wow. Where'd you get this girl?"

153

"Molly could always think on her feet," I replied with a mixture of pride and surprise. "Have you any idea what to ask?"

"I'll Google it while we're on our way to the morgue," replied Molly.

Candace high fived her. Even Chad nodded, buying into her idea.

Odd man out, I reluctantly gave in, but not without a promise from Chad to keep her safe.

"Don't worry Mrs. C, she'll be by my side at all times." The two young friends rose to leave.

"Oh Chad, before you go, could we borrow the key to your apartment?" I asked. "We need to check if the crime scene people left that book *Flash* Drive there."

"Also, the flash drive." Candace tossed in.

"Sure," he said, pulling out his key ring from his jacket pocket. He unhinged one and handed it to me. "I don't know if you'll find anything. CSI is pretty thorough, so I'm told."

"Ah, but they won't know what to look for."

"True, but there's caution tape over the door, and they may have it padlocked if they're not through."

The talk of crime scenes and caution tapes were beginning to play on my confidence. "This new information from Chad worries me to the point of scrapping our plan." I held up the key. "On second thought, maybe we ..." I started to give it back to Chad when Candace, sensing what I was about to do, swiped it from my hand.

"No worries," said Candace, suddenly taking charge. "We'll figure out what to do once we get to your place." There was a mischievous twinkle in her eyes.

*Oh good lord! She's thinking of breaking into Chad's apartment padlocked or not. I hope I'm wrong. I could only wish.*

"Now, run along you two. We'll all meet back at the hotel this evening, say around sixish?" Candace looked at me to confirm. I nodded.

When the two were out of earshot, I grabbed her by the arm. "Tell me we're not going to do something as stupid as breaking into an apartment and risk getting arrested for interfering with a crime scene."

"Oh pooh Kate, you worry way too much. If we have to use another method of getting into the apartment, we'll simply wear gloves, no fingerprints to trace back to us." Candace smiled. "Come, loosen up, let's live on the wild side for a little while. Remember you wanted some adventure in your life."

I knew those words would somehow come back to bite me. What I should've done then and there was to stand my ground and stop this foolishness, but I couldn't put my curiosity to rest. Lydia had spun her story, and like a spider, she caught us in her web. We had to find the flash drive. Chad's was the most likely place to search. Really the only place, as far as we knew.

"Okay, yeah, let's go." Candace signaled for the waitress to bring the bill. She signed the tab, latched onto her purse, linked her arm with mine and maneuvered our way out of the restaurant.

Approaching the lobby, I suddenly remembered what I wanted to ask her. "Why were you in such a hurry to drag us into the restaurant? Did you think we were being watched?"

"Yes and no. I'm not sure," she answered, a bit bewildered. "There was a young man standing near one of the huge vases by the concierge's desk. He kept staring at us … and I guess I kind of panicked."

I nervously glanced around the area. "Do you see him, now?"

"He's not here. I even checked in the restaurant after we were seated, but he didn't follow us. Sorry to say this, Kate, but we've got to be on guard at all times."

"Whew, well good thing you didn't mention it to the other two." I checked my watch. "Goodness, it's almost one o'clock. We've got to be going. What time will the rental car be here?"

"Ah, not until 3:30," Candace answered, avoiding my eyes.

"Huh?"

"Well, I sort of made a hair appointment with Lawrence for 1:15 pm."

"Candace, you didn't."

"Now don't be mad. Chad's apartment isn't going anywhere. Besides, I told you I had a list of things to do … and that was one of them."

"Now I understand why you were so prompt this morning." I narrowed my eyes at her.

"Honestly, I just couldn't come to Vegas and not have my hair done by the most marvelous stylist ever. And he's squeezing me in, such a dear man." She checked her reflection in one of the glass windows of the shop next to the restaurant. "Besides, I want to look good even when facing the enemy."

"Damn it Candace! I should've known something like this would happen."

"Oh tut, tut, what's the big deal?"

So many angry words came to mind. I wanted to spew them at her all at once, but it wouldn't have done any good. With the last bit of patience left in me I asked, "So what, pray tell, my dear Candace, am I supposed to do while you are otherwise engaged?"

"Oh, I don't know, get your nails done, read a magazine, play the slot machines, roulette … or call Harry. I'm sure he'd like to hear from you," she finished, nearly out of breath.

Between clenched teeth, I sputtered, "All right, meet me in the lobby at 3:30 sharp. I don't care if you have a curling iron hanging from your head, hear? I'm not waiting."

We separated, Candace tripping lightly to the hairdresser, me stomping to the elevator.

# Message in a Jacuzzi

THE AFTERNOON RAYS of the September sun began to slip behind the huge hotels as we finally pulled out of the Bellagio and headed to Chad's apartment. I had little trouble maneuvering the bright red Chrysler Sebring convertible through the main thoroughfare. I had to give credit to Candace for the rental. It felt pretty darned classy. I exited onto the freeway and drove southward to Paradise, a small town a few miles south of Las Vegas. A dark cloud whisked by, sprinkling a few drops of rain, making little cat prints on the windshield.

"Oh dear," Candace wailed, swatting the two or three drops that fell on her heavily sprayed coiffed tresses. "I just knew we should've started out sooner. Maybe you should put the top up?"

I glared at her. If I weren't behind the wheel, I'd have throttled her. Instead, I tossed her my scarf. "Here, throw this over your head."

Candace flipped it lightly over her hair and held the two ends under her chin for a brief moment. By then any threat of a torrential rain vanished. She was driving me insane, gushing about the fabulous Mr. Lawrence.

"He's so utterly charming. What that man does with a drier, a brush and a pair of scissors is simply marvelous." She pulled the visor down and admired his handiwork in the mirror. "I think he made me look ten years younger. Don't you think?"

"Yeah, guess you got your $250 worth," I scoffed.

"You should try him before we leave. He could do wonders for you. A little trim here, a tint there. He'd work his magic and turn that outdated style of yours into—" She stopped mid-sentence catching the murderous look in my eyes.

I gripped the steering wheel, willing myself not to turn off the highway and toss her to the curb.

After a bit, I glanced sideways and saw that she'd slunk down in her seat. My fury subsided. I softened. "I know you mean well, but there are times when you drive me plum crazy."

"Sorry," she apologized, her face lit up at my apology. "So now that I'm forgiven, and if we're friends again, would you let me call Lawrence and—"

"Don't push your luck, kiddo!" I quickly cut her off.

The rest of the drive was quiet. Candace carefully rearranged the scarf over her hair and loosely tied the ends together. I was deep in thought when the voice on the GPS announced something. "Did she say Exit 13 was a mile away?"

"Um, maybe we just passed … no, yes, it's coming up right about … quick, get in the outside lane." Candace cried out.

I swerved, barely missing a burly looking man with long white hair riding a Harley. I was thankful his eyes were hidden by dark glasses. *I don't need another adventure.* "I hope you're right." Luckily, the apartment was only a few blocks off the highway. I swung into a slot marked for visitors.

Chad's place was on the second floor. The yellow caution tapes that had been strung tightly across the front door was slightly sagging. Tiny fingers of fear gripped the back of my neck. Someone had been there earlier, and it wasn't the police. "Candace, we need to get in and out quickly before anyone else gets an idea to check out the place."

I tried to open the door with the key Chad had given me. Nothing happened. Perhaps the manager changed the lock. Lucky for us it wasn't padlocked. Candace stood closely behind me. I knew she was itching to help but afraid to open her mouth for fear of having my foot stuffed in it.

"Crap! Now what'll we do?" I turned around, almost bumping heads with her. "You look like a horse ready to fly out of the gate." I stepped aside. "I suppose you know how to get this door open."

"Uh, huh!" Candace popped her head into her enormous bag and came out with a small silver case. She opened it and pulled out a slender piece of metal that looked something like a crochet hook.

"What is that?"

"It's a skeleton key."

My eyes narrowed. "Candace…!" I tempered my outdoor voice.

"Now Kate, don't ask questions. Step aside," she ordered.

Candace inserted the key into the lock and twisted it while simultaneously turning the knob. The door opened. "Presto, there you are my friend. After you." She bowed low, waving me into the apartment.

Candace didn't notice the small throw-rug in the hall. Head held high and sporting a confident smile, she tripped on it, head first into the living room.

"Way to go, Grace. Always making the grand entrance." I sighed and bent down to help her up. "Are you hurt?"

"Don't know yet." Candace batted my hand away. "I can get up by myself, thank you very much." She rolled onto her knees and pushed up to a standing position. She straightened her clothing, picked up her purse, and dramatically limped to the nearest chair.

I stood in the middle of the room, surveying the surroundings. A desk was situated in front of a side window. *That's as good a place as any to start.* A bit of late afternoon sunlight was almost enough to search without turning on the desk lamp. I used the pen light I bought while browsing through the gift shop waiting for Candace.

"Oh darn!" Candace burst out, looking down at one of her shoes. "I tore the strap off my new Jimmy Choo's." She looked toward me for sympathy. "Now how am I going to get around?"

I was exasperated "You figure it out. I told you to bring a pair of flats."

"Well, you rushed me after my hair appointment, and I didn't get a chance to go back to our room," she retorted.

"And, besides, these were the only ones that went with this outfit." Out came the pout.

"God forbid you should wear something that could go with everything."

"You know, I just can't go out in public without everything matching."

Seeing the forlorn look on her face, I managed to choke down all the terse words stuck on my tongue. There was no use arguing. Instead, I pointed to her purse and said, "You must have something you could use in that satchel on steroids - a bobby pin, paper clip, glue, bubble gum, shoe repair man."

"I'm offended by your attitude." She continued to pout, holding up her purse. "This so happens to be a marvelous Jimmy Choo bag, too."

"Choo, schmoo, I don't give a damn what's on your feet or slung over your shoulder. Just do the best you can and hurry it up, will you? We don't have much time. Find something, please."

I continued pawing through Chad's desk drawers, looking for the flash drive *nothing*. I spotted a book on the end table next to the sofa and cocked my head sideways, attempting to read the spine. I jumped when Candace let out a small cry.

"Ouch! Damn it!" She held up a chipped a nail.

I answered with a disgusted look. *No sympathy here.* Candace gave me a sheepish grin. "I'll fix it." She rummaged through her purse, pulled out a nail file. "Oops!"

"Now what?" My patience at level roaring red.

"My nail file fell between the cushion and arm of the chair. Don't worry. I'm getting it." She reached inside the crack. "Wait, I feel something else down there." She fished out the article. "It looks like a tube of lipstick. Probably fell out of one of Chad's girl friends' purses," she giggled. "Hmm, I wonder what color she wears." She open it. "Oh, I don't think this is a lipstick."

"Oh, for heaven's sake, bring it over so I can take a better look."

Candace closed the tube and hobbled over to me, still wearing the one good shoe. I stared at her feet and then at her face. *No, I won't comment.* I grabbed the item and studied it for a second then pulled it apart.

"It's a flash drive." We gave each other wide-eyed looks.

"Do you think that it's *the* flash drive we're looking for?" Candace asked.

"Maybe Stanford was in a hurry to hide it here before being caught."

A sudden noise outside the apartment stopped Candace dead in the middle of the room. We heard the rattle of the front door knob.

I jumped up and whispered, "Oh God, I forgot to lock it when we came in. Quick, we've got to hide!" I motioned to Candace to grab her stuff.

She picked up her purse, the damaged shoe and shuffled toward me.

"For God's sake, take off that other shoe," I hissed.

"Okay, okay," she whispered back.

I turned off my pen light, tossed the flash drive into my purse, and signaled for Candace to follow me. We headed down the hall and into the first open door, which happened to be the bathroom. There was a shower stall and a small Jacuzzi with a lid secured on top. I fumbled with one side, got it part way open, and reached inside to see if there was any water. *Good it's dry.* "Quick, get into the tub."

Candace threw her shoes and purse in first, then sort of slithered in. I followed behind whispering, "Hunker down as low as you can." I grabbed the open end, pulled it over us, and scooched next to her.

"I feel like such a cliché hiding in here," Candace mumbled.

"If you don't shut up and keep your head down lower, you'll be a dead cliché," I hissed into her ear. More than one set of footsteps entered the living room. Sounds of furniture scraped the floor, drawers emptied, cabinets opened and slammed shut, and papers ruffled.

Near the hallway, a male voice called out, "Hey Bernie, what're we s'posed be looking for, again?"

The second voice responded gruffly, "Hell Ralphie, don't ya remember anyting? It's some kind of a computer gizmo the boss wants us to find."

"Geez, ya don't have ta be a shitface about it."

"Shut up. Just keep lookin'."

"Hey, Bernie, I gotta take a piss!"

"Well, find the can, go. An' hurry back. We ain't got all day."

Alarmed, we huddled closer together as the man called Ralphie entered. He began singing, "Whenna da moon hitsa yer eye like a biga pizza pie," off key while doing what he came in to do.

I shoved my fist in my mouth, stifling the urge to laugh hysterically. I didn't dare look at Candace, who was beginning to shake up and down, ready to burst. When a disgusting odor penetrated the room, we almost lost it.

Suddenly we heard the voice of Dean Martin singing "That's Amore" floating in from the living room. The music stopped, and the man called Bernie started talking.

"Dat's my man Deano,"said Ralphie, singing along with Martin, finishing with a final squirt, and a flush.

"Hurry it up will you," yelled Bernie. "No boss, we ain't found it, yet. Huh? Oh yeah, I see it, but you said to...ok, ok, I got it. We're on our way."

"Hey Ralphie, git your ass back in here. The boss wants us back, now! Capisce?"

"Okay, okay! I'm comin'." He flushed the toilet. We heard him zip up his pants and stroll out of the john … without washing his hands.

Candace and I looked at one another. "Eew," we both gagged. There was more noise of papers crunching underfoot, and then we heard the door open and slam shut.

We waited for a few minutes, pressed against the bottom of the tub, not willing to take any more breaths than necessary. When we thought for certain that the men had left, I inched the lid up. My heart finally left my mouth and drifted back into my chest.

"Boy that was close! That Ralphie, what a jerk! Didn't even wash after peeing. Yuk!" said Candace. "I hope we never have to meet him in person."

"Better hope we don't have to shake his hand," I added.

I peeled my body off the porcelain and pulled myself up. My legs had gone to sleep, so I stood for a minute, knees bent, holding on to the edge of the tub until the tingling stopped. I looked back at Candace. "You ok?"

"I think so. Give me a sec to unkink the kinks." Candace tossed her purse and shoes out first, then climbed over the edge. "Oh, oh. I think I might've broken another nail." She took a minute to assess the damage.

"Come on, Candace. We need to get out of here."

The living room looked messier than when we first came in. I went straight to the table where I'd first seen the book, but it was gone. *Drat!* Candace had interrupted me with her nail issue before I got a good look at the spine. "I'm not sure, but I think they took the book Lydia mentioned she'd given to Chad."

"Flash Drive?" She asked.

"That's it. Looks like Bernie and Ralphie took it. Stanford must've told the Busonis he had some information hidden in the pages."

"Well, ha, ha, Bernie and Ralphie, we did better than you two, *we've* got the flash thingy!" Candace thumbed her nose at the imaginary thugs.

"I wouldn't count them out," I cautioned. "We don't know which one of us has the right info. There've been way too many twists and turns in this double-crossing scheme. For all we know, Lydia may still be lying to all of us, Stanford included."

"You're right. We need to get access to a laptop and find out what's on this drive," said Candace.

"We're wasting way too much time talking. Let's get out of here before anybody sees us." I took her arm and maneuvered her out the door, down the steps, and to our car.

I was ready to pull out of the driveway when my cell phone beeped. It was a text message from Molly. I read it to

Candace. "Mission accomp, pic sent, heading bk to hotel. Mo."

I texted back, "Gd job! On r way. See u soon, m."

On the way back to the hotel, Candace busied herself doing shoe repair. I couldn't begin to guess what she found in her 'duffle' bag to use as a Band-Aid, but in a few short minutes she waved the finished project at me. It was a Band-Aid!

"There, look see, I did it. Hope it holds until we get back to our room."

"That's great, Candace. Now remove that spikey stiletto from my face before we become another Nevada statistic." I batted at it like it was an annoying fly. Thirteen hundred dollar purse, $850 pair of shoes, $250 hair job, $400 pair of Armani sunglasses that she uses as a head band. Jeez, the woman's a walking designer groupie.

She dutifully slipped the shoe back on her foot, testing its strength by wiggling it a bit. Satisfied, she leaned back in her seat. We rode silently the rest of the way back to the hotel.

We drove into the entrance at six o'clock, the exact time we were to meet Chad and Molly. We rushed up to the concierge's desk so that Candace could request a laptop to be sent to our suite. "Thank you, Henri," she purred.

*Bet his name is really Hank from Hoboken* "Hurry up." Candace tucked her arm through mine. "We need to get to the elevator fast. I feel my handiwork is coming apart."

Molly and Chad were already seated comfortably on the sofa, watching the local news. "Quick, come look!" Molly motioned us to the TV. "The anchor's talking about the homicide in Chad's apartment."

Aside from what we already knew, the reporter had little to say. A banner with a phone number was running at the bottom of the screen for anyone with information to contact the police.

"Good," I said, relaxing a bit. "Apparently we managed to get in and out without anyone seeing us."

"Even Bernie and Ralphie," Candace added, applying hand sanitizer from a small bottle she pulled from her purse. "Anyone else want some? Kate?" She held out the vial.

"Who's Bernie and Ralphie?" Molly wrinkled her brow.

"We'll explain after we hear what you two accomplished at the morgue." I put a finger to my lips and stared at Candace to keep quiet.

"We didn't have any trouble at all. It was a breeze," Molly began.

"That's because the entire department from the guy at the front desk to the medical examiner were completely under your spell," teased Chad.

Molly punched him in the arm.

"I explained that Molly was studying Criminal Justice. She asked if she could come with me to see the corpse."

"I smiled sweetly at the M.E., that's what they call him in cop talk," said Molly, "and kept him busy with questions while Chad took a couple of pictures with his cell phone. Actually, Mom, it was quite exciting seeing my first dead body." She paused. "As a matter of fact, I'm thinking of changing my major," she announced, and then burst out laughing at the astonished look on my face. "Gotcha."

"Thanks a lot," I said, grabbing my heart before it flew out the window. "With everything that Candace and I've just been through, that would've topped it!"

"I'd say that's a job well done. Bravo!" Candace said over her shoulder as she wandered to the bar and drug out four glasses. "I don't know about all of you, but this air conditioning is making me dehydrated. Anyone for a cool glass of H2O?" Without waiting for an answer, she filled and distributed the drinks to us.

Candace's interruption gave me a chance to regain my composure. I turned my attention to Chad. "So, did your mom call you back?"

"Yes, but her voice sounded a little strained. Mom told me the dead man might've been Leo's business partner, but she wasn't sure because she'd met him only once while in Tunisia."

165

"That's strange. Lydia never mentioned meeting anyone else. The only other person she told us about was the handsome doctor." Candace and I exchanged worried looks. "I'm sorry to say this, Chad, but I think she's lying, or covering for someone. I bet the Busoni brothers have—"

A knock on the door interrupted her sentence.

"Good lord, don't look so startled," said Candace glancing at our worried faces. "We've got to stop getting all flustered when someone rings or knocks. I'll get it."

We heard her flirtatious banter at the door. Soon Candace returned, proudly holding the laptop high above her head as if she had won the Mirror Ball on Dancing with the Stars.

I had to admit that this whole situation was beginning to play heavily on me. I settled my nerves enough to motion for Candace to set the laptop on the table. "Chad, you do the honors."

We crowded around while he fired it up. It was a Windows PC. "Dad uses Word and Excel, so we should be able to click into his documents." He slipped the flash drive into its port on the side. A message appeared on the monitor. "Oh great! It's password protected."

"Can you think of a word or list of numbers your parents would use for one?" I asked.

"I'll give it a try." He began to type in birth dates first forward, and backward, people's names they knew, even Jasper the cat. Nothing worked.

"Any music, books, movies that they both enjoyed?" I asked. "I know, you've probably never paid too much attention to their likes. But…" I was beginning to lose hope.

Chad's brow furrowed. He chewed on his lower lip. "There's one tune on the soundtrack from Xanadu that Mom played a lot, especially when she was distressed about something. When Dad and I heard the music playing over and over, we knew she was in one of her moods. The song had a calming effect on her."

"Well, give it a go," Candace urged.

He typed in Xanadu and hit the enter key. The password was accepted.

"Bingo!" shouted Candace.

We now knew for a fact that this flash/thumb drive belonged to the Whitetowers'. Two yellow folders appeared on the monitor. One was simply called NUMBERS, the second one BENTON.

"This looks like a no-brainer. The combinations to the safe are obviously in the first one," he surmised. "This should be easy enough." Chad opened the file and found two columns of numbers with corresponding dates for each. He scrolled down to the last one listed.

The entry was made the day before Stanford left for Vegas. "Guess I spoke too soon," Chad's earlier optimism wilted. "That certainly won't help Mom at all, unless Dad was in such a rush, he didn't get a chance to change the code on the day he left."

"Or … he did but didn't put it in the flash drive," Candace worried the beads of her necklace with her fingers.

"What about the second one, Chad? Does BENTON mean anything to you?" I asked.

"Yes, that's Mom's maiden name," he answered. "Maybe we'll find a clue in there."

"Good," Candace said. "Open it up while I get the vodka you brought. Something tells me we may need it."

*She may be right.* Weariness was beginning to show on all of us.

Candace hurried to the bar for the bottle and snagged a bag of chips. I followed her and picked up the bucket of ice and tonic. We returned to find Molly and Chad staring wide-eyed at the monitor.

"What the…?" he puzzled. "I didn't expect this."

Candace and I peered at the screen.

"It…it's a poem, I think, or maybe a riddle," said Chad.

"What could it possibly mean?"

"Maybe one of us should read it out loud," said Molly.

Chad nodded. "You do it." He moved to the side so that she could get a better view. The poem/riddle was typed in big print and took up the whole page.

Molly began:

167

" 'Two flowers, one vase
New fragrance escapes
Two people involved in a loving embrace.
A tick of a clock
Its hour does chime
Could it possibly be three, seven, or nine?' "

"There must be a series of numbers in the riddle. It looks like some kind of cryptic message that Lydia could—"

"What a minute," Chad interrupted me. "There's a second page." He scrolled down. "There's one line" He read it to us. "Casa - Blanca – Henderson – 6500."

"Oh my God!" Candace dropped the bag of chips she'd just opened, spewing them all over the table. Her face paled. I saw fear creeping into her eyes. "The Busonis...li...live in H...Henderson," she stammered, "at 6-5-0-0 Casa Blanca Circle." Her right hand clutched her throat. "Oh dear God, they've taken Stanford to the mansion! If he's double-crossed them in any way, they'll torture him. And..." her voice shriveled to an inaudible whisper.

I tried to ease the panic that filled her face. "We don't know that for sure."

"But, if...if he talks, lord knows what he'd tell them. You and I could be in grave danger."

"Why would Stanford tell them about us?"

"Because they know you're his neighbor. Besides, Beefo, or whatever you called him, pretty much gave you a veiled threat."

"But what about you? How would they connect you to the Whitetowers?"

"Don't you think they've spotted me at your house? Come on, Kate, these guys are real pros. They don't let too much get by them." She started to stand then weaved slightly, putting her hand on the chair to steady herself.

I hurried to her side and slipped my arm around her. "We don't know that for certain," I said, trying to keep my voice calm as I led her to the sofa.

"Yes, but do you want to wait around to find out?"

168

Thoughts of what that family was capable of sent shivers throughout my body. We needed to think rationally.

Fear continued to spread over us like a heavy blanket.

Chad slumped in his chair, shaking his head. "There's no way Dad could survive any torture." He was about to say more when his cell phone beeped. "It's Mom!"

"Be careful what you say to her and try to sound hopeful," I cautioned.

"Chad," Candace called out, "tell Lydia to stay put at my house until we get back. She's really the safest there…at least for the time being," she added quietly.

Chad nodded, cleared his throat and picked up his cell phone. "Hi, Mom."

To give him space, I meandered to the big picture window. Molly joined me. We watched the sky turn from various shades of red into a myriad of neon lights typical of a Vegas evening. The Dancing Waters began to rise up and sway in sync to the music being played.

The strange expression on Chad's face was difficult to read after talking to his mom.

"Chad, you look puzzled. What is it?" I asked.

"What did Lydia say? Is she all right? What about Stanford's messages?" Candace hailed him with questions.

"Please," he stilled our voices with a wave of his hand. "Give me a chance to sort it out." Chad motioned for us to sit. We circled around him waiting for some answers like hungry animals waiting for our next meal. The suspense was killing us.

Finally, he drew a deep breath and began. "I really thought I knew my parents pretty well, but somewhere between adolescence and adulthood, I must've been too busy with my own life to notice they had changed. I can't believe…" He ran his fingers through his blonde wavy hair.

"What happened, Chad? What did Lydia say to you?" Candace asked impatiently.

I elbowed her. "Shush! Give him some slack."

"It wasn't what Mom said, it was the tone of her voice that caught me off guard."

169

"What do you mean?" asked Molly.

"Well … she was eerily calm; her voice a monotone. It sure didn't feel like a mother - son chat, more like an exchange of information between two peers."

"Wasn't she surprised at what we found?" I asked.

"Not really. She wasn't too upset about the riddle. Apparently she knew how to decipher Dad's cryptic messages."

"What about the one sentence on the second page?"

Chad shrugged his shoulders and flayed his hands. "She said it wasn't important. But here's the real puzzling part. I asked Mom when she had last heard from Dad. She paused a moment, then said matter-of-factly that it was yesterday. He told her the job was done and that he'd be home soon."

"That's it?" Candace's eyes opened widely. "Doesn't she care that her husband may be coming home horizontally?"

"She didn't seem to think he'd be in any trouble if he gave the real artifact to the Busonis."

"I didn't think Lydia would be so callous." Scheming I could believe, but heartless? Especially about her very own husband. "Was that all she said?"

"That's about it. She seemed to be in a hurry to end the conversation, but then as an afterthought asked me to thank you and Candace for all your help. She said that she could handle everything else on her own from now on. There was a brief goodbye and she clicked off." His face conveyed a mixture of confusion and disapproval with sadness thrown in.

"Well, guess Lydia has written the two of us off," murmured Candace. "Shoot! She fired us just when we were getting close to solving the case."

I stood abruptly, shoved my chair against the table, and paced back and forth from the window to the table, muttering to myself. As much as it angered me at the way Lydia used us, my heart broke for Chad. The bitch didn't even tell her son she loved him.

I stopped abruptly and turned to the group. "I don't know how you all feel, but I've had it with this ever- changing mystery merry-go-round. It's been way too draining. This last incident in Chad's bathroom with Bert and Ernie nearly catching us just about did me in."

"It was Bernie and Ralphie," corrected Candace.

"I don't give a rat's ass what their names are." I stunned them by my outburst. I turned to Chad, "I'm so sorry you have to go through this experience, but I don't see how we can be of any more help. Lydia has pretty much written us off. Apparently, she's gotten what she wanted."

"And you…" I cast my eyes toward Candace. "You were even kind enough to give Lydia a place to stay. This is the thanks you get, Wow!" I was on a roll. "It didn't really matter to her that we, especially you, opted to come to Vegas. Now we're here, out of our comfort zone and smack dab into Busoni territory. It's not fair to expose you any further." I shook my head. "I'm afraid the odds are stacking up against both of us."

Exhausting the adrenaline that had raged through my body a few minutes ago, I sank into a chair, rested my head against the cushioned back, and closed my eyes. A headache began to gain momentum over my right temple. "If Harry were here, he'd be wagging and pointing his *I told you not to pry into other people's affairs* finger at me."

Candace slowly circled the rim of the empty glass with her finger. "You're probably right, Kate. Even though it'd be nice to see the Busonis on the other side of the receiving line, it's probably for the best that we give it up."

Silence fell like a dark cloud covering the entire room.

Molly was the first to burst through the quietness. "*No. No!*" she exclaimed. "We can't stop now. It just wouldn't be right to leave Chad all alone to deal with this. I want to do whatever it takes to get this cleared up." She reached over and grabbed hold of my hand. "We've got to see this through, Mom."

"That's very noble of you, Molly," said Chad, humbled by her insistence to continue, "but you've all done too much already. The police should probably handle it. Besides, Mom doesn't seem to be too worried about anything happening to Dad."

171

"Yeah, but why would Stanford leave a cryptic note unless he realized he was in over his head. What if it was a cry for help?" Molly posed the question to all of us.

She had picked up the gauntlet for Chad and led us into a heated discussion. We argued. We listed the pros and cons. We compromised. We rescinded the compromise. We changed sides. We swayed to the right. We swayed to the left. We were all talking and wildly gesturing at each other when the house phone rang.

Molly happened to be closest and picked up the handset "Just a minute," she said into the phone, then put her hand over the mouthpiece and hissed, "Shush I can't hear."

"Sorry for the noi...oh ... hi, Dad," she said loud enough for us to hear her salutation.

We froze in our spots like characters in a stop-action film.

Molly's face turned the color of a ripe tomato. "Here." She handed the phone to me.

I stared at the handset as if it was a grenade ready to go off the minute I touched it. I placed it against my chest, willing it to help me breathe. I plastered a smile on my face, mustered up all the courage I *could* muster, and put the receiver to my ear. "Harry, what a surprise...now, before you start yelling, I..." A strange feeling struck me. "Ah, why didn't you call my cell? Oh, you did. I guess I didn't hear...you're where?" My composure crumbled. "In La...Las Vegas? In the l...lobby?" I stammered. "Okay, we're in Suite 1031. I guess you already figured that out. Okay." My hand shook as I placed the handset back in its cradle.

"You all heard?" I barely whispered the words.

They nodded like three bobble heads.

"He's on his way up."

"Well then," declared Candace as she walked to the mini bar and opened it, "we better have it restocked. Looks to me like we're gonna be in for a long night."

# Heeere's Harry!

WE SCATTERED ABOUT the room, bumping into one another like Keystone Kops in an old silent movie, until I called a halt. They stopped in mid-action to listen.

"Look, we all want to help Chad any way we can, right?"

All nodded.

"At first, Harry will mostly likely be more upset finding out that Molly has been with us. We'll let him have his furor over that, but while he's ranting, I'm sure we can come up with some kind of a working solution to satisfy him. If he offers any advice, we'll take it under consideration. Are you with me on this?"

"I'm in your corner," Candace replied.

"All right, just follow my lead. Chad, stand by the door and be ready to open it at the first knock. Molly, you'll greet him."

"Yeah, throw the child to the lion." Candace muttered.

"What was that?"

"Um, just waiting for my orders. What do you want me to do?"

"Do what you normally do," I replied anxiously.

"Like?"

"Oh, hell, just sit at the table and pretend to do something, file a nail, read the hotel menu. I don't care, just do it and fast."

"I'm sure glad he's not *my* husband," she muttered to Molly.

A few minutes later, we heard a firm rap on the door. Chad answered immediately, and Molly rushed to her father, hugging him before he had a chance to put down his carry-on bag

"Hi, Daddy." She wrapped her arms around his neck, kissing him on the cheek, and purred sweetly. "Now, don't go blaming Mom. It was my idea to come here." The words spilled out of her mouth so fast, Harry didn't know what hit him.

"Hi sweetie," he said, giving her a peck on the cheek and at the same time launching daggers at me. He gently unwound himself from Molly's grasp. Chad shook his hand and quickly grabbed his bag. In his haste, he fumbled with the handle, almost dropping it on Harry's foot.

"Oops! Sorry." Chad set it on one of the chairs and plunked down alongside Candace.

"Hi Harry! Want a Frito?" Candace cheerfully waved the bag at him.

He rolled his eyes, ignoring her offer, and aimed straight for me.

"Hi hon, what brings you here?"

"I cannot believe…" Harry started, then paused a moment. I could see him trying to control the anger forming in his throat before it spewed out of his mouth. No way could I figure out how to put a stop to his anger. I was sunk before I could begin. *Somebody just shoot me!*

"What in God's name were you thinking, agreeing to bring our daughter into this, this stupid … idiotic … adventure-slash-mystery?" He tossed the words into the air like tennis balls, slamming them directly at me.

Recovering slightly, I volleyed back. "Molly's fine and having a great time. After all, she is an adult. I could hardly forbid her to come."

Candace attempted to deflect one or two of his missiles. "Yeah, she's been hanging out with Chad who's been showing her some of the sights. Kate and I've been doing my favorite thing … shopping."

"But, the two of you could've dissuaded her," Harry said, catching Candace and me in his sites.

"Oh, Dad, Mom tried to talk me out of it," she admitted, "but since I had a week before classes started, I thought, why not go with them to Vegas. It's been fun catching up with Chad." She winked at him. "He's been the perfect bodyguard." Molly's eyes flashed at Chad, and sported a big smile. "He's even getting tickets for us to see a show."

Chad nodded, his mouth cemented into a convincing grin.

Not fully convinced, Harry shrugged out of his wrinkled jacket, and rolled up his shirt sleeves. He pulled out a chair, turned it around directly in front of me, and straddled it. He rested his arms on the back.

I started to speak, but he stopped me, pressing a finger to my lips. "We'll discuss Molly later. Let's talk about this Whitetower business. What's been happening with that?"

I crossed my arms and leaned into his face. "You haven't answered my question, Harry. Why are you here? Weren't you supposed to be helping Jerry with the deck?"

He shot back. "We finished earlier than I thought, so I figured since I didn't have anything pressing at home, a little vacation for me would be nice, too."

"You could've called to tell us you were coming."

"I wanted to surprise you." His eyes belied the smile on his lips.

"Hah! I think you were more curious about how we were managing." I watched the smug expression drop off his face.

"And now, to answer your question about the Whitetower business, we've been looking into several plans to figure out exactly how we're going to approach the next step."

"I'd like to hear them and perhaps give some sound advice." Harry slipped back into his authoritative voice.

"We'll take it under consideration," I countered.

"Under consideration," Candace mimicked me, stifling a laugh.

I chose to ignore her comment, and began to relate almost everything that happened since our arrival, up to a few minutes or so before he called.

Harry listened to the events as they tumbled one-by-one from my mouth, an alarming shade of red forming on his cheeks. He sat up abruptly when I casually mentioned Molly and Chad's trip to the morgue. He swiveled his torso toward Chad, raising a questioning eyebrow.

Chad gasped in alarm, but Molly shushed him. "It's like this, Dad. We had to find out if the dead guy was Stanford's partner, Leo Viorsky. The only person who could identify the corpse was Chad's mom. So I came up with the brilliant idea to—"

"Just get to the point, Molly." Harry's reserve appeared to wane quickly.

"Okay. While I was asking the coroner a boatload of questions, Chad took a picture of the body with his cell phone and immediately sent it to his mom. It was really quite simple," she sighed, then added, "And by-the-way, it wasn't Mr. Whitetower's friend Leo."

"Are you sure that's the whole story?" Harry's tone was still skeptical.

"I can attest to the fact that Kate has told you the fine points," Candace confirmed.

I gave her a funny look.

She said sotto voce, "You know, the incident in Chad's apartment."

I felt heat beginning to rise up from my neck. I grabbed a magazine off the table and used it as a fan. "Just a little hot flash," I said, waving it briskly in front of my face.

Candace tried to stifle a chuckle but it got caught in her throat. She quickly choked down a glass of water.

*Serves you right.*

Harry noticed the strange interplay between us and started to speak before Molly put things back in perspective.

"Bottom line, Dad, we need to find Stanford."

"So, have you settled on one plan?"

"Well…" I hesitated,

"You don't have one, do you?"

"Actually we do. We were beginning to put it together when you rang."

"Kate, Kate!" he exclaimed. "For weeks you've put a deaf ear to my advice about meddling in other people's business. Can you see what you've done? You've gone and managed to involve three other people in this madcap adventure."

I glared at him. "We are all adults, Harry. I didn't strong-arm anyone. It was all volunteer. We couldn't leave Chad alone in this horrendous situation."

176

"I see. So from everything you've told me, it looks like you've dug yourselves into a hole with not enough rope to pull yourselves out."

"Far from it. We're working on the details," I huffed.

"Do you mind telling me what they are?"

"Only if you can keep from trying to control everything."

"Okay, let's hear what you've got so far."

I knew it would be hard for Harry to hold his tongue, but I couldn't let him hold my hand forever. This was our mystery to solve.

"Candace, you start, and please don't go off on one of your tangents," I said.

"I promise I won't." Candace placed her hand over her heart and crossed her fingers behind her back.

"If only I could believe you," I sighed.

# And the Plan Played On

HARRY ROSE FROM the straight back chair and stretched his arms above his head as he walked to the bar. He pressed his hands on the granite countertop and faced the mirrored wall. He listened quietly while we outlined our plan. When someone mention police involvement, Harry's ears picked up. "Ah, now that's the best thing I've heard, yet."

"Harry!" I scowled at him.

"I can't help it. You are all playing amateur detectives. The police are trained in this stuff. Surely you're smart enough to realize the seriousness of this situation."

I raised my hand.

He raised his voice. "I haven't finished."

I waved him on to continue.

"As I understand it, you all agree that Stanford is your first priority and that's as it should be. Personally, I don't care for the man … sorry, Chad," he squeezed out a small apology.

Chad nodded understanding Harry's gesture.

"However, he is your father, and the sooner you get the law involved, the better chance you have of finding him alive."

Chad flinched at Harry's last comment.

"If the Busoni family is behind Stanford's abduction," Harry continued, "there ought to be a hefty dossier on them down at the station. Chances are, they've begun investigating them already."

Candace raised her hand. "Ah, Harry, there's something about the Busonis you need to know."

"What about them?" The irritation in his voice matched the expression on his face.

"Candace, you don't have to do this," I pleaded.

"Yes I do," she responded. "Harry needs to know everything."

"What more does Harry need to know?" His earlier relaxed manner stiffened as he pushed off the counter, and

178

fired a questioning look at Candace. "I thought we had true confessions a few minutes ago."

"We did, Harry. Kate told you all the Whitetower stuff, but not the part that affects me and the Busonis."

"Now I'm really getting confused." He ran his fingers through his hair, then slowly moved toward us. "You've already mentioned you knew one of them from the pictures Kate showed you."

"I think you better sit down." She patted a chair next to the sofa. "It's complicated."

"Okay," he grumbled, sinking into the soft cushions, "let's have it."

"You see, I know the Busonis...*intimately*." Candace paused to give Harry a moment to let that piece of information sink in.

"Go on," he nodded. His face was solemn except for a slight twitch in his right eye. "You might as well drop the other shoe."

"I didn't tell you about my association with them because I made Kate and Molly promise, even pinky swore them into silence." Her lips quivered.

"I don't understand pinky swear, Candace. Just get to the point."

"I'm getting to it." She succumbed to the impatient look on his face. "You see, I was married to Nicky, the son of Gino, one of the notorious Busoni brothers. It was a ... a wonderful, yet terrible period in my life. I can tell you for certain how they handle people who double cross them." Shivers rippled through her shoulders.

"What does that have to do with you now?" Harry questioned, although his tone softened a little.

"We ... Nicky and I ... had a child, a son." Candace related the rest of the story, but watching her tell it again was like reliving the whole heart-wrenching episode in her life.

Harry's facial expression changed from irritation to mild interest and finally, to jaw-dropping amazement.

Chad jerked his head at Candace's last words. Nervously fiddling with a pen, he dropped it on the table. The small noise was loud enough in the quiet room to draw our attention to it. We watched it slowly roll to the edge and nose-dive onto the floor.

Harry's words shattered the silence. "My God, Candace, if those bastards are the ones Stanford double crossed, and they have a sense that you're somehow mixed up in this, not to mention my family and Chad, then it's imperative that we call the police."

"The police can't help me, Harry. The Busonis have somebody in the LV Police Department on their payroll."

"How do you know that?" Harry's anger began to rise.

"It makes sense, Harry. Those brothers are always one step ahead of the law. They've had the ability to essentially get away with murder. Plus, they have a bevy of crackerjack lawyers. That I know … first-hand." Candace brushed away the tears welling in her eyes. "I'm quite certain they know I'm in town. I can feel it." She rubbed her hands up and down her folded arms.

"Candace, that's more reason to get help." Harry bolted off his chair and began mumbling to himself while pacing up and down the length of the room.

Before any of us had time to respond, he stopped abruptly and tossed out more questions at us. "Don't you see? Everything you've told me points to calling the police. This whole business is way beyond your capabilities. Let the professionals handle it, for God's sake."

He turned his attention to Chad. "This must be hard for you, son, but you realize that when your father is found, he needs to be accountable for his actions. I'd rather they'd be the ones to handle his part in this ugly mess."

"That's your answer, Harry," Candace declared. "But before you call the police, there is a chance that my friend Sammy may know if Stanford is still alive and where he's being held."

"Sammy?" questioned Harry.

"Yes, the only one of Busonis men who felt I'd gotten a raw deal. I could try—"

180

"No, you can't." My heart was beating as fast as my mouth. "We nixed that idea earlier."

"Well then, that's the end of it." Harry started to pick up the Las Vegas phone directory when Candace jumped off the sofa and pulled it out of his hand, holding it firmly across her chest.

"Hear me out first, Harry."

He let out an exasperated sigh. "Okay, but this is the last time, Candace."

"After my abrupt departure from the Busoni Bastille, Sammy made a promise to keep me posted about my son. He was always careful and used a public phone and later an untraceable cell phone."

"But Candace, you'll be putting yourself deeper into the midst of all this," I cautioned. "I hate to admit it, but maybe Harry has a point."

"Kate's right," he agreed. "The danger's too great."

"I think it's worth a try," Candace replied. "Look, I still have some friends here in town who know Sammy. All I'll do is make a couple of phone calls. If I come up empty, we'll do it your way, Harry. Okay?"

Before he could object, Candace rushed past him toward her room. "It won't take long." She flung the last words over her shoulder before closing the door to her bedroom.

To avoid any more pressure from Harry, I pushed up off the couch and bustled about the bar, tidying up the countertop. I washed and dried the glasses, placed them in a row, and began filling them with ice. *It's time to pour the vodka.*

"I need to jot some things down," said Harry. He rummaged in the desk drawer and found a notepad with the Bellagio's insignia on top, picked the fallen pen off the floor, and slid into the vacant chair next to Chad. "Can you give me the name of the officer who questioned you about the victim?"

"Ah ... yes, I think I have his card somewhere." Chad searched his pockets and found it a bit wrinkled, but legible. He glanced at the name before handing it over to Harry.

"Sorry, must've been clenching it pretty tight when I was being interviewed."

Harry read the name out loud. "Hmm, Detective Dan Warren, good. He'll be the first one to call." He jotted the name and phone number on the pad.

When Candace appeared twenty minutes later, we were reviewing facts and sipping vodka with whatever mixer on hand.

"Ta-da!" She stood at the counter, draped one arm on the bar and drew the other to her hip, striking a dramatic pose. *I know that pose.* "Looks like she made some headway," I whispered loudly to the rest.

"Indeed I have," she said with all the authority of one whose confidence preceded her. "I spoke to my old friend Lorelei St. Cyr." Candace pronounced the last name with a French accent. "She and I worked together years ago at the old Sands."

"Lorelei St. Cyr." Harry smirked. "Now that sounds like a name we can trust."

"Was that her real name?" asked Chad, suppressing a smile.

Molly snorted.

Candace wagged her finger at the four of us "Do you want to hear what I found out, or are you just going to sit there making fun of me?" She tapped her finger on the counter, waiting for a response.

I gave Chad a swat on the arm and directed a stern look at Molly. "It doesn't matter if the name's a stage one or real. That's of little importance right now. Go on Candace."

"Thank you, Kate," a smug smile formed on her lips. "Now, to continue. Liz, I call her that, was my best friend - actually, the only friend I had left in Vegas after … you all know so I won't repeat it." Candace pulled away from the bar, crossed over to the table, picked up the last full glass, and slid into the chair closest to Harry. She toyed with her drink.

*Even in the height of danger she can be such a drama queen.* "And?" I asked.

182

"Yes, I did get hold of Liz. She agreed to try to contact Sammy. No promises. I told her to tell him we'll be at the show tomorrow night."

"Show? What show?" Harry sat upright, straightening his spine. "Is this one more item you've managed to avoid telling me?"

"I told you Chad was getting us tickets. Apparently, you weren't listening very well," chided Molly.

"You were able to get tickets, weren't you, Chad?" Candace shifted her attention to him.

"Yes, right." He nodded. "With all the stuff going on, it slipped my mind. I got good seats, close to the front."

Harry stared wide-eyed from one to the other. "Could this be any more confusing? Would someone please tell me why the hell you're going to a show when Stanford's life is at stake? It doesn't make sense."

"I admit it's a little complicated, Harry." Candace answered. "But there's a really good reason for going to this concert."

He shook his head. "With you, everything is more than a little complicated."

"Harry, listen!" I took a shot at convincing him. "It may sound strange to you, but going to this show is really an essential part in helping Chad find his dad, and definitely not something you might think is whimsical."

"Sorry, it's not logical to me." He shook his head. "As I see it that'd be slowing down the whole process."

"Does everything in your world have to be logical?" My composure took a detour.

Molly took a shot at defusing her father's temper. "I guess telling you that Bonasera - that's the group playing tonight - is one of my main reasons for coming to Vegas."

"Bongo who?" Harry shot her a perplexed look.

"Oh Dad, if you'd kept up with the music of the day, and not stayed stuck in the dark ages, you'd know that Bonasera's one of the hottest groups around," she retorted.

"But, sweetie, regardless of how wonderful this...this Bono group is, it's hardly the time to go off partying."

"Seeing a show is not *partying* Dad. It's Bonasera, not some punk rock band," she exclaimed, mildly irritated.

I started to come to Molly's defense. But before I opened my mouth, Candace figuratively stepped in the middle of the battling Creightons.

"Enough you three," she blurted out. "The reason is simple, Harry. The lead singer of the group is my son, Jimmie Busoni."

"I … your … son?" Harry's mouth dropped open, stunning him into silence.

Candace nodded. "Now do you see why going to this show is so important? Everything's falling into place. We go to the concert. I meet up with Sammy and find out if he knows anything about Stanford. And, while all this is happening, I get to see my son perform for the very first time." Her confidence rose with each thought she spelled out. "It's like getting two birds with one stone. Now if that doesn't that fit in with your logic, I don't know what does." She smiled, satisfaction dancing all over her face.

Finally recovering from yet another surprise, Harry bellowed, "Are you serious? Can't you see how dangerous this whole idea is, especially for you? Myriad things could go wrong." His tone softened. "Now with the police there…"

"Nonsense, Harry," Candace countered with a flip of her hand. "With a room full of people, I should be pretty safe."

He leaned back in the cushion chair, arms folded across his chest. Seconds ticked slowly by while he studied each of our faces.

We had rested our case. *What is he thinking?*

Harry exhaled deeply. "Well then, since you're all dead set on going, I'd better go along with you to the show. I still don't like it one bit, but I wouldn't feel comfortable knowing you're there and I'm here."

"No!" My shout escaped so loud, I had to dial it back a notch to continue. "I mean, we'll be fine, dear. No need for you to spend a couple of hours listening to music you pretty much hate." I motioned to Molly and Candace for assistance

"I'm sure you can find something else to do while we're gone, Harry. We'll call you when it's over and you can meet us for a drink," added Candace.

"I think it's sweet that you want to be our big hero, Dad, but it really isn't necessary."

"Is there another reason why you don't want me there?" He eyed her skeptically.

"Of course not," Molly replied, giving her father a quick peck on the cheek. "We'll be fine. Chad'll know what to do if there's any problem. Don't you worry about us."

"Look Chad," Harry said rather pompously, "I mean no disrespect, but my presence with the ladies will offer a lot more security. I'll just have to suck it up and suffer through the concert."

Chad cleared his throat. "Then, ah, I guess I'll get another ticket." He looked at me for conformation.

"Well, if you must, Harry. But don't start complaining the moment we get there," I scolded.

Harry rose from his chair and headed straight for the bar, hesitated, then turned quickly around. A suspicious look crossed his face. "Just one last question before I take this vodka and drink it straight from the bottle. Are there any more *minor* disclosures you might've forgotten to tell me?"

"No, Harry, We've told you everything you need to know," Candace replied, placing her hand over her heart and crossing her fingers with the other behind her back.

He shook his head while rolling his eyes upward. "I'm not taking any bets on that last remark."

# Shopping … Don't Interrupt Us

THE NEXT MORNING, Candace and I curled up on the sofa sipping cups of strong coffee and noshing on Krispy Kreme donuts that Molly had picked up after a swim in the hotel pool.

"So, were you finally able to get Harry to change his mind?" Candace asked.

"No," I sighed deeply. "When we were alone, he was more adamant on going. I had hoped he would only offer some suggestions, not take over the whole thing." I flipped my hand in the air. "We are now under his masterful arm of analytical reasoning."

"There must be a way to convince him otherwise." Candace gave me a seductive smile. "Of course you could—"

"Uh uh, I've tried that, remember?"

"Let me see what I can do," she said.

"Can do what?" Harry shuffled into the living room before she could finish her thought.

"Bring you a cup of coffee in the bedroom," I quickly masked our conversation. "But since you're up, there's the pot on the counter behind the bar."

He poured the hot brew into a mug, ambled back, and settled in the chair adjacent to the sofa.

"Here Harry, have a donut. They're Krispy Kremes." I shoved the box at him.

"Kate and I were discussing what we're going to wear tonight. I suppose you didn't bring any evening attire." Candace commented nonchalantly.

"Huh?" He gave her a curious look, not quite awake.

"Yes," she surmised, "I didn't think so. I'll give Ari at Giorgio-Armani's a head's up and let him know you'll be needing something appropriate to wear for tonight's performance. Believe me, he does know how to dress a man. Winston always asked for him when we stayed here."

"Wa…wait just a damn minute, Candace," Harry's temper resurfaced. "Under no circumstances will I … I…" he sputtered and muttered a few choice words under his breath. He looked at me for support. "Help me out, will you, Kate? She's *your* friend. Please make her stop this madness." He reached for a donut and sagged back in his chair.

"Harry, she's only trying to help. I know, she can be a little over the top at times, but you have to admit, she does have her moments of clarity." I laid my hand tenderly on his arm and spoke soothingly. He rolled his eyes and kept eating.

"I know you think that we're going a roundabout way to find Stanford, and you may be right. But at least it's worth a try. Like Candace said, there'll be lots of people surrounding us," I pleaded. "It's all right if you decide not to go. Honestly, I'm sure we'll be okay without you for a couple of hours."

"No way out of this, sweetheart. I'm going but not decked out like some fashion magazine prick."

"What's all the noise about?" Molly asked as she entered the room fresh from a shower, wearing one of the hotel bathrobes and a towel wrapped around her wet hair. She plopped down between Candace and me. "Good, you left the maple bar." She captured it and took a bite, savoring the flavor. "Mmm, my favorite."

"Oh honey, I was just telling your father where he could get something to wear tonight. I merely suggested he meet Winston's man Ari at Giorgio-Armani's store in in the hotel, and he kind of loudly scoffed at the idea," Candace huffed.

"I'll take care of dressing myself without anyone's help thank you very much," he snorted. He reached for the remote, turned on the TV, and channel surfed until he found the one news program he liked.

"Now then, since Harry has had his little say, we need to make our plans for today," Candace announced. "We've got some serious shopping to do for tonight."

"We? Why? I'm pretty sure I brought something that'll do. And I know for a fact that you did," I said.

"Yes, of course. Well, that was back home clothes. We need some snazzy outfits, Kate. This is Las Vegas," she lectured. "It's my town and WE are going to shop."

"Hey," Molly piped up. "Am I invited to this shopping extravaganza?"

"You bet, honey child," purred Candace.

"Okay, okay, I'm outnumbered. Give me a minute to psyche myself up for one of your lengthy trips," I groaned.

"Who says it'll take long?"

"It's you, Candace. I know you, remember?"

Candace flashed us a big smile and headed for her bedroom. I wished she would've said something before I took the last bite of donut. *Oh well, what's one more pound?*

"Hurry up," Candace yelled. "There're wonderful opportunities outside waiting for us."

\*\*\*

I was surprised to see Candace all ready to go when I entered the living room. She was dressed in a pair of off-white linen slacks. Her sandals and purse complimented one of the colors in her print silk blouse. I was no match for her, but at least I wasn't wearing a T-shirt, sweats, and rubber flip flops.

She stared at me for a moment, then sighed, "Yes, well, I think we should do a little extra shopping. I fear you'll be needing more than just a dress."

Before I could defend myself, Candace's cell phone rang.

"I've got to get a better ringtone. The one that guy Bernie had was pretty neat. Oh, it's Anita. Hi, what's … wait, hold on you're talking too fast. I'm going to put you on speaker so we can all hear. Okay, now tell us again, and speak slowly. "

I signaled Harry to mute the volume on the TV and join us at the table. "It's Anita," I whispered.

"It's Mrs. Whitetower … she's …she's gone." Anita's voice started to break.

"Gone? Did she tell you where she was going? Did she say anything to you?" I asked.

"No, only that someone was coming here to pick her up. Sh … she just left a few minutes ago."

188

"Did she tell you when she'll be coming back?" asked Harry.

"She didn't say." Anita's voice faded a bit.

"How did she look? Was she nervous, afraid?"

"Oh no, no! She was very happy." Anita sniffled into the phone. "Oh, I'm so sorry, Miss Candace, I know I was supposed to make sure she stayed here until you got back." She began to cry. "I didn't know what to do."

"That's okay, Anita. She wasn't a prisoner," I said soothingly. "Was it a man or woman that came to get her?"

"It was a man, tall, nice looking, very polite. He had kind of a foreign accent. Mrs. Whitetower was all smiles and ready at the door when he came for her."

"Did you get his name?"

"No, they were in such a hurry to leave. I tried to ask if there was any message to give you, but they were down the steps and to the car before I could open my mouth. And … and," she sobbed into the phone, "she left that awful cat of hers here. Oh, Miss Candace, I don't know what to do."

Candace and I exchanged shocked glances.

"Anita, please calm down. I'm not upset with you. You did your best," Candace said softly.

"Y… yes, ma'am," she replied.

"Anita, would you do us a favor and check the bedroom?" I asked. "See if there is anything Mrs. Whitetower may've left behind."

"Yes, ma'am."

"Oh, also look around the computer area and the wastebasket, too," I added.

"Let us know if you find something. Call us either way," Candace put in. She reassured Anita once again not to worry then clicked off. Raising her arms in the air she added, "Now what could possibly happen next?"

The answer came a few minutes later with a fast rapping at the door.

The sudden sound raised the hair on the back of my neck. Candace and I swapped worried looks.

"I'll get it." Harry headed off to answer it.

189

Chad rushed in waving a newspaper.

"Have you read the morning news?" he asked, neglecting the usual formalities.

"Oh crap, I forgot to bring in the paper when I got back from my swim," Molly apologized.

"Here, take a look at the picture on the first page of the metro section!"

Puzzled, we did as Chad told us. "What's this all about? Who is this person?" Harry asked.

"Just read it, Mrs. C," he instructed. "Out loud."

I did as he asked.

"'DEAD BODY IN PARADISE APARTMENT IDENTIFIED.'"

"The body of the victim found strangled in the Paradise apartment of Chad White has now been identified as the internationally notorious art thief Arturo Santini. Santini had been a person of interest in connection with the theft of a priceless chalice recently stolen from the Cathedral of Monreale in Monreale, Sicily. Interpol had been trailing Santini for the past few months. According to Sicilian police, the chalice was one of a set, donated to the cathedral by the Italian explorer Giovanni Medina around the early 15th century. Interpol traced Santini's movements to Las Vegas. Both Paradise and Las Vegas police are coordinating their efforts with the Sicilian Policia and Interpol to continue the ongoing investigation. If anyone has any information, please call…'"

I stopped reading and laid the paper on the table, carefully doubling it in two like a manila folder. The silence was so profound it seemed to shove the air right out of the room. "Oh, crap," I exclaimed, "Can this mystery get any more convoluted?"

Chad's brows furrowed. "This just doesn't make any sense."

"You said that the last phone call you had with your mother seemed strange. How? In what way? Do you think she knew anything about this Santini person?"

"Her voice was flat," he answered. "There was no expression of surprise, worry, or fear." Chad hesitated, scratching his head, trying to remember the conversation. "She reacted to the news to both the dead person and Dad in the same manner, unruffled. I really thought her comment was the residue of the medication she'd been taking." He slowly shook his head, disappointment cloaked his body. "I don't really know my parents at all."

Placing a motherly hand on his arm, I murmured, "Chad, honey, I'm afraid Lydia may have twisted us into a noose so tight that we could all be left hanging before this mystery or whatever we call it gets solved."

"Wow, that's some metaphor." Candace clutched her throat in dramatic fashion.

"Looks like we have even more to think about," said Harry.

I picked up the paper and read the story again, hoping some clue would fall out of the page. Failing that, I rolled it up like a bat and began tapping it against the open palm of my free hand as I paced back and forth. "Chad your mom told you that she would be seeing your dad soon, right?"

He nodded.

"But that doesn't match with what Candace's maid Anita, told us."

"I don't understand. What do you mean by that?" he asked, puzzled.

"Anita called a few minutes before you got here. She said your mother left with some man, and it wasn't your father."

"Maybe, it could've been a person she knew and trusted; someone that would take her to get the diamond and put it in another safe place." A shred of hope perked him up a bit.

"That may be true. But she left without leaving any message or letting Anita know when or if she'd be coming back. And that doesn't make any sense at all," I puzzled.

It didn't take a mind reader to see how all this affected Chad. Worry and distress drew lines across his handsome face. His hand trembled as he reached for the arm of his chair.

"I've no idea what we're supposed to do now," I continued. "Stanford could've gone home to meet Lydia and this man, whoever he is. If that's what happened, then there's really nothing more for us to do. "

"But there's those dreaded Busoni brothers," added Candace.

"And," Harry tossed out, "That's why I'm going with you to this concert tonight."

"Well," said Candace, picking up her purse, "if we can't do anything about it, we can still go shopping. Harry, are you sure you don't want me to call Ari and—"

"I appreciate your help," he briskly cut her off, "But, I'm sure I can find something suitable without anyone's help."

Before another scene erupted, I grabbed Molly's hand and quickly ushered her and Candace toward the door. "Okay, enough chit chat, let's go. See you later, boys." I waved goodbye and shut the door behind us.

Candace pushed the down button on the elevator. "Let the shopping begin!"

"Lead the way." Molly grinned.

***

Candace and Molly were two feet in front of me chatting away in animated conversation. I couldn't believe their stamina. They bustled in and out of stores so quickly, I hardly had a chance to see what was on the mannequin, let alone what was inside the place. The two continued to look as fresh as when we first started. On the other hand, glancing at my reflection in the mirror, I looked every inch the number of miles we traveled along the Strip.

"Hey, you two," I shouted above the din of shoppers' voices echoing off the expanse of marble in the forum of Caesar's Palace, "Could you slow down a bit? I'm not the heavy-duty shopper you are, Candace," I puffed. "Don't you think we could use a breather … or at least find a place to sit and have a drink?"

"Can't keep up, huh?" She laughed, stopping to wait for me. "But, you're right, and I know the perfect place. Think you can manage a few more steps?"

What I managed was a sneering smile. "Lead on."

Molly slipped her arm through mine, and we strolled along following Candace. "This place is some piece of work. The Fall of Atlantis, and the moving statues are magnificent. It takes my breath away," she gasped.

"There's a whole lot to process everywhere in this city," I agreed.

Molly's tone turned serious. "I'm thrilled to be here, Mom, but I can't help feeling a little guilty about why we came to Vegas in the first place. I feel so sorry for Chad."

"I understand, Molly. I hope we can find his dad and get the rest of this mess cleared up soon."

A few feet ahead of us, Candace made an abrupt stop in front of a shop. "Ooh, I haven't seen this one before. It must be new, and oh so cute. Maybe we could—"

"Step away from the boutique, Candace," I ordered. "And keep moving."

"Geesh, don't go military on me, I just wanted to take a little peek inside." She put on a pouty face.

"I know your peeks…they turn into full bore inspections of every article of clothing."

"Oh well, guess I'll have to check it out another time." Candace picked up the pace and we trudged behind for several more minutes until she stopped in front of the entrance to the Mesa Grill. "Ah, here we are. I'm told that they serve some of the best margaritas in town, and in several different flavors. I'm dying for one. Shall we sit at the bar?"

"I don't care where, just as long as we're not standing." I spied the first empty seat and eased my aching body slowly into it.

"I hope everyone's happy with their purchases," Candace murmured after placing our orders. "Molly you'll be smashing in that strapless red sheath. And Kate, I do think Harry's eyes will pop out when he sees you in that black low cut gown with the sexy slit up the side."

"I'm afraid there'll be a lot more eye-popping when he sees the bill," I replied. "I probably won't have another chance to wear it again."

"Oh pooh, just make him take you somewhere snazzy." She took a sip of her drink. "Or, maybe he'll win big gambling tonight and won't mind paying for it."

"One could only hope," I quipped. "Mmm, this *is* a very good margarita." I took time to enjoy the icy cold liquid flowing down my parched throat.

Feeling a little more relaxed, I turned the discussion toward what else? The Whitetowers, and the concert tonight. "By the way, Candace, wasn't Anita supposed to call you back? I hope nothing's happened."

"I'll call right now." Candace pulled out her phone and tried to turn it on. "Drat. It's dead. I forgot to charge it this morning. She probably already did and left a message."

"Here." I handed her my cell. "You talk."

Candace's conversation was brief. Handing the phone back to me, she gave us a short account. "There was nothing in the room that might've given us any clue as to where Lydia was headed or with whom. Anita, the poor dear, is still nervous about the incident and hesitated answering the phone until she saw your name pop up on the caller ID. I do hope she'll be all right while we're away."

"Speaking of being away," said Molly, pointing at her watch, "It's about time we head back to the hotel. Drink up, ladies. We need to hustle."

We gathered our things and headed for the front entrance. "Candace, I know it's a short distance to the Bellagio, but could we take a cab?" I pleaded. "I don't think I can take another step." Candace immediately requested a taxi from the valet. *God Bless her.*

"I take it I'm back on your good side?" she asked, as the driver put our packages in the trunk.

I tossed her a weak smile as I crawled into the back seat.

# The Music Begins and the Fat Lady's Humming

THE MINUTE WE returned from shopping, and before I had a chance to put down my packages, Harry grabbed hold of my arm and marched me into the bedroom. "We need to talk."

*Oh man, now what did I do?*

"What's this all about?" I asked sharply, wrenching my arm from his grip.

"There's something I need to tell you, and you may not like it." He caught the familiar expression of defense in my eyes. "Now, don't look at me that way," he said.

"What way is that?" I huffed as I busily set about placing my purchases on one of the chairs farthest from him.

"That way you do whenever we have this kind of conversation." He sat down on the edge of the bed and motioned for me to sit next to him.

"Not until you tell me what's going on." I stood my ground.

"Please, just listen to everything I'm about to tell you before you start erupting like that volcano over at the Mirage."

I started to refuse but reluctantly eased over to the bed, keeping a sizeable space between us. "Okay, Harry, what have you done this time?"

"Look, I'm not going to beat around the bush. Chad got hold of Detective Warren."

"Oh God," I gasped. "What did you do?"

"Hear me out, Kate." Harry reached out and pulled me back to his side.

"Traitor," I shot at him, yanking my arm free. "You're right. I'm probably not going to like whatever it is."

"Just listen, please."

The seriousness in his voice disturbed me.

"I know I promised Candace, but I kept thinking about the Busoni brothers. I was concerned about not having a plan B in case A doesn't work out, or worse, if it causes more trouble for her."

"So, what is this plan B?"

"Chad and I met with this Detective Warren and told him everything from the beginning."

"Oh Harry, how could you?" I started to back away.

"Please Kate, let me finish." He touched my arm. "Detective Warren agreed that going to the concert tonight without police protection was foolish. But after I told him about Candace's association with the Busonis, he decided that using the concert as a set up might give the police enough evidence to make an arrest."

"So, how involved will they be?" I asked. Candace would be crushed to know that Harry had gone against his promise to let her do it her way first.

"Detective Warren intends to be at the show tonight. His men will be stationed about the room. He and I will be in touch by cell phone if, and/or when Candace hears from her friend." He took my hand in both his. "Kate, honey, you know deep down that it's the right thing to do."

I had to agree. "But how will I tell Candace?" I could feel the guilt churning inside my stomach.

"We can't tell her or Molly anything right now. They must know nothing about our visit with Detective Warren or where they'll be at tonight's concert."

"That's absurd, Harry. I don't see why—"

"Look hon, if what Candace says is true about Busoni's men keeping a watch on her, the police won't want her tipping them off."

"How do you mean?"

"If Candace is being closely watched like she claimed, she might get a little nervous, and unconsciously communicate to them by body language that they're being set up. Hopefully, Candace will be able to get the information we need to find Whitetower before they … well you know."

I grimaced at his last statement.

"It's better if fewer people know what's actually going on," Harry reasoned. "It's for Candace's own good, Kate ... and the rest of us as well."

We were quiet for a moment, each thinking about the evening ahead.

A horrible thought struck me. "Harry, did you say anything to the detective about Jimmie Busoni being Candace's son? We pinky swore."

"Well, *I* didn't pinky swear," he answered, "but no, it wasn't my place to tell him that."

"That's a relief." I sighed.

"I told Warren enough to make him understand why Candace is so involved in this case. He was actually quite impressed with her desire to bring down the Busonis." A bit of surprise seeped into Harry's tone of voice.

"I hope he tells her that after this evening's over. She could use a little praise once in a while," I offered.

"I'm kinda beginning to admire her myself. Although, she does drive me crazy most of the time." A grin creased his lips. "Don't tell her I said that!"

"I think you really don't mind it as much as you say," I chuckled, beginning to relax.

A knock on the door broke the softening moment. "Hey, in there," Candace boomed, "we've got to get ready. No time for other activities."

"Okay, but we'll probably be waiting on you," I called out. I turned to Harry. "Just be your usual snarly self with Candace. She won't suspect a thing. Got it?"

He smiled and nodded as he walked to the door and locked it. "You want to shower first?" he asked, tossing me a seductive look.

*I swear, men can change their attitude at the drop of a towel.*

Harry was the first to emerge from the bedroom. "Hurry up, before I change my mind," he called out to the rest of us. I heard him pacing anxiously about the room.

"Why is the man always the first to be ready?" he grumbled loud enough for people in the next suite to hear.

197

"Oh Dad, you look terrific." Molly's cheerful voice rang out as she walked past my bedroom door. I'd shoved Harry out before he could see my whole ensemble. I had to hide the tags on everything I bought. He'd see the bill anyway, but I'd rather he be surprised later ... much later.

I picked up the black and silver lamé stole, took in a big breath, and made my entrance. Candace was right. Harry's eyes nearly popped out of his head. "You...you look stunning," he stuttered a real compliment.

I took a turn and struck a pose, leaning lightly on the counter. The dress showed off my *Spanxed*-body. *Thank God for the slit on one side of the dress.*

"Okay, Candace. We're waiting on you."

"Coming." Her voice rang out. She made her usual grand entrance, looking dynamic, dressed in a floor-length bare back long-sleeved silk teal creation. "Here I am everybody—" She stopped in mid-sentence in front of Harry, eyeing him up and down and shaking her head in disapproval. "I must say, that's *so* not very Armani."

"You're right, it *so* isn't," he countered.

"But—"

"Look, you didn't think I'd really follow your advice. I told you, I'm not an Armani clone. Chad took me to one of the places he frequents. It was more in my price range." He was wearing a light green silk, open collar shirt, tan slacks, and soft brown leather loafers. He did a model's turn, tossing a beige linen jacket over one shoulder. "Less is More. You like?" he smirked at her.

Candace gasped.

"Dad, you didn't."

"Of course not. I just wanted to get Candace's reaction." He sported a satisfied smile.

"Oh, very well." Candace scowled at Harry. Composure restored, she picked up her gold satin purse and raised it high in the air like a majorette signaling the start of a march. Heading for the door, she called out, "Hurry up now people. We've a show to see."

Bonasera was performing in one of Caesar's Palace's smaller venues. Chad met us at the entrance. We were ushered to a small round table—barely enough for four let alone five—one row behind center stage. After drinks were ordered, Chad tried to take some of the stress off our minds with talk about the band's recent surge in popularity.

"The secret to their growing success is their ability to hook into the mainstream and play almost everything from hip-hop to jazz. Right now, they're a top ticket."

"Ah, the fickleness of youth," Harry commented.

"Actually," Chad continued, "they've been booked on some of the late night talk shows. Saturday Night Live is interested."

While waiting for our beverages, I noticed a striking redhead moving toward our table. I nudged Candace.

She immediately rose from her chair. "Liz! What a pleasant surprise!"

We all stood to welcome her.

"Candace, darling, you look absolutely marvelous!" Lorelei St. Cyr gushed while they exchanged air kisses, Hollywood style.

"My, my, who is this tall handsome man?" She eyed Harry. Her voice was deep and husky.

"*Him?*" She tossed a dismissive shoulder his way. "Oh, that's just Harry, Kate's husband. Let me introduce you to my party."

We all shook hands.

"Lovely to meet you all," Lorelei replied, focusing her attention mostly on Harry, stroking his hand seductively.

I noticed how thoroughly pleased he seemed to be enjoying the extra attention. I was not amused. "Isn't she gorgeous?" Molly whispered to Chad.

"Huh? Oh, yeah, for an older woman, I guess."

"When I saw you come in, I just had to come over and say hi." She grasped Candace's arm. "Will you be in town long? We must get together and catch up."

"This is just a short visit, dear friend. We'll be leaving the day after tomorrow."

199

"Well, perhaps we can all meet after the show for a drink."

*Not in your lifetime!* "Yes, perhaps we could." I smiled over my clenched teeth. Harry just stood there with a stupid grin on his face. I poked him in the ribs.

"What?" He jumped.

"Never mind." I rolled my eyes. "Men." I declared to no one in particular.

The two old friends continued to fill the air with idle conversation until Lorelei announced, "I must get back to my table. Again, it was lovely to meet you all." She smiled and winked at Harry. Giving Candace a quick hug, she wiggled her way back to her friends.

When we were seated, Candace leaned behind Harry and touched my shoulder. "We need to meet Liz in the restroom in a couple of minutes."

"I hope she's got the information we need." The butterflies in my stomach were doing a tap dance.

"Be careful, you two," Harry warned as we headed out of the room.

Candace passed swiftly in and out of the tables, and I followed behind checking to see if she was being watched which was futile because she always draws attention wherever she goes. Before entering the restroom, she stopped and faced me. "From the look on your face, I sensed you were a bit miffed with Liz' obvious flirting with Harry. Don't pay any attention to her. She's really harmless."

"Sure." *I disagree.* Lorelei was waiting for us inside.

"We're the only ones in here right now, but we need to hurry."

"Where's Sammy? Why didn't he come? Has anything happened to him?" Candace fired the questions at Lorelei with rapid pace.

"No, he thought it better that I come instead. It wouldn't be a good idea for the two of us to be seen together at the show, especially when your son is performing." Lorelei speed dialed Sammy's cell number and waited for the ring then hung up. "That's his signal to use one of those throw away phones that he'll dump after we talk to him."

We waited nervously until Lorelei's phone beeped, "It's him." She nodded turning on the speaker.

"We're all here Sammy. Tell us what you've got." Candace spoke into the phone.

"Candace, sweetie, sorry I haven't been in touch. Things are pretty crazy around here."

"Sammy, do you know anything about Stanford Whitetower?"

"I know the name, not much about him, honey-girl, except he's in a world of shit."

"Sammy, this is Kate, Candace's friend and Stanford's neighbor. Do you think he's still alive?"

"Not sure."

"If he is, would you know where they'd be keeping him?"

"Not specifically, although the usual place they take double-crossers like him, is to—"

A sudden burst of background noise nearly blotted out Sammy's voice. "What's going on? I can hardly hear you." Fear seeped into Candace's voice.

Sammy's spoke quickly in a whisper. "Look, sometimes they use one of the boss' boats in the marina on Lake Mead."

"Do you have a name?" Candace urged.

"Ah, La Dolce Cara, Mia Amore, or maybe Del something, hell I can't ..." The phone went dead.

"Sammy!" Candace shouted. "Damn it!" She turned anxiously to Lorelei and me. Sammy's abrupt ending unnerved us all. What happened? Visions of doom circled us like hungry vultures waiting for our demise.

We were struggling to calm our nerves, when the door to the restroom suddenly opened, causing us to scatter. Two young twenty-somethings rushed in giggling and tittering about Bonasera and the lead singer, Jimmie B. They barely noticed the surprised expressions stretched across our faces. Gathering our composure as best we could, we rushed to the mirror, fished in our bags for lipstick, and applied a fresh layer with hands still shaking.

"Darlings, hurry up now," announced Lorelei, spritzing perfume behind her ears and between her breasts. "We must get back before the lights go down. You know how hard it is to find your table in the dark." Her calmness made me think she'd been in a similar position like this once or twice in her life.

Lorelei left first. Candace and I slowly wove our way around the tiny tables to our seats.

"You look a little pale, Kate. What happened?" Harry handed me the drink I'd ordered.

I gratefully took a sip of the cold beverage then relayed the information to him. Harry immediately texted Detective Warren.

"Now, you and Candace have done your part," he said. "It's time to leave the rest for the police to handle."

Candace caught the tail-end of Harry's comment. "What about the police?" She flashed him a questioning look.

The lights dimmed. "I'll tell you later," I answered. "Look, your son is up on the stage. Sit back and enjoy."

"Hush, guys," Molly whispered excitedly, "the show's about to begin."

At the end of the first set, chatter buzzed about the table. Everyone commented on how well the group played, and especially Jimmie B. His voice was as rich and smooth as his stage presence. I could understand why he was such a hit.

An emotional Candace dabbed at her eyes, tears of joy welling up. "My heart is pounding so hard it's about to come out of my chest. I'm so proud of him."

"They weren't too bad," Harry admitted. "Better than I expected."

"I told you to give them a fair chance, Dad." Molly laughingly nudged him.

As one of the servers approached their table, Chad rose and turned to Molly. "Order me another, would you, Mol? I'll be back in a few minutes."

I watched him head toward a door on the far left side of the stage. A funny feeling caused a shiver to race up spine..

Candace basked in the joy of hearing the audience reaction, especially to her son. Eventually, she shored up her tears, and blew her nose. "So, what was Harry saying about the police, Kate?"

Harry spoke up. "While you were out shopping, Chad and I got in touch with Detective Warren."

"Why? I thought …" Questions immediately clouded over her happy face.

"I know what you're going to say, Candace. Yes, I agreed to let you go ahead with your plan first before bringing in the police, but it seemed logical to have them get involved as soon as possible. God only knows what would happen if there was some kind of altercation, especially with your son on the stage."

"You … you told the detective about Jimmie?" She glared at Harry. "You promised not to. It was a pinky-swear."

"*I* didn't pinky swear."

Candace paled at his response.

Seeing her reaction, Harry hurried on. "But we didn't tell Warren anything about your connection with Jimmie B. That's personal. However, we felt he needed to know about Whitetower's involvement with the Busoni brothers."

I tried to intervene on his behalf. "Harry wanted to have us all be doubly protected, especially you, because you have more at stake in this than any of us. There are plain-clothes detectives scattered around the room watching Busonis'men."

"I would've been able to carry it off, without their help," Candace sniffed, nose in the air. Then her brow furrowed as she stared at me. "You knew what was going on all along and didn't tell me."

"I wanted to, but Harry begged me not to say anything, which is saying something for him." I pleaded for her understanding. "He told me just before we got ready for the concert. I'm really sorry about keeping this from you."

Harry continued. "You've told us that Busonis' men keep a close watch on you, even more so when you're in their territory. Wouldn't you feel a lot safer knowing the police have your back?"

"I guess so," she reluctantly agreed, "but I'm not quite ready to forgive you for not trusting in me and my plan."

"You were a big help, Candace," Harry readily admitted. "It was a brave thing that you did, and I'm very proud of you." He reached over and gave her a hug which surprised her as much as it did me.

The gesture left her flustered. Slowly her coolness toward Harry lifted. She immediately regained her lighthearted attitude and replied, "Yes, I did quite well, didn't I?" She flashed him a big smile and said, "You know me ... can't stay mad for long."

"Detective Warren's men are checking out the marina as we speak," Harry disclosed. "If your friend Sammy was right, they just might get to Stanford in time."

Chad came back a few minutes before the start of the next set. I saw him whispering something to Molly, causing her to choke on the ice from her glass. "You can't!"

"Why not?"

Their voices rose so loud, they overlapped, breaking up our conversation. We stopped to listen.

"It's too risky," Molly fired back. "Candace can't meet Jimmie after the show. Besides, I don't think Jimmie even knows if she's alive or dead." She vehemently shook her head. "It'd be a disaster waiting to happen."

"But after all these years, how would Jimmie know who she was? He hasn't seen or heard from her since he was little baby. We'd certainly keep Candace's identity hidden," Chad argued.

"Hey, over there," Candace yoohooed to get their attention, "I heard you mention my name. What are you two talking about?"

Chad explained that he'd set up a backstage meet with Jimmie B. "Don't you think with all of us surrounding you, the Busonis would leave you alone?"

"Nice thought, Chad, but it won't work. None of us is safe at this point. We're like walking targets with bulls-eyes on our backs. Trust me, I know," Candace responded. "Busonis' men are probably scattered all over the place. One could be sitting at the next table over and we'd never know it."

"Yikes!" I quickly glanced around our area.

"I can't risk putting all of you in their cross-hairs."

"Oh God. You're right." Chad slapped his forehead with the palm of his hand. "Candace, I'm so sorry. I wasn't thinking. I just figured ..." He started to jump off his chair. "I'll let him know we have a change in plans."

Candace stopped him and gently cupped his chin so that his eyes met hers. "No need to apologize, sweetie. What you've done tonight to make it possible for me to see and hear my son perform was something I'll never forget. I can't thank you enough for this night."

"I ... I" Those were the only two words he could squeeze out of his mouth.

Molly and I blinked back tears. Harry turned his head to one side to clear his throat.

After a short pause, Candace regained command. "Look, before the band returns, why don't we old folks leave, and let the young'uns stay for the rest of the show. We'll catch up with them at the hotel later."

"No, we'll come with you." Molly started to rise, but Candace stopped her.

"Nonsense! I know how much you wanted to see Jimmie. I don't want you to pass up the opportunity to meet him in person."

"But ... I ... you ... oh, please stay for the rest of Jimmie's performance," she begged.

She wagged her finger at Molly. "Now, don't argue with me."

"Candace, don't you think we should stay. I'd hate to leave them unprotected," I intervened.

"They're better off without me sitting in their midst," she insisted. "I'm sure that one day we'll finally meet, but not now, not in these surroundings."

"I'll let Detective Warren know what we're doing," Harry said while texting.

Within seconds the reply came. "He's putting a couple of guys nearby. I think it'll be safe to go."

"But, Candace, your son …!" I implored her to wait until the end of the second set.

"No, I've put you all in enough danger. I'm quite ready to go, but Chad, do you think you could get his autograph for me, even if it's on a napkin?"

"Sure thing. But what if he asks who it's for?"

"Give him my middle name, Mae." With that said, Candace stood up, flipped her blond hair back in typical Hollywood style, plucked her gold mesh stole off the back of the chair and with a *whoosh*, wrapped it around her shoulders. She motioned for us to follow.

"I'm with you, Candace." Harry was right behind her. "Where to?"

"I'm itching to do a little gambling. You two game?" Without waiting for an answer, Candace pulled me up by the arm. "Come on Kate, there's gotta be a blackjack table or a slot machine out there, calling our names."

Our exit was timed perfectly. Bonasera had just entered the stage. Candace turned back for one final look before we left the theater.

# Does the Thin Man Sing Instead?

AFTER LEAVING CAESAR'S Palace and hitting several other casinos along the strip, we stopped to admire the Dancing Waters in front of the Bellagio. We could hear Sinatra's voice crooning above the colored waters as they rose and fell with his every crescendo. The evening air and mist from the spray helped to ease some of the tension we'd experienced the past couple of days.

Candace broke the silence. "Now wasn't that a fun way to take our minds off the Whitetowers?"

"Well yes, if we'd all been as lucky as you," Harry grumbled.

"Can't help it," she chirped. "Maybe you'll have better luck tomorrow. You did all right, didn't you Kate?"

"Yeah," Harry scoffed. "Betting the way you do doesn't win you much."

"Oh Harry, you're such a killjoy." I kissed his cheek, hoping to stem his grouchiness.

"I'll share some of my winnings with you," Candace offered.

"Harrumph!" He started to make a snide comeback when his cell phone beeped. "It's Detective Warren."

Candace and I hovered around Harry. "Put him on speaker," I urged.

"Hold on just a second, Detective." Harry hit the button. "Go on."

"Thanks to Ms Carrington-Jones information, we were able to find Stanford alive, but pretty badly beat up. He's been taken to the hospital ... one moment." Warren paused to speak to an officer. "I just got word that one of Busonis' men has been captured, but the other one dived into the water before he could be caught."

"That's great news," we chorused.

"What's next?" asked Harry.

207

"I'll want to talk to all of you at the station tomorrow to take your statements. Someone will call in the morning to arrange a time."

"Sounds good. We'll see you then." Harry clicked off.

"Imagine that," Candace beamed, full of self-pride. "Detective Warren even thanked me for all my help. See, I always come through when it counts." She did a little happy dance on the sidewalk.

"Oh man, there'll be no living with you for a while," I snickered. Then my cell beeped. "It's a text from Molly. Warren called them. They're on their way to the hospital now."

"Chad, poor boy, he must be so confused by this whole ordeal." I sympathized. "I'm glad that Molly's with him. She's strong and stays calm in tough situations."

"So, I guess we have our orders," Harry said.

"That shouldn't be a problem. We don't have anything to hide," I replied, wrapping my shawl tightly around my shoulders. The night air was beginning to cool.

"No?" Harry's eyebrows rose, practically hiding his forehead. "You're going to have quite a time explaining why the hell you and Candace got mixed up in this Whitetower mess!"

"Don't be so snarky, Harry. I thought you told them everything."

"All that you told me. No doubt there's more you've both either forgotten or selectively chose not to reveal." He flashed his all-knowing eyes at the two of us. "And Warren said he needed to take everybody's statements, and I'm sure he means individually."

I was ready to take issue with him when Candace stepped in.

"OK, ok. Come on now you two. Let's not spoil the rest of this lovely night."

"But, he's insinuating that—"

"You know," Candace continued, avoiding my outburst, "I think that since we were so ah,-*incidental* in helping the police find Stanford, we should have a drink to celebrate our part in this, don't you?"

"The word is instrumental, not incidental, Candace." Harry shook his head.

"Oh, po-tay-toe, po-tah-toe," she flicked the words in the air as if they were pieces of lint. "Doesn't matter. One way or the other, we definitely should be proud of ourselves."

"If you say so, Candace," he conceded. "And, you may be right about that drink. A nightcap sounds pretty good right about now." He nudged her. "Are you buying?" He grinned.

We were sitting in a booth at the Pool Bar, sipping Irish coffees and listening to some cool jazz, when Molly and Chad entered the restaurant. Molly had her arm linked through his, her head bent toward him in intimate conversation. I caught the exhausted look on Chad's face. Candace scooted over to let them slide in next to her.

"Were you able to see your father?" I asked Chad.

He let out a huge sigh. "Yeah, they beat him up pretty bad. His face was bandaged. His jaw may be fractured."

"My God, how awful!" Goosebumps traveled up my arms.

"It wasn't a pretty sight, Mom," Molly replied.

"He was so heavily sedated, he kept drifting off. I'm not so sure he knew it was me."

"You two look like you could use something to drink." Candace waved the waitress over and ordered the same drinks for them.

"Did you talk to Detective Warren?" Chad's voice was a mixture of disappointment and sadness.

"Yes," said Harry. "He'll call around 10 o'clock to confirm a time for us to meet with him. It'll probably be sometime in the afternoon."

"Do you think we'll be able to see Stanford?" I wondered.

"I don't know. It'll depend on what the detective says." Chad put his head in his hands and closed his eyes for a moment. "I tried calling Mom, but her cell was not in service. You'd think she'd be worried about Dad and give me a call." He slumped against the booth's cushioned back. "How did they ever let themselves get so caught up in a mess like this?"

No one knew the answer or what to say to console him. Finally Harry broke the silence. "Well, there's not much we can do now. I guess we should probably call it a night."

"Dad, I think Chad and I will stay for a while." Molly put a reassuring hand on her friend's arm.

"Sure, honey, but don't be too late. We've got a big day coming up." Harry kissed his daughter on top of her head and squeezed Chad's shoulder. "These things have a way of looking better in the daylight, son." He motioned to Candace and me. "Let's go ladies."

As we walked through the lobby, I questioned Harry's comment to Chad. "Do you think it was right to give Chad false hope about things looking better in the morning?"

"I had to say something. That kid was so distraught. He's got a hell of a lot to process. I just wanted to give him a little encouragement."

"You know Harry, inside that rough shell, you're not such a bad egg after all." Candace gave him a little pat on the back.

"Yeah, but don't go broadcasting it!" he responded, ushering us into the waiting elevator.

***

The next day we sat around the dining table nervously awaiting Detective Warren's call. Chad arrived a few minutes before ten and helped himself to some coffee.

"I need a jolt to keep me awake." His hands shook slightly as he carried the cup to the table. "I didn't get much sleep.I Spent a lot of time trying to sort through everything from the last few days."

Even though we were prepared, we jumped at the first ring of Harry's cell phone.

"Yes ... yes ... fine, we'll see you then." Harry signed off. "We're to be at the station at one o'clock."

"That's three hours away. Whatever will we do until then?" Candace moaned.

"We could go over everything that's happened up to this point," I suggested.

"That's no fun. I've a better idea. Let's go to the mall. That'll eat up an hour or two."

"How can you think of shopping at a time like this?" I almost shrieked.

"It's what *I* do to calm my nerves," she answered, lips pouting, and one shoulder shrugging.

"Okay, you two," Harry's voice rose above us. "Quit your bickering. Let's do what Kate said and go over the events that led up to last night." He turned to me. "You've been involved in this thing since the time of my retirement party, let's start with you, but please keep it short."

"Okay, but tell that to the drama queen as well," I flicked my head at Candace, who responded by sticking out her tongue.

I ran through the incidents from the time of the party to Lydia's frantic phone call that some men were coming for her.

"Don't forget about the letter," Candace interrupted. "That happened before she made the call."

"I don't know if that's important," I hedged.

"Everything is important, Kate," Harry insisted.

"Oh, okay, I'll tell him, and after that is when I'll need help from Candace and you."

"Warren will most likely have questions throughout your statement, so be prepared to answer the best you can," suggested Harry.

Candace fidgeted in her chair, waiting for me to finish my account. She frantically waved her hand to get his attention. "Since the next event happened at my house, I'll go next."

"Have at it," he said.

"Well, I thought I recognized one of the men in the photo that Kate took, and sure enough it was one of the Busoni brothers." She discussed Lydia's change in her behavior after settling in. "We caught her in another lie. Lydia confessed that she hadn't told us the truth, then turned around and lied about that lie. We were pretty shocked when they found the big diamond inside the chalice."

"At that point we were beginning to wonder what was really the truth or another one of her convoluted fabrications," I added.

"I'd say she told one lie too many. What did you do next?" asked Harry

"You already know the rest. Do I have to go into it?"

"I realize that, Kate, but the police don't. So yes, continue."

"Oh, all right, Mister Interrogator." I let out an irritated sigh. "Lydia told us that Stanford had put the diamond in a safe place, she didn't know where, exactly. But the answer was in the safe in their office. Stanford diligently changed the combination daily, and recorded it in a document saved on a thumb or flash drive, whatever. Unfortunately for Lydia, Stanford took it with him to Vegas without giving her the new number. The last time she heard from him was two days ago. He was in Chad's apartment."

"That's when you decided to go to Las Vegas."

"Yes, we thought it'd be too dangerous for Lydia. She was to stay at Candace's house while we searched Chad's place. The only clue we had was a book, *Flash Drive*, which, as you know, is another name for thumb drive. We found one hidden in an easy chair and—"

"I was the one who found it, Kate," Candace interrupted, claiming victory.

We glared at each other. "Okay, so *she* found it, and we brought it back to the hotel. Chad plugged it into a borrowed laptop from the hotel. The last entry was a strange poem. Chad called his mom with the info."

"So tell me, how does Molly figure into any of this?" Harry switched his interrogation from us to his daughter.

"She's completely innocent, Harry. Why do you ask?" His question took me by surprise.

"Hey, I'm just playing devil's advocate. I'm sure the detective will want to know how she got involved in this mystery."

"Dad, I think my part isn't much more than being a tagalong to Vegas." She paused, her brow furrowed. "Oh, but do you think I should tell the police about the morgue visit?"

"I'll tell them that," Chad offered. "I don't think it's too important. If anything, I can say that I wanted to let Mom know if she recognized the body. We had to take a picture to send to her. That should do it."

Time passed quickly. Harry glanced at his watch. "It's almost time to go. Detective Warren is sending a car to take us to the station. Don't forget to stress the fact that we were merely helping a friend in need, and not signing up to be accomplices to any alleged theft."

We nodded.

# The Confession or...Whose Lie is it Anyway?

LAS VEGAS POLICE station was a hub of activity. The desk clerk took our request and buzzed Detective Warren. Within minutes, a tall, blond-haired woman of slight build met us. "This is Officer Irene Saunders. She will escort you to one of conference rooms," said the deputy.

The coldness of the bare room bounced off the gray metal table and chairs. The monochromatic walls were naked except for a large clock and a black phone. I don't know why, but we stood when Detective Warren entered. He offered a friendly greeting and motioned for us to sit. We women centered ourselves in the middle with the men anchoring us.

I'd armed myself with a strong dose of confidence expecting to be interrogated by a gruff, take no prisoners investigator. Instead, the detective was open and congenial. I figured him to be somewhere in his late forties or early fifties. The weariness in his dark brown eyes, and the lines on his rugged face, traced his many years working in the justice system. A pair of reading glasses peaked out from the top of his curly salt and pepper gray hair.

Chad was the first to speak. "Did you get to talk to my Dad?"

He nodded. "I was able to ask a few questions, but he was still pretty sedated. I'll be seeing him later today."

"What about the guy at the dock? What's his name? Did he tell you anything?" asked Chad.

"His name's Ralph Bacigalupo, not one of Busonis' sharpest knives in the drawer, but smart enough to lawyer up when we told him we found his fingerprints at the crime scene."

Both Candace and I gasped. I choked on my saliva which led to a coughing fit. She gripped my arm. Harry threw me a puzzling look. *It couldn't be our Ralphie of the bathroom scene that we sort of neglected to reveal in our mock interview with Harry?*

The detective eyed me curiously.

"I'm fine, now." I apologized. "Please go on."

Warren slipped his glasses onto his nose and reviewed the notes in his folder. "Now, what I have so far are sketchy pieces of information regarding the alleged theft and sale of a chalice stolen from the cathedral in Monreale, Sicily. I'll be taking your statements, one at a time." He peered over his glasses, eyes resting on me. "Mrs. Creighton," I jumped at the mention of my name, "I'll start with you."

As the detective's attention centered on me, my confidence began to flounder under his scrupulous stare. I felt that I had nothing incriminating to hide, but those darned pesky butterflies kept playing ring-around-the-rosy in my stomach.

Harry reached for my hand. Feeling the iciness of my fingers, he gently massaged them, relaying his support.

"Officer Saunders will escort you to one of the interrogation rooms. If the rest of you need anything, please use the wall phone next to the door. Press in the numbers 451, that's Officer Sander's extension."

\*\*\*

The large clock in the conference room ticked away the minutes. We were like swinging doors, one coming in, one going out. The investigation exhausted each of us to the point that hardly a word was exchanged.

I thought the interview I had with Detective Warren went pretty well. I stumbled a bit on one or two questions, but he seemed to understand my nervousness and appeared satisfied.

When all the interviews had ended, Officer Saunders brought in some cold bottles of water, and set them on the table.

"What happens now?" asked Harry, reaching for a couple and handing one to me.

"Detective Warren is going through your statements with his team. He'll be in shortly." She turned and left abruptly before anyone else could pump her with more questions.

I took a few sips of water, letting the coolness run down my parched throat then pointed the bottle at Harry. "You were right. Many times Warren would stop me in mid-sentence asking for clarification. I was anxious at first. I kept losing my train of thought and stumbled over my words, but after a while I relaxed. I think I did all right in the end."

"I didn't flub up at all," Candace gloated. "I simply dazzled him with my excellent repartee. He only interrupted me once."

"I suppose he wanted to stop you from wandering off a cliff into obscure trivia like you do so well," I taunted.

"Yeah, sort of ... but after I finished, he thanked me graciously for helping them find Stanford. So there!" She fluffed her hair.

"Oh please!" I wanted to douse her with the rest of my water, but a look from Harry quickly settled me down.

I looked at the clock. A half hour went by. We spent the time pacing about the room, suppressing yawns or nervously drumming fingers on the table.

"This place is worse than a doctor's office." Candace muttered to herself. "At least *there* they have magazines to look at."

Fifteen more minutes went by before Detective Warren returned. We stood up, but he waved us back to our chairs then placed a folder on the table. He spent a few minutes viewing its contents. The suspense was killing us.

Finally, he settled back in his chair, cleared his throat, and began. "We've gone through all of your statements. Most seem to be in order. However," his glance fell directly onto both Candace and me. "I'd like to question Mrs. Creighton and Ms. Carrington-Jones again. There seems to be a little detail that needs clearing up before I make my final report."

"We? Us?" Candace looked at me. At that moment I was suffering one of my worst hot flashes to date.

"Yes, you two." The detective gave us a no-nonsense command. He called in Officer Saunders. "Please show Mrs. Creighton and Ms. Carrington-Jones to room 105."

Clamminess engulfed the back of my neck. I looked at Candace.

"Okay. What *did* you tell the Detective?" I cautiously asked.

"Me?" she muttered back. "*I'm* perfectly innocent."

She seemed too nonchalant, and I wasn't buying it. "You must've alluded to something in your statement that triggered a question."

"Allude? Why I most certainly did not," Candace huffed, nose in the air. "I never allude ... at least I don't think so." Confusion clouded her face.

*Maybe she's innocent. I shouldn't be so hard on her. But then...*

Officer Saunders shuffled us into another cold room. Candace spent time studying the latest manicure that hid her broken fingernail, while I searched my brain, trying to find something that could've raised a red flag.

Detective Warren arrived shortly and took the chair facing us. He began thumbing through the same folder. If I wasn't nervous before, my level of panic was now at the point of explosion.

Tapping his pen on one of the pages, he stated in a somber tone, "There seems to be a time conflict in both of your stories. You stated here that you were at Mr. White's apartment two days ago. If that's true, there would still be caution tape covering the door, correct?"

"Well, y...yes there would," I stammered, "b...but, it was hanging loose from the door handle, so we assumed that it was okay to go in."

"Wasn't the door locked?"

"Um, yes and no," Candace fidgeted with her necklace.

"How could it have been both, Ms. Carrington-Jones?" he snapped. "It's either one or the other."

She jumped. "Ah, we ah, jiggled the knob, and with a little help we got it open."

"A little help?" He leaned on the table, moving his face closer to her. "What kind of 'little help?'"

"Okay, okay, I picked the lock." Candace confessed, all flustered. "How else would we've been able to get inside and find the thumb, er flash drive?"

"So then, that would be breaking and entering. Do you understand that it is a serious offence?" It was a pop up question for either of us.

I caught it and answered, "I … I suppose so, but if we knew who the person was living there—that would be my neighbor's son, Chad—and if it were his mother, Lydia, asking a favor of us, surely it wouldn't actually be the same as breaking into an apartment of someone we didn't know."

"That certainly wouldn't be the same, now would it?" Candace batted her eyelashes at the detective.

There was a slight raise of his eyebrows. I saw a hint of a grin before he pressed his lips tightly together. He shoved his glasses upon the bridge of his nose and began writing. A moment later he asked, "Now then, after you *helped* yourselves into the apartment, what did you do next?"

"We were hunting for that drive, which I found, by-the-way, when we were interrupted by voices outside the door. Then we heard the knob rattle." Candace gained a bit more confidence. "We needed a place to hide, so we ran … well I hobbled because you see, I'd broken the strap of my Jimmy Choo shoe and—"

"Get to the point, please," Warren sighed.

I wanted to clamp my hand over her mouth before we got arrested for excessive boring. Instead, I clutched her arm forcefully and hurried on. "We headed for the bathroom, hopped into the Jacuzzi, pulled the cover over us, and scrunched below the rim. We heard two men's voices talking and calling each other by their names, Bernie and Ralphie. When you told us that you arrested a man called Ralph Baccia something, we thought he might've been that same person."

That got Detective Warren's complete attention. He jerked his head up, "Did you get a look at their faces?"

"Well, not their faces, exactly…" Candace's voice faded into the handkerchief she pulled from her pocket.

"Well, what then?" He was clearly puzzled.

"What she's trying to tell you, detective, is that while we were in the tub, the one called Ralphie decided to ah, use the facilities."

"And he didn't even wash his hands afterwards," Candace replied disgustedly.

"All right, I've heard enough." Detective Warren stifled a cough and cleared his throat. "So you can't really identify either one, only by voice and—"

"Right," I quickly answered. "We waited a few minutes to make sure they'd left before getting out of the tub. When we got back to the living room, we saw that the men had messed up the place even more. One of them took a book off the side table. You might get good prints off it, if you find it."

"As you can see, Detective, we hardly disturbed a thing," Candace concluded.

Warren made some more notes, closed the folder, and stood up. "I believe I have everything I need." He held the door open and signaled for Officer Saunders to lead us back to the others.

We followed behind like two convicts marching to our cells.

"Do you suppose he'll put us in jail?" wailed Candace. "Oh, dear, I'd look so awful in that horrible orange jumpsuit. Maybe they'd let us accessorize."

"Shut up and keep walking," I barked. It'd been a long, nerve-wracking afternoon, and my tolerance had sunk to a level beyond coping with her screwball ideas. *Accessorize? Puleease!* Everyone greeted us with a barrage of questions. I tried to talk over their anxious voices. Finally, Candace put her two fingers together and let out a whistle loud enough to stop a train on its tracks. "Thank you," I grudgingly acknowledged her assistance. "We had to clear up a small detail about when and how we entered Chad's apartment."

"Like, how small was it?" Harry wondered.

"Oh, nothing to bother with."

"Nothing?" Candace nearly screamed in my ear. "Easy for you to say, but the fact is you just might be seeing the two of us be—"

"No, no. Candace is just being well … Candace." I tried to act casual, but inside, I harbored a small fear, that there'd be some kind of penalty for our alleged crime.

At that moment, Detective Warren stepped into the room carrying that dreaded folder. We sat quietly, suppressing our nerves, waiting for him to speak.

He slid on his glasses and studied something in the file then began. "We have concluded that in the matter of Mrs. Creighton and Ms Carrington-Jones failure to notify the authorities first before attempting to solve this case is not subject to arrest." Like a scolding parent he continued. "When amateurs try to be detectives, they make it difficult for us to do our job. I hope you remember this in the future." He stressed the last line.

We answered in a collective yes, and sighs of relief bounced off the walls of the conference room.

"Just a moment, I'm not through." The sternness in his voice sent our highs crashing down to a thud at our feet. "There is still the matter of breaking and entering into Mr. White's apartment." Warren focused his attention on Candace and me.

*Oh crap, he didn't believe us, and we were almost free and clear.*

I could feel the noose tighten around my neck. I managed a quick glance at Candace. Her face looked as pale as mine felt.

The detective flipped to a page in that damned file and studied it for a few moments.

*Maybe he'll let us off with a slap on the hand and a fine. The suspense is killing me. Come on Warren, stop making us sweat. If we're guilty, cuff us.* After what felt like forever, he raised his head. "Mrs. Creighton, Ms. Carrington-Jones…"

"That's it," whispered Candace. "We're toast."

"After reviewing your latest testimony, outrageous as some of it sounded, I've concluded that it couldn't possibly have been made up. And since you were given permission by Mr. White to be in his apartment, we've chosen to drop the charges of breaking and entering."

220

Candace and I hugged. "We're free!" she shouted in my ear.

Yes, we were, as far as the justice system was concern. But Harry hadn't heard about the Jacuzzi incident, and I had a feeling there'd be a lot of explaining to do. *God help me!*

"I want to thank you all for coming. This has been quite an interesting afternoon." Warren collected his pen and folder and stood up to leave.

We followed his lead and started heading for the door when he suddenly stopped and turned back to us.

"There's one more thing about this case that has me puzzled."

We searched each other's eyes, equally confused by his statement. Tension reared its ugly head.

"It's this bit about the diamond. In all the reports we received from the Monreale police, there was never any mention of a diamond or anything else sequestered inside the chalice."

"That's what Lydia Whitetower told us," I declared. "We believed it at the time. That is before her yarn started unraveling inch-by-inch."

"Well just in case, I'll have my team check further into it."

"You said you'd be seeing my Dad again," Chad spoke up. "Could we go to the hospital with you?"

Harry concurred. "Maybe Whitetower might have that answer we're looking for."

"Possibly." Warren checked his watch. "I'll be leaving for the hospital in a few minutes. Why don't you come up around seven? That should give me enough time to get his statement."

"Will do," Harry agreed. "I, for one, would certainly like to see this whole mess done once and for all."

Detective Warren thanked us again for our help. Officer Saunders escorted us to the front entrance. A blast of heat and a taxi pulled up in front of the door. She had told the desk clerk ahead of time to call for a large cab.

Harry, Molly, Chad, and I took the back and middle seats of a black Cadillac Escalade. "Vegas seems to be top heavy

221

with these cars," I mused out loud. Candace slid in the front seat.

"Where to?" asked the driver.

Candace turned to face us. "I don't know about you all, but I'm famished. There used to be a little Mexican place a few blocks from the hospital. They've got the best enchiladas and margaritas this side of Vegas."

"I thought you said the one in Caesar's Palace had the best ones," I uttered.

"Those were the best on the strip. These are much better," she explained. "Now let me finish. The place is called *El Cerrito*. Is it still there?" she asked the driver who gave an enthusiastic nod. "Sound good to you guys?"

"Great idea, Candace," Harry licked his lips. "My mouth's already watering. What're we waiting for? Let's do it!"

Candace's suggestion was a hit. The Mexican food, authentic and delicious, was welcomed by five hungry stomachs. The stress of the last few hours melted into our icy margaritas. Cheerful Latin music moved our mood to a more pleasant beat. Time was spent unwinding and renewing our energy. After dinner, we women freshened up in the small restroom while Harry paid the bill.

When we arrived at the hospital, Detective Warren was still in Stanford's room. The officer guarding the door instructed us to wait in the sitting area near the elevators.

"Sure seems like it's been a day of sitting and waiting for the next thing to happen," Candace remarked.

"I wish I was a fly on the wall to hear what Stanford had to say to the detective, especially about the diamond," I wondered out loud.

"Well, looks like you don't have to wonder anymore." Harry gestured to the open door.

Detective Warren stepped out of Stanford's room and eased himself into an empty seat next to Chad, who gripped the arms of his chair, bracing himself for news of his dad.

Seeing the worry in Chad's eyes, Warren laid a hand on his shoulder. "There's no easy way to put it, but I'm afraid that we have to take your father into custody as soon as he's released from the hospital. He'll be charged with attempting to sell stolen property. However, he's ready to implicate his partner, Leo Viorsky, so that may help in his arraignment."

"Did he say anything about the diamond?" I asked.

Detective Warren took a few seconds before responding. A semi-smile curved upward on his lips. "I'm afraid that his wife told you another lie, Mrs. Creighton. Stanford Whitetower was as amazed as I when I asked him about a diamond in the chalice. It was the first he'd heard of it, and he swore that there wasn't anything like that inside."

A muffled groan escaped my lips. "That bitch!" I uttered to Candace, sitting next to me. A sudden rage propelled me off the chair. "That conniving, no good, lying bitch. She played us all along. Damn her. I should've known that last story about the diamond was nothing but a big fat lie."

Everyone stared wide-eyed at me. Even Detective Warren was startled at my abrupt outburst. I could feel my face turn the color of an over-ripe tomato. Realization hit me. *Yeow! I just called Chad's mom a bitch. Twice.* "Oh God, Chad, forgive me for what I just said about your mother. It's—"

"That's okay, Mrs. C, no offense taken."

"I'd say Lydia was a pretty good actress," Candace admitted a little admirably. "I don't think I could've done it with as much conviction … well maybe with more practice I could've—"

"Candace!" I made a slicing move across my neck with the side of my hand to silence her.

"Good God, will this Whitetower craziness ever end?" groaned Harry.

"Well Harry, it was your idea to come to Vegas." He was such a grump. "If you think about it a little, we've had quite an adventure."

"So, Detective, if there wasn't a diamond in the safety deposit box, did Whitetower tell you what was in it?" asked Harry.

He paused a moment, assessing the mood of the group. "I think it's best that Mr. Whitetower tell you. You all deserve to hear the truth from him."

"What if he's lying, too?" asked Candace.

"I believe there's nothing left to lie about." Warren rose wearily from his chair. "Come, he's expecting you."

We entered the room. Stanford's wrist was handcuffed to one side of the railing. His face was covered with bruises. We circled the bed. Chad clasped his father's free hand and Stanford gripped it for a moment. Shame marched across Stanford's face. "I'm so sorry, son." His jaw was heavily bandaged making it difficult for him to speak and for us to understand him.

Chad bent closer to his face. "Dad, how, ah, what made you and Mom get involved in this scheme?"

"Money, son. It was all about money. There were rumors that the university would be downsizing and combining classes. Your mother and I weren't sure about our future. This plan of Hamadi's looked like an easy way to increase our income." He cleared his throat and motioned for the glass of water on the stand.

After a few sips through the straw, Stanford continued. "You must believe me, Chaun…Chad, I didn't know the chalice was actually stolen in the beginning. I had no reason not to trust Hamadi's word. Then Leo got greedy. He found another interested buyer who was willing to pay a lot more for it, so he had a replica made. He'd sell the fake to the new buyer and the real one to the Busonis. Leo was quite convincing, so your mother and I went along with it." He coughed to clear the phlegm in his throat.

"How did the Busonis find out about the fake chalice?" Harry probed deeper.

Stanford's tone sharpened a bit toward Harry, attempting a haughty response. "I'm not certain. Either someone tipped them off, or it was Arturo Santini. They are both in ancient artifact acquisitions," he finished.

"I'm confused. Did Leo try to sell the fake to Santini?"

"Ah, yes. Leo didn't know that Santini was traveling under a fictitious name. At first Leo thought he was a two-bit con artist who wouldn't know a fake artifact from the real item. But, as you already know, that wasn't the case."

Stanford was beginning to tire; his voice became raspy. He held his free hand to his bandaged jaw.

"How did Leo find out Santini's true identity?"

"Santini told him. He knew of the chalice's authenticity by a small marking at the base. The person Leo commissioned to make the replica either missed it or may've thought it had been scratched in the handling. Unfortunately, Leo's idea of a double sale backfired. Santini threatened to tell the Busonis if we didn't sell him the real artifact. So we made arrangements to meet him at Chad's apartment the next day to seal the deal."

"Okay, you satisfied one buyer, but how did the Busonis find out that you were selling them the fake?" Harry kept pressing him for answers.

"I don't know." Flashes of anger darted from his eyes. "We weren't close friends."

"Was it Leo?"

"Yeah, Stanford," Candace chided. "Did they put the muscle on Leo to squeeze the truth out of him?" A collective gasp filled the room. She stopped suddenly eyeing us. "Sorry guys, but you forget I lived with those people, and *I* know first-hand what they do to … oh never mind. Go on, Harry." She shot an attentive nod at him.

"Thanks." Harry threw her an exasperated glare. "Now Stanford, if what Candace told us is possibly true, do you think Leo could've been the one to confess in order to save his ass?"

Stanford grimaced as he shook his head. "No, not at all. Leo was in a state of shock when we met at Chad's apartment the next day. He said a reliable source told him that the Busonis' had been tipped off to our scam. We needed to move quickly before Santini arrived to collect the chalice."

"Was the real chalice with you?" Harry asked.

Stanford coughed. His thin hand trembled, his answer softly spoken. "Ah, no. It's in the safety deposit box back home."

*Ah, so it was in the bank all along. But what about the diamond?*

225

Stanford's lips were dry and cracked. Chad held the glass of water while his father took several sips. "What happened next, Dad?"

"Leo left first. I started to follow him then remembered I had the thumb drive in my pants pocket. I was wasting precious time, but I needed to find a good place to hide it. There was a loud knock on the door. I was frantic. There wasn't a moment to spare, so I shoved it in the crack between the cushion and side of the easy chair. Then I quickly dialed Lydia to warn her, but before I could finish, Busoni's men marched in and ... you know the rest." Stanford slumped back onto his pillows. Exhaustion played upon his pale face. His eyelids fluttered.

Stanford's frailness caused an uncomfortable pause in our questioning. Detective Warren studied something on his cell phone. Molly leaned into Chad and softly rubbed his back. Harry stared at the ceiling. Candace fidgeted with her necklace. And I chewed on my lower lip. There were still things not answered. Even though Stanford told the detective that there wasn't a diamond, we needed to hear it from him.

*Somebody say something!* My eyes darted from one to the other.

Finally, I broke the silence. "Stanford, do you think Leo could've come back to the apartment later and killed Santini?"

Stanford's eyelids popped open. He raised his head. "That's pure nonsense. If you would've seen the frightened look on his face, you'd have known that Leo was incapable of killing anyone."

"He's right." Detective Warren spoke up. "We're pretty certain it wasn't Leo. The hit was professional, the kind we've seen before. The Busonis handiwork was all over it."

"See, I told you so." Candace nudged me.

I rolled my eyes. *I'll never hear the end of it.*

"My deputy just sent me a text regarding Mr. Viorsky's whereabouts," continued Warren. "They've checked all the departures out of Vegas and found that Viorsky had purchased a one-way ticket to Phoenix at approximately the same time the murder occurred. The police at the Arizona airport have been alerted. Leo will be extradited back to Vegas for questioning."

His admission caught us all off guard.

*Leo in Arizona, and not with Lydia?*

"Then who—?" Candace began.

She took the words right out of my thoughts. I quickly grabbed her arm and whispered, "Let's not say anything just yet."

Suddenly, Stanford reached out to Chad, tugging at his hand. "My God, Lydia! Your mother? Is she all right? Does she know what's happened to me? I tried to tell her she was in danger but … the men …" He frantically searched Chad's face for answers.

"Before he says anything," I interrupted. "There's something we need to clear up."

A curious expression crossed Stanford's face. "What do you mean?"

"It's the diamond, Lydia told us about it."

"What diamond? What are you talking about? There was no diamond. I told the detective that." He focused his attention on Warren. "Didn't you tell them?"

I answered for Warren. "He did. But Lydia told us something different, Stanford. She seemed pretty convincing to us that you found a large diamond in a red velvet pouch inside the chalice."

"That's ridiculous. Why would Lydia tell such a story?" Stanford appeared perplexed.

"We don't know. That's why we're asking you."

"What else did she tell you, and why should you be so interested in something so preposterous?" His tone raised a notch.

"It's like this, Stanford. At first we were quite concerned about your wife's safety. I'd even been threatened by one of Busonis' men, so when Lydia called me for help, I believed she was in grave danger. We decided that Candace's home would be a safe haven for her to stay. And that's when things didn't seem to add up. Lies started to fly out of her mouth." I paused to assess the effect this information had on him. "I have to admit that Candace and I were intrigued by this whole scam even though we could detect a lot of holes in her story."

"Lydia went into great detail about finding the diamond in the chalice. When she got your last message, she believed you were in trouble and was upset that she couldn't find the flash/thumb drive with the latest combination to the safe. She figured you took it to Vegas. She seemed more intent on getting it rather than being more concerned for your safety. Lydia wanted us … well no … Candace and I offered to go to Vegas and find the flash drive. Even though we questioned her innocence in all this, we still felt it would be too dangerous for her to go. We found it where you said you put it, opened it and sent the information to her."

Stanford took a few seconds to digest what he heard. He shook his head slowly in disbelief. "I already told you that the real chalice was in the safety deposit box."

"Anything else in there, Dad?" asked Chad.

"Only our passports, and a large sum of money." He caught sight of disappointment on Chad's face.

"Was it the Busonis, money?" he asked.

"Yes, a partial payment. I didn't trust Leo to hold onto it, so I told him I'd put the chalice and the money in a safe place. Gino Busoni had seen the real one when he was at our house this summer."

"You know, I'm beginning to wonder if Lydia had something to do with informing the Busonis about the fake chalice," wondered Harry.

"How can you think that?" Stanford retaliated, quite agitated at his suggestion.

"Looks to me like your wife left you to suffer the consequences," I added.

"What are you saying?" Stanford tried to sit up, but pain from the beating, and his handcuffed wrist, slapped him back down.

"Oh, let me tell him," Candace said, pushing me aside. "My maid, Anita, called yesterday and told us that your wife left my house with a strange man. She didn't say who he was, where they were going, or if she intended to be back at all."

"Apparently it wasn't Leo," I weighed in. "And since Lydia had the right combination to get the key to the safety deposit box, I wouldn't be surprised if she and this mysterious man emptied it, leaving you with nothing but a jail sentence."

"Why, that's preposterous," he spluttered

"Anita told us that the man spoke English with a foreign accent. Stanford, do you know who that might be?" I asked.

"Oh, I bet it was the nice French doctor in Tunisia. The one who took *such* good care of her." Candace jabbed the knife in a little further.

The revelation shook Stanford's whole body. He tried to return a rebuttal, but the words wouldn't materialize.

"Yes! I'm certain he must've been the one who wrote the letter to her." I directed the comment to Candace.

"And Lydia lead us to believe it was an *old friend,*" She replied.

"Ly…Lydia, and DuBois!" Stanford stammered, his eyes darting about from face to face. "Wh…why that's absurd. Lydia wouldn't abandon me!" His voice cracked.

"I'm afraid it must be so, Dad," responded Chad. "We haven't heard a word from Mom since she left Candace's house. It doesn't seem like she cared what happened or will happen to you."

The last bit of news was too much for Stanford. Tears tumbled down his sunken cheeks.

There was a time when I would've gladly given him a well-kept piece of my mind, but after watching a defeated man reduced to uncontrollable sobs, I found little satisfaction. Instead, I stated resolutely, "That should answer all *your* questions, Stanford, and ours as well." I turned to Detective Warren. "I think we're done here."

"I'd like to have a little more time alone with my father, if that's all right." Chad directed his request to the detective.

"Fifteen minutes."

"Thank you."

"Well, that's that," said Harry, following Warren out of the room. "There's nothing left to do but pack up and get the hell out of here."

The rest of us fell in step behind him. I stifled a yawn. "You know, Harry, I'm with you one hundred percent. I can't wait to get home to sanity."

"Aw, the night's young," insisted Candace. "We can still do a little more gambling and maybe catch a late show."

Our silent response answered her suggestion. "You two are turning into old fogies," she sniffed. "Well then, I'm sure Molly has some enthusiasm left. You want to take in some more hot spots?"

"I think I'll wait for Chad. I don't want to abandon him," Molly's solemn answer matched the caring tone in her voice.

"Maybe he'd want to unwind. He could do with a little fun, maybe some little casino hopping," she urged.

"Oh for goodness sake, Candace, what are you thinking? Chad must be pretty worn-out after all that's happened to him. His family's just fallen apart in a matter of days!" I chided her.

The red in her cheeks indicated a trace of embarrassment. "Oh my ... yes, you're right, Kate," she answered contritely. "Drat! I hate when you do that."

"Do what?"

"Make me stop and think!"

Chad emerged a few minutes later, sadness and disgust written all over his face. He headed for the elevators. "I'm done here. Let's go."

Molly moved quickly to his side. We rode silently to the main floor. I was about to speak to Chad, but Harry stopped me, shaking his head. He was right. Silent support was what Chad needed now.

The ride back to the hotel was quiet. An idle comment bounced off someone's lips from time to time, but the sentences were short and the replies a mere grunt. The taxi pulled up in front of Chad's temporary quarters. Detective Warren had told him that he was now free to return to his condo anytime. But he wasn't ready to go back just yet. Chad got out of the cab and leaned on the door, thanking us all for being there for him. "This would've been a monstrous thing to have to take care of alone."

Feeling a mothering urge to comfort coming on, I reached out and touched his cheek. "I think I can speak for all of us, Chad, when I say just how sorry we are that this horrible thing happened. I just wish that—"

"No need to go into it, Mrs. C. I'll check in with you guys in the morning." He closed the door and walked slowly up the path to Mike's door. Like Atlas with the world on his back, Chad carried the weight of his parents' grave mistakes on his hunched shoulders.

The night lights of Las Vegas seemed dim due to our somber moods. When we reached the hotel, Candace tried once more to rally the troops but failing she succumbed to calling it an evening.

"You know, after experiencing the high level of energy this city puts out, I'm really looking forward to the simplicity of life in a small college town." Molly sighed.

As soon as we entered our suite, Harry went directly to the laptop to make reservations for our return. Flights to the town nearest to Molly's school were limited, but after a long search, he was able to book four seats leaving around noon. "I'm afraid that it's not a direct flight, but there should be enough time to get you settled in, Molly. We, on the other hand need to hustle to get home before midnight."

"Harry, you could've booked yourself a direct flight," I said as we gathered our bodies and headed off to bed.

"Too late now. Guess you'll have to put up with me for a few more hours."

"Hope he sleeps all the way home," I whispered to Candace.

"See you all in the morning," Molly yawned.

The next day was a rush of dressing, packing, gulping down coffee and noshing on bagels room service sent up. Chad called to say he would meet us at the airport to say his goodbyes.

With Harry in the lead, we made it there in plenty of time. Chad reached us before we queued up for inspection.

"Dad asked me to fly up in a few days to check on the house, and Jasper. Does anyone know what happened to him?" he asked.

"He's at my place. Anita was a little upset that Lydia didn't take him when she left. The cat made her a bit jumpy," offered Candace.

"Yeah, Jasper can be strange at times, but I can't worry about him now." Chad shoved his hands in his pockets examining the floor. When he raised his head we could see a mixture of sadness and worry in his eyes. Questions poured out. "What's going to happen in the days to come? What about the plans *I* have? Am I being terribly selfish to think about me?"

"Take it one day at a time, son," advised Harry. "No one here thinks you're selfish. Look, if it'll help, we'll keep an eye on the house and see about Jasper until you come up."

"Thanks, Mr. C, I really appreciate that." Chad held out his hand to Harry, but Harry drew him into a hug, as if he were comforting one of his own sons.

I was so moved by Harry's offer that I burst into tears. Candace and Molly followed suit.

"Oh great!" Harry exclaimed. "Now I'll have to contend with three emotional women for the next couple of hours." He took a clean handkerchief from his pocket and handed it to me. "Sorry, I only have one. You'll all have to share!"

"Oh Harry, you're such a nut sometimes," I blubbered, taking it and dabbing my eyes.

Molly kissed her father on the cheek and murmured, "You old softie." She grabbed a tissue from Candace, who of course, found a packet in the endless bottom of her purse.

In a fit of emotion, Candace pulled Harry into a hug.

"Enough already!" he blustered. He disengaged himself from her embrace. "Hate to break up this love fest, but we better get a move on. The gate is at the end of the concourse, so we've got a bit of a hike to make it in time."

"Chad, let us know when you'll be coming up," I said, giving him a big hug.

Candace kissed him on the cheek and thanked him again for his part in giving her the opportunity to see her son.

"You all go ahead. I'll catch up. "Molly said. "I want to spend a few minutes alone with Chad."

Molly made it to the gate just as the attendant finished the last call before the door closed. She hustled down the passage way, into the plane, and squeezed into the empty seat between Candace and me. Harry had wisely taken the aisle seat across from us. It didn't take a rocket scientist to know not to break up three of a kind.

"Hey Molly-oh, what's going on between you and Chad? You were looking mighty chummy," needled Candace.

"Could there be a romance in the offing?" I added.

"Come on you guys!" Molly laughed.

"Ooh yes, the boy who longs for the girl next door," cooed Candace.

"That's so sweet," I agreed.

"Forget it, you two!" huffed Harry.

"Maybe she's simpatico to Chad's situation. He's at first grateful to her, and next—"

"Their long-standing friendship blossoms into love," finished Candace.

Molly watched us batting her life back and forth like players in a ping pong match. She tried to interrupt several times, but we kept on planning her life down to the number of grandchildren. At that point, she stopped us by grabbing hold of our arms. "Listen to me. It won't work!"

"Why not?" we asked, a bit surprised by her insistence.

"Because, he's gay!"

Dead silence followed Molly's announcement. I glanced sideways at Harry, who had caught the gist of the lively conversation. He rolled his eyes and continued working on a crossword puzzle he'd found in the airline's complimentary magazine.

An embarrassed Candace turned away from Molly and gazed out the window. "Why are the nice good looking ones always gay?" she sighed.

As the plane taxied to the runway waiting for permission to take off, Harry leaned across the aisle and poked me in the arm with his pen.

I let out an irritable sigh. "What is it now, Harry?"

"What's a five letter word for 'meddlesome', beginning with the letter 'N'?"

# Pirates, Princesses...and Adeline? Oh My!

OCTOBER WAS ONE of my favorite months, mostly because Halloween was in it. I loved the mix of fall colors that blended well with the decorations for the big event. Harry had two jobs. One was digging the boxes out of the attic every year. The other was carving a couple of pumpkins to put out on the front porch. He actually got a kick out of making mischievous faces on them. That was one job he tackled with gusto. I wrapped twinkling orange lights around the front door and placed a giant neon pumpkin face right in the middle. It winked at youngsters as they bounded up the steps to trick-or-treat. Since no one else was here to help this year, the rest was left up to me to finish.

A few years ago, Kenny had burned a CD of haunting noises and eerie music. He set it up near the pumpkins to surprise unsuspecting Trick-or-Treaters. The neighborhood kids looked forward to being scared silly. This year, we added one new item to our chilling Halloween night. An eerie black cat was perched on the back of the living room sofa; a soft light outlined his presence as he peered into the darkness watching everyone passing by. Yes, we acquired Jasper. It took a while for Romeo and Juliet to accept him, but they all seemed to have plotted out their territories and kept pretty much to themselves.

This year I dressed up in black tights and an oversized sweatshirt with a big orange pumpkin on the front with the word *Boo!* printed underneath. I used to be more creative, but after all that had happened the past few months, I opted for unfettered simplicity.

Harry, Jr., his two children, and Meg's twins stopped over to show off their costumes. Harry took pictures of the spirited group. The children sprinted out the door armed with a good start of treats nestled in pillow cases and pumpkin pails.

"Thanks, Mom, for adding to their sugar high," Meg scolded playfully as she rushed to catch up with the group.

"A grandparent's prerogative," I hollered out.

Romeo happily accompanied me to the door as soon as he heard the bell ring, announcing the arrival of a bevy of costumed children. The Findley kids were our first trick-or-treaters. They were almost as excited to see Romeo as they were about getting their candy.

"Can't we take him with us around the neighborhood?" asked Haley.

Romeo was wagging his tail so hard it nearly tossed the candy bowl off the small table. I thought he might've understood the question. I shook my head. "There's way too much excitement out there. He's better off inside with me."

"OK, but can we come over Saturday and play with him?" asked Charlie.

"Sure, he'd love it."

At 8:30 p.m. the stream of children dwindled down to an occasional one or two. I was about to turn off the porch light when the doorbell rang. I opened it to a very tall princess in a frilly pink chiffon, floor-length dress, layered with a mountain of petticoats. A sparkling tiara peaked out atop her blonde hair. Her arms were covered with a shimmering stole. She carried a wand with a glittered silver star at the tip.

"Aren't you a little old to be trick-or-treating?" I couldn't resist the remark.

"Never," said Candace, sashaying into the house sideways, her petticoats barely making it through the opened door. "I've just spent an hour reading to the children in the cancer wing at St. Mary's Hospital, plus handing out books and candy at the library. I was told I had to come in costume, so I just went into my closet and *voilá!*" She did a little pirouette then stopped abruptly, giving me a disapproving eye at my meager attire. "Well, you sure went all out for the occasion!"

I ignored the comment and bowed lowly, swinging my arm out in a welcoming gesture. "Follow me into the family room, your highness. Harry's been reclining on the sofa watching some news program for the past hour. I'm sure he'll enjoy the diversion." We both laughed. We knew him so well.

Once in the family room, Candace tossed her stole on the back of the couch and plopped down next to Harry. The skirt of her dress spread out and over part of his lap. "Greetings my good man," she said with an air of royalty.

"Ah, yes," he sighed, turning down the volume on the TV. "Is your royal pumpkin parked outside?" he asked, one eyebrow lifted.

"I do hope that I'm not interrupting your quiet evening." She smiled sweetly, batting her eyes.

"No more than usual." His nonchalant remark covered the near grin he tried to suppress.

"I'm ever so parched ... you know, tending to my little subjects for *sooo* many hours." She placed her hand over her brow in dramatic fashion then tapped him on the shoulder with her wand. "Would you have some kind of Halloween beverage to quench my thirst?"

Harry gave her a sideways glance then looked down at the glitter from the wand that fell on his sweater. Brushing the sparkles off, he inquired, "Well, your royal-pain-in-the-butt, what did you have in mind?"

"Oh, I don't know, something warm and cozy, I should think."

"Sounds good to me," I added, sliding into an easy chair next to the couch. "I'm exhausted from being the resident dispenser of sweets this evening. Maybe some hot spiced cider would be nice, or I think there's mixings for hot buttered rum. Hmm, that's even better. But anything you'll find will do, hon."

Harry shoved the mountain of chiffon off his lap and pushed off the couch. He ambled toward the kitchen muttering, "What I do for those two women."

While he was off conjuring up drinks, we made idle chatter, but the talk always came back to the Whitetowers. Suddenly, Candace sat straight up. "Quick, Kate, look! Turn up the TV."

The breaking news banner ran across on the bottom of the screen. "Harry, come in here. Hurry! You've got to see this," I cried out.

He rushed back in yelling, "First you want me to fix drinks, now you ..." He looked at the screen. "What the hell?"

*"Fifteenth century artifact reported stolen from the Cathedral of Monreale, Sicily several months ago found early this morning ... more to follow."*

"What do you think, Harry?"

"Let's wait and see what our crack anchor, Lawnsdale, has to say."

As on cue, the newsman abruptly interrupted his regular commentary to continue with the breaking story.

"This just in from Monreale, Sicily. A 15th century chalice stolen a few months ago from the Cathedral of Monreale has been found. A cleaning woman discovered it underneath one of the pews at the rear of the church. According to Father Francis Sanpietro the chalice, one of a set donated to the church by the Italian explorer Giovanni Medina, will be thoroughly inspected to detect any damage and determine its authenticity. The chalice was thought to be stolen by the notorious art thief, Arturo Santini, found dead last month in Las Vegas, Nevada...We'll bring you more information as it comes into our studio."

"Wow! Who do you think had the guilty conscience, Lydia, the doctor, or both?" I wondered. "Of course we really don't know for sure, if the chalice *was* ever in the safety deposit box in the first place."

"Well, it's back now." Harry reported. "The people of Sicily are happy. The priest is happy. You two should be happy. End of story. And as far as I'm concerned, I don't give a rat's ass what those two were thinking. Maybe now we can put this final episode to bed once and for all." Harry went back into the kitchen.

"Aside from all that's happened, I'm so glad the chalice is back where it belongs," I said to Candace.

"On the other hand, Kate, I kind of miss all the excitement and chaos, don't you?"

"Well, to tell you the truth," I spoke softly out of Harry's range, "I really do too. At first I appreciated getting back into the same old grind, but lately, I've been thinking about our adventure. It was certainly quite exciting." I smiled, thinking about the bathtub incident.

Harry returned carrying a tray with three glasses and a bottle of rare cognac. "To hell with the cider and rum, this is far better and will certainly warm us faster." He poured a small amount of amber liquid into the three snifters. We were toasting the rightful return of the chalice when the doorbell rang.

"Oh my God, it's well after nine. All the kids should be through by now," I groaned.

"Don't answer it," advised Harry.

Rapid knocking on the door followed more ringing.

"Well, whoever it is must not have had their share of candy," said Candace. "I'll go and zap them away with my wand." She started to get up off the couch, but I stopped her.

"I'll take care of this late comer." I was a little concerned about the insistent knocking. *Who could it be?*

"I'm coming. I'm coming," I called out.

Harry caught up with me. "I'll get it." He threw the door wide open. "What the ...?"

"Adeline!" I gasped.

As surprised as I was to find her standing all alone on the porch, I was more shocked by her appearance. Adeline McHenry never left her house without being impeccably dressed; even a trip to her mailbox was cause for full makeup. But tonight she must've thrown on whatever clothing was handy on her body. Her slacks were wrinkled; her silk blouse partially tucked in, her open-toed shoes unsuitable for fall weather, and to top it off, she was coatless. Mascara was smudged below her lower lids. She shivered in the crisp night air, arms clutched tightly to her chest.

"Come in, come in," said Harry, cupping his hand under her elbow and drawing her inside.

"You must be freezing to death." I ushered her into the warm family room.

Seeing Candace, Adeline abruptly turned to leave, "Oh dear, I didn't know you had company."

239

"She's not company, just our resident princess," offered Harry.

I steered Adeline to a cozy chair next to the fire, pulled the comforter off the back of the couch, and wrapped it around her shoulders. "Here now, let me get you something to drink."

"Just a glass of water," she murmured, and then as an afterthought added, "and, maybe a shot of bourbon on the side." Adeline scrunched deeper into the chair, hugging the throw to her shivering body.

An uncomfortable quiet settled over the room. I sent Harry a worried look. I prayed Adeline's request for alcohol wasn't a prelude to the near-catastrophe at Harry's retirement party last summer when she nearly took a header into the fish pond.

"Turn off the TV and get her to talk while I'm in the kitchen," I whispered to Harry. He gave me a 'why me' look, and motioned for Candace to do it. "Well, one of you take care of it. I'll be right back." I hurried out of the room just as Harry mumbled something.

I grabbed a tray and put an empty shot glass and tumbler of water on it. I hesitated bringing the whole bottle, but decided to keep it at my hand and not hers. I entered the room just as Candace attempted to pick up the lagging conversation.

"So, ah, Adeline, been to any fun parties this Halloween?"

"Christ, you could've been a little more discreet," Harry hissed at her.

She shrugged her shoulders. "Well, at least *I* didn't mutter something incoherent like you." She batted him with her wand.

I poured a jigger, handed it to Adeline, and set the bottle next to me on the end table.

Adeline swallowed the whiskey in one gulp and followed up with a sip of water. "Thank you." She offered a weak smile.

"You look so distraught, Adeline. What's troubling you? Are you ill? Is it Ed? Is it your family?" I asked.

"I'm not finc," she answered, then quickly added, "I mean my health is good. It's …" She reached into her pants pocket, retrieved a handkerchief to pat her wet lips. A piece of paper followed and tumbled to the floor. She quickly bent down to pick it up and clutched it tightly in her hand. We watched her, our curiosity heightened, waiting for her to speak.

"It's...it's Ed." She blinked. A tear escaped one eye and rolled down the side of her cheek.

"What about him? Is he sick, injured?" asked Harry, immediately concerned about his former boss and close friend.

"No. Well yes, sick in a way." She looked at Candace, not sure if she should continue.

I saw Adeline's questioning stare and eased her concern. "It's okay, Adeline. Candace is family. Go ahead and tell us what it is."

"All right," she wiped her cheek with her hankie. "You see, ever since Ed was forced to retire from the bank he hasn't been the same. For a while he hid his feelings, especially around others, but with me it was constant bickering. Oh, I'm sure he probably told you that the problem was me, Harry." She nodded to him.

Harry shied away from her comment by taking a sip of cognac and swishing the contents around in his glass.

Adeline raised the small glass. "May I have another?" She watched me pour the second shot but she let it sit, continuing on. "Ed became very depressed. He vetoed any activity I suggested. Perhaps a change of scenery would help, so I proposed that we take a trip to the coast for a few days. He finally consented with little argument." She let out big sigh. "Unfortunately, my bright idea turned into the biggest nightmare."

"What do you mean, Adeline?" I asked, all sorts of thoughts whirled around in my head.

She reached for the shot-glass and downed its contents. The combination of a warm fire and the alcohol gave her cheeks a rosy hue. She stared into the flames for a minute, then at us. "The first night there we had a quiet dinner at the casino. Afterwards we wandered into the gambling area. Ed decided to try his luck at one of the five-dollar slot machines.

I was a little nervous about the amount, but he said, 'Addie, if you're going to play one of these things, might as well start high.' Ed began to relax. He even won a few hundred dollars. And the winnings seemed to invigorate him. The depression that had hung over him for the past year was beginning to recede."

"Well now," said Harry, "that doesn't sound so bad."

"Playing a little for pleasure would've been fine, Harry, but Ed got the gambling bug." She drank a little water. "After the slot machines, he moved to the blackjack table, the roulette, and soon he was playing poker with the high rollers, betting really big money. At first it was just the weekends, later he'd go to the coast a couple of times during the week. When I told him I was getting concerned that maybe he was becoming addicted, he said I should be happy that he found an activity he liked and to quit my nagging. "

"I see where this is going. Ed's gotten himself in over his head, right?" Harry asked.

"Yes!" Tears cascaded down both cheeks. "He's used up nearly all of our savings, even mortgaged the house."

"Oh dear," I gasped.

"He's also borrowed money from some loan sharks who have been calling several times this week wanting their money."

"Is it a lot?" I winced not wanting to hear the amount.

"About a hundred thousand and counting."

"What so you mean, counting."

"They're tacking on interest for every day it's not paid in full."

The news stunned us into silence.

"But that's not all." She wiped her the tears away with her the back of her hand.

"What more could there be?" Harry asked.

"I was going through the pockets of Ed's old jackets to give to the homeless and found *this*." Hand shaking, she gave the paper to Harry.

He spread the creases out and read the contents. His eyebrows shot up. "Oh!" he exclaimed.

I took the note from him. "Apparently, it must be something big to reduce you to one word … oh goodness!"

Candace snatched it from me. "You two are making me crazy with your … oh my … not Ed?"

"Yes Ed," Adeline shook her head. "My once faithful husband is having an affair."

"Now, now, Adeline, you don't know that for certain." Harry tried to calm her.

"Oh, come on, Harry, give me a little credit. I'm not naïve." Anger crept into her voice. "When a person signs her name *Cyndi* with little heart over the 'i' along with her phone number, she's not selling him time shares in Mexico."

"Did you call the number," I asked.

"Yes. It's some kind of business called Executive Assistance. There's a sexy automated voice that says if you know the extension number of your representative, to dial it now, or stay on the line and an operator will assist you."

"Holy crap!" yelped Candace, banging her wand on the table, "that's one of the most expensive escort services in town."

Our mouths dropped open at Candace's knowledge of the business.

Candace continued, ignoring our astonished faces. "You're right about your suspicions, Adeline, Ed could either be having an affair or paying big time for—"

"Okay, that's enough," barked Harry. "We don't need to go into that in detail." He turned the subject back to his missing friend. "Do you have any idea where Ed might be?"

"I don't know for sure. The last thing he said to me was that he was going to the coast and that was two days ago. I tried to call and text him, but he wasn't answering his cell phone." Adeline sank back in her chair, her posture matching the crumpled paper. "I thought of calling the police but was too embarrassed." Her eyes exposed the hurt and humiliation she felt. "I didn't know what to do or where to turn."

"I'm glad you came here, Adeline." I replied consolingly.

Candace pulled her many layers of petticoat out from under Harry and rose off the sofa. She swished about the room, waving her wand, making little dots of glitter flutter in the air.

"What *are* you doing?" I asked.

"I'm thinking."

"About what?" That worried me. *God only knows what goes on in her mind.*

"There's four parts to Adeline's problem. One, her husband's missing; two, he could be at the coast losing more money; three, he could be with this Cyndi person with a heart shaped 'i' somewhere at the coast; and four, Adeline needs our help stalling the loan sharks."

"I think you can consolidate it all into one, Candace. But, you've summed it up pretty well." Harry spoke cautiously. His eyebrows formed a mustache across his forehead. "Do you have something in mind?" he cringed, waiting for an answer.

I careened out of my chair, and grabbed Candace's wand. "I know what you're thinking," I exclaimed looking directly into her eyes.

"ROAD TRIP!" we squealed together, giving each other a high five at the same time.

Harry pressed a hand to his forehead and moaned, "*That's what I was afraid of!*"

\*\*\*

Made in the USA
San Bernardino, CA
18 April 2016